REVENANT

A Novel

by David Hanna

For Natasha

Revenant: French. Present participle of *revenir*, to return.
    1. To return home
    2. To return from the dead; a ghost; a spirit

PART I

Berlin – Spring 1863

I

THE CONGRESS OF THE HARTENSTEINS

The streets, bathed in brilliant sunlight, were festooned with blazing banners, a lively breeze whipped pennants hanging from every lamppost, and gleaming ribbons of many colors streamed from triumphal arches. An impassioned throng, standing ten deep along the *Kaiserstrasse*, cheered what seemed to be an endless procession, as the troops of the thirty-eight Germanic states swept by to the staccato beat of drums.

They were resplendent in spectacular uniforms: the Württemberg dragoons in powder-blue jackets with gleaming rows of buttons down the front, the Silesian *Schutzen* battalion wearing dark green tunics with black collars piped in gold, the Nassau infantry in madder red, Magdeburg in light blue. They wore red fezzes topped with tassels. Brass eagles, cockades, and plumes topped their chacos. Their towering bearskins and spiked *pickelhaubes* were emblazoned with crescents, death heads, and triple-flamed badges.

Cavalry squadrons swung by on prancing chargers – helmets, swords, lances, and gold epaulettes flashing in the sun.

Blaring trumpets heralded a parade of gleaming black-lacquered landaus carrying the day's principal figures: the kings and princes, archdukes and dukes, barons and electors of the Germanic states grand and small. In the leading carriage, drawn by eight cream-colored horses, rode Kaiser Wilhelm I of Prussia, wearing a white tunic edged in gold embroidery, a crimson sash across his chest, the Order of the Golden Fleece at his collar. In a passion of pride, little children waved flags wildly, handkerchiefs fluttered in women's hands, and men flailed the air with their hats. The monarchs were gathering.

•

A few streets away, in the *Victoria-Allée*, with somewhat less pomp but with hardly less exuberance, the family Hartenstein was also assembling. A parade of carriages drove up to the door of Baron Judah Hartenstein's pink granite town house. Each landau, victoria, and brougham shining and glistening, the horses' coats lustrous in the sunlight. They carried the cream of Hartensteindom. Across the road, peering through the gates and clambering as close to the door as the gendarmes would allow, gathered those scrutineers of the Berlin streets who appear whenever the "someones" gather. They gaped with eager eyes, hoping to be rewarded with a glimpse of what to them would pass for royalty.

The leaders of the Hartenstein banks – fathers and sons, brothers, cousins, in-laws – had traveled to Berlin from all over Europe, from Asia, and the Middle East. Some were there as advisors to their clients – the rulers of the 38 independent states of Germany – who were gathering to consider unification. A family that was ever forward-looking, the Hartensteins saw this as an opportunity to take the measure of the economic prospects in the newly burgeoning realms of science and technology.

Judah Hartenstein stood in the entrance hall of his home, greeting the members of his family as they arrived, searching their faces with his inquisitive eyes, bestowing upon them his luminous smile, taking their hands affectionately in both of his, as if receiving a precious gift. A charming, vigorous man in his fifties, Judah Hartenstein was of medium height and build. He had fine gray hair, dark blue eyes, and a neatly trimmed beard. His dress was, as usual, in unostentatious order, his posture erect, his steady eyes glowing bright with enthusiasm. His demeanor, striking in its composure, radiated a confidence that spoke of his authority. A leader in the community, active in many charities, he was a generous supporter of the Berlin library, the opera, and the museum. As a Jew, he could never aspire to nobility, but he had received from the emperor the highly coveted title of *Kommerzeinrat* – privy councilor – which entitled him to the honorary title of baron, and with it a desirable decoration, the Red Eagle, which he never wore, except in the presence of the monarch, because the base of the medal was emblazoned with a cross.

The family accepted without question his patriarchal rule. He and the other family elders constituted an informal council that governed the conduct, not only of business matters, but of any family affair of consequence as well: major personal investments, assignments at their banking houses scattered around the world, and alliances by marriage with other prominent Jewish families. This was a tradition that had served them over many generations, seeing them through wars, pogroms, revolutions, and the rise and fall of nations. They had thrived over the years, even as hundreds of other influential families had passed into obscurity. This was a family of fabled affluence at the zenith of its power and influence.

In all of them there was a self-assurance that sprang from generations of authority, which they had wielded for so long that they were barely conscious of it. Power and influence came naturally to them – by birth, breeding, and a subtle, unassuming awareness of their place. They made the most of their position quietly, with dignity, inspiring admiration among those they dealt with in the opulent halls of royals of many nations and in the solemn salons of businessmen the world over.

On this day the assembled family had a more than usual poise, a radiant correctness, a swelling of importance; there was a more than ordinarily elegant appearance and a flawlessness of attire. London, dapper in his fawn-gray coat and striped silk cravat, stood close by the windows, conferring with a subdued Paris. Mustachioed, hearty Hamburg gesticulated assertively to Amsterdam, who had Constantinople by the sleeve, waiting impatiently to interpose an urgent thought. Earnest, studious Bombay was perched delicately at a small, marble-topped table, fretting over his papers. Vienna, his crystalline blue eyes intense, was patiently explaining to Berlin why Prussia and Austria would, under no circumstances, ever be bound in a united Germany.

The only woman present was the eldest of the Hartenstein family, Amelia Oppenheim, Judah's sister. An austere woman in her late sixties, she was straight-backed and tall. She was a solemn eminence in deep-red bombazine, with a velvet ribbon around her slender throat. The wife of Sandor Oppenheim, the son of the Vienna banking family, she was a brilliant businesswoman who spoke several languages, and she had quite a reputation for saying what was on her mind in all of them. She wrote poetry and published commentaries in the satirical magazine *Kladderadatsch*, under a *nom de plume* of course. Every day, always escorted by her secretary and footman, she attended to the business of the All-German Women's Society, which promoted education and equal work opportunities for women and girls. She also found time for her various charities for the sick and the poor.

Standing in the midst of the assemblage, she was greeted effusively by the cousin from Constantinople, a petite, swarthy man in a black swallowtail coat, his handlebar mustache stiff and glossy, his black hair slick with pomade. He bowed over her lace-gloved hand.

"A rare pleasure, Madame," he whispered.

"I am not Madame," she replied. "I am Cousin Amelia."

Then she was off on her rounds, repeating as she made her way around the room, her lush soprano echoing above the hum of the crowd, "I am Cousin Amelia."

•

Judah Hartenstein contemplated the variety of his exuberant family: wan and hearty, swarthy and pale, woolly sidewhiskers over high stiff collars, mustaches clipped and trim or full and flaring, cravats in billowing bows, waistcoats of velvet and silk brocade, spectacles attached to long, black silk ribbons.

"Is it possible," he mused, "that any group of individuals assembled in a single chamber could be more diverse in their appearance?"

They were substantial and diminutive, portly and slender, theatrically handsome, and unfortunately homely. Though their physical differences were pronounced, certain dynastic characteristics neatly divided the family into its two major components: the Hyams and the Hartensteins. The Hyams – olive-skinned and dark-eyed – had long, arched noble noses that betrayed their oriental origin. The Hartensteins – taller of a lighter complexion – had noses of the middle European type, sharp-tipped with flaring nostrils that imparted a supercilious, beaky, birdlike air. Almost all of them could be identified by a certain prominence of chin – always referred to with pride as the "Hartenstein chin."

Notwithstanding their obvious physical differences, there was something that mysteriously united the Hyams and the Hartensteins, something deep-rooted in their psyches, something that rendered them so formidable. Both families were a miscellany of complex personalities. Some were imperious, haughty, and vain; others were benevolent, considerate, and self-effacing. A few were boisterous and demonstrative, most were contemplative and reserved. They had immense charisma and dexterous charm.

They sailed, skied, raced horses, scaled mountains, collected paintings, and indulged in a passion for music, attending the opera and sponsoring orchestras. Several were accomplished amateur musicians – violinists, cellists, and pianists. Their children created theatricals and musicales. The adults put on productions of Shakespeare and Moliere in English and French. They were secure in their penetrating intellect, confident in their competence, and unconstrained in their enthusiasms.

Herschel Hartenstein, at sixteen, was the baron's youngest son. He was overjoyed to be included in a meeting of his elders. He stood at the fringe of the gathering, observing the members of the Middle Eastern branch of the family with delighted curiosity. His sense of the romantic was stirred. He thought they were mysterious and exotic.

Not so Herschel's brother Kurt, who gazed at his Hyam cousins with disdain. Kurt looked at his Turkish cousin, Aaron Hyam, a slender, diminutive man, who wore a gold scarab with eyes of tiny seed pearls pinned to his cravat. Petite replicas glinted at his cuffs, and a large diamond flashed on his left hand. Kurt thought of the swarthy Hyams – with their ostentatious jewelry and flamboyant mode of dress – as *shvartzes*. But to Herschel they were colorful and exhilarating.

The Hyams were direct descendants of the founder of the Hyam-Hartenstein dynasty, Sheikh Amam Hayeem. Aaron had green eyes flecked with rust and a dark bushy mustache above full lips. He and his brothers Reuben and Hyam who, as Hyam Hyam, was known as "Twice", oversaw the bank's interests in the Middle East and Asia.

A fourth brother, Abdullah, known as Albert, lived in Bombay. He was a distinguished botanist whose work in orchidales consisted of painstakingly removing delicate pollen sacks from one plant and gingerly depositing them onto the stigmatic surfaces of pod parents to form an admirable column – an original orchid. Despite a frail physique and a sickly aspect, he traveled widely, often at his peril, to study the uses to which primitive peoples put the orchid - as a cure for poisoning from fish in the West Indies, to prevent sickness after childbirth in Malaya, as a diuretic in Chile, and to treat broken bones in Ecuador. The orchid was to Albert an intricate phenomenon, as was Albert to his family.

As a young child, Herschel would often sit in his father's library, holding in his lap a leather-bound volume of *The Thousand and One Nights*. On the frontispiece there was a drawing in faded pastels of a city of golden domes and lofty minarets, surrounded by crenellated walls, surmounted by billowing clouds. This, in his imagination, was Baghdad, the home of his Hayeem ancestors. In his mind's eye he saw Sheikh Amam Hayeem's sons congregating with other merchants, greeting the arrival of camel caravans from Kabul and Bombay, carrying cotton and gold and silver ornaments. Into the teeming bazaars and *souks*, silks and trinkets came by sea from Java, Singapore, and China.

In the often-recited saga of the Hayeem family, Sheikh Hayeem and his sons traded in wool, cotton, copper, spices, and sugar. They transported slaves, silk, swords, castor, marten, and other furs. They loaded their goods on the backs of camels and went by land to Kolzum. They embarked from the Red Sea and sailed to Medina and Jeddah. They traveled in great caravans from Spain and France to Rabat, Cairo, Damascus, and Constantinople.

The family legend recounted that in the early 1700s, when Baghdad fell into economic disarray, Amam Hayeem made for the Holy Land with his sons David and Moses, his daughter Leah, and members of his extended family. Some Hayeems went on to India, to Bombay and Calcutta. Others went to Constantinople, the heart of the Ottoman Empire. David, Moses, and Leah eventually made their home in

Germany, in Lübeck, in the duchy of Schleswig-Holstein, where they adapted their name to Hyam.

The Lübeck branch of the Hyam family – along with Leah's husband, Mordechai Hartenstein, a pawnbroker – funneled loans from their family connections in the Orient to a throng of cash-hungry kings, princes, dukes, and bishops. By the dawn of the nineteenth century, they had established a family bank in Berlin, with branches in Frankfurt, London, Paris, and Amsterdam. Their cousins had opened counting houses in Bombay and Constantinople, and trading posts in Shanghai and Canton.

Judah turned his gaze to the long table looming before him. Banners of sun streamed though the lofty windows, dazzling the pendants of the crystal chandeliers, dancing off the mirrored walls. Anticipation throbbed in the room.

• • • •

2

THE GATHERING OF THE CLAN

Judah looked down the table to the two eldest of his four sons. As different as the two brothers were in so many respects, they had, to a greater degree than their contemporaries in the family, that vital attribute of determined and vigilant insight into "affairs." They were both capable financiers and shrewd businessmen. But, their father wondered, are they statesmen? Did they possess those rare, indefinable qualities so highly prized among international bankers: sensitivity, finesse, and mature judgment?

Alone among the Hartensteins, Elias, the eldest of the four brothers, had been permitted by the government to enter the army reserves, though, of course, as a Jew he had been denied a commission. He considered this to be a great misfortune, because it was as a *bügerlicher Offizier* that one achieved access to the most lofty social circles and to the pinnacle of social distinction: acceptance into court society. This deficiency, however, did not prevent him from assuming the bearing and adopting the manner of a Prussian cavalry officer. He was fervent in his belief that the cavalry charge was the noblest expression of a gentleman's character –

a sentiment that encouraged in his father the belief that Elias was a *schlemiel*. Judah believed that by a daily routine of schnapps and a weekly fall on the head from horseback, the cavalry remained in that state of numb confusion that he believed was the aim of every cavalry officer.

Judah's second son, Kurt, ran the London bank. Kurt's angular face was baby-smooth. His valet often shaved him twice a day. In his appearance Kurt was self-satisfied and serene, but secretly he yearned for the one distinctive badge of honor he would never wear: the dueling scar. Even as the practice of dueling was falling into disrepute, Kurt defended it.

"Personal honor," he said solemnly, "combined with a manly, courageous character and zeal in defense of honor, constitutes one of the most wonderful aspects of our whole modern culture."

He was *mashuga*, thought his father.

Simon, the third son, and Herschel's much-loved brother, was twenty-one. He stood quietly at his place at the table. He was as unlike his brothers as a sibling can be. Tall, spare, reserved, he was a serious scientist who had worked on the development of steel-production processes with both William Siemens in Germany and Henry Bessemer in England.

Judah's eyes came to rest on Herschel, who was five years younger than Simon. Herschel sat silently at the far end of the table.

"Why is the boy so shy?" Judah wondered. "Why is he always so tense? Why can't he sit still? His body is always wandering."

Herschel felt his father's gaze. His fingers flew to his lips, and as if through a tremendous force of will, he brought all movement to a halt. He trained upon his father a look of commiseration. He knew that he was an annoyance to him.

Judah considered the pathetic condition of his youngest son's life.

"But why now?" Judah thought. "Why now, when I should be focused upon the urgent matters at hand?"

Judah faced the tall draped windows. His eyes narrowed against the sun, the sounds of the throng drifting up to him from the streets below. He heard the muted strains of a marching band. Church bells tolled in the distance. The room was warm. He felt an unaccustomed ennui. An immense weariness had descended upon him.

He wondered if the years of sustained labor were finally taking their toll. He had succeeded in bringing the bank through a potentially disastrous period - the Crimean War, a precipitous devaluation in commodity prices, the collapse of several American banks and railroads, and panic on the stock exchange. Failure had threatened rival banking firms, but under Judah's leadership the Hartenstein Bank had flourished. From his baroque marble and granite building in the heart of *Behrenstrasse,* Berlin's financial district, he looked out upon a sprawling enterprise that embraced banking, investments, and brokerage.

At last they opened the portfolios placed before them and they began to deal with the lengthy agenda. Restless and uneasy, Judah toyed with his spectacles. He leafed through his papers. Voices came to him as if from a great void. His mind was adrift.

Before his eyes the image of his wife Helena materialized. When she came to his study a week ago she had been downhearted, her face tear-stained.

"Not at all herself," he had thought. "No, not at all herself."

"What can we do for Herschel?" she had cried. "He is miserable, morose. Sending him to that school was a terrible mistake." She was in tears. "He has no friends. He is lonely, desolate. He can't possibly go on this way."

Judah groaned.

"What is wrong with the boy?" he wondered. "Why is he so quiet, so sensitive, so withdrawn? Sometimes, in his silence, he is almost surly."

Judah often stared at the boy without seeing him, as though he were an apparition.

His son Kurt's voice intruded on his thoughts: "The Polish rebellion against Russia…." he heard him say. "Mobilization of Prussian forces…"

But Judah's mind remained fixed on Helena. He and Helena had always been in perfect harmony. They had always refrained from disagreements. Their rapport was complete. But on the question of the Herschel they were divided.

With uncharacteristic impatience he had said to her, "You must pull yourself together, dear lady. You are overwrought."

Now he heard Aaron Hyam saying, "Schleswig-Holstein is flaring up again… the business community is terrified… Denmark is threatened."

Judah heard Hyam's voice, but not his words. He was lost in remorse. He regretted that he had responded to Helena in platitudes, that he had cast aside the enormity of her anxieties and belittled her fears.

Judah's brother Avraham's voice drifted to him as if from a great distance: "Austria's efforts to obtain help from the international bankers have been unsuccessful."

His cousin Eric replied: "The Rothschilds will certainly step in to help."

Avraham disagreed, "The Vienna Rothschilds have already refused outright, and Austria needs ninety million gulden immediately!"

A ray of light flashed for an instant through the window – the sun dancing on a button or the hilt of a sword. Judah was suddenly enveloped in a blur of color. A veiled memory was stirred. It is 1814 – the Congress of Vienna. He and his father are strolling hand in hand. Together they walk along the broad tree-lined boulevards. He feels the comforting firmness of his father's grip. He savors the fragrance of new leather gloves. The aroma of roasting chestnuts is in the air. Noblemen, promenading arm in arm with sumptuously attired ladies, nod respectfully to his father, the financial advisor – the Court Jew – to many in the Prussian imperial family.

The royalty of Europe is on display: the Tsar and his empress, four kings, a queen, two crown princes, three grand duchesses, and three princes. In all, more than two hundred heads of princely families, decked out in splendid uniforms, adorned with glittering decorations.

Judah's heart swelled with memories of his father. He remembered how, as a child of eight or nine, he would slip noiselessly into his father's library, crawling into the knee-hole of his father's massive desk – now his own – to eavesdrop on his father's business gatherings, often held in the evenings at their home. Judah remembered the clamor of greetings and footmen's arms piled high with cloaks and hats. Guests, hale and hearty, ascending the sweeping staircase to the book-lined room in the northwest corner of the house, finding seats on the leather sofas surrounding the marble fireplace.

Judah had viewed his father through a prism that splintered his life into many enthralling shades of brilliance. He had constructed an icon of a father that was sacrosanct. He saw him as an exemplary man, wise and virtuous. He had held him in awe.

But now his thoughts returned to his son.

"Could it be that I have undervalued my boy?" Lamentably, he had not taken the time to befriend him; he had not made an effort to understand him, to know him.

"Collaborate with the French Rothschilds," his brother-in-law, Sandor Oppenheim, was saying, "Take a leading part in founding the Darmstadter Bank..." Oppenheim droned on: "...the Thuringian Railroad," he heard him say. "...the Cologne-Minden and Rhenish railroads..."

Judah heard only disconnected words, fragments of sentences. His mind wandered in reminiscence. Images of

Herschel's childhood passed before Judah's eyes – evenings when he carried the boy to bed. Dark nursery. Flickering light of candles in the windows, reflected in the shimmering lake. Stroking the boy's head, soothing him in the dark, consoling a small, terrified creature.

He was lost in the vision of himself and little Herschel, father and son, walking up the *Kaiserstrasse* together. It was a picture of grace and charm, of beauty. He saw it with such clarity that it summoned forth an agonized murmur.

Now he beheld himself in the kaleidoscope of the ballroom mirrors. He was awed by the alien eyes that returned his stare. His appearance, always alert and energetic, had dulled to a state of troubled weariness. A morose preoccupation had dropped like a curtain between him and the realm of his emotions.

"Is this what I have come to?" he grieved.

Although, of course he could never have given voice to these thoughts, he had always believed himself to be a tireless, resolute leader. And wasn't he always the devoted husband and benevolent father?

"But now," he reflected sadly, "I am weary."

His thoughts turned to Homer: *"Alla ti e moi tauta philos dielexato thymos"-* "Why does my own heart dispute with me thus?"

• • • •

3

THE WIDER WORLD

She appeared out of the shadows, drifting into the tranquil garden. She was so near that he could sense the gentle throbbing of her heart. He could hear her breathing, inhale her fragrance. She leaned toward him, smiling, her lips parted. She held out her arms to him, beckoning. But she hovered just beyond his reach.

Then – as suddenly as she had appeared, she vanished. She vanished, melting into the still iridescent forest.

He struggled to hold tight to his dream, but as always it drifted from his grasp. Nothing remained of it but vague shreds of emotion. A pale, sickly light filtered through the shutters. He pulled the eiderdown closer, drawing his legs up to his chest, awaiting the sounds of the awakening city. The unavoidable day was once more approaching.

Herschel Hartenstein's pale face was grave behind his wire-rimmed spectacles. He lamented that it was not a face that would cause a girl's gaze to linger. On walks through town he saw lovely, vivacious young women sitting in cafés or promenading the boulevards arm in arm with men not much older than he. Herschel longed to appear carefree, to dress like the dashing, debonair young students of the university. His adolescent flesh was under duress. He felt that life, true life, the essential life of the soul, had eluded him.

•

Each dark dawn he arose from his bed and dressed hurriedly. Downstairs, in his father's library, he joined the prayer service. Every weekday morning his father's *minyan* assembled here. The *minyan*, a quorum – ten or more observant Jews of Berlin, and often visitors from other cities – bustled in. They entered the lofty, marble-colonnaded room, bringing with them the winter on their clothes, the scent of snow-damp wool. There was Jacoby the tailor, a short, round-shouldered man with a large hooked nose and ears that hung from his head like pendants. He bowed to Gettinger the notary, a tall, thin, stiff-backed man with a goatee trimmed like a spade and a mustache curled in a spiral. Seven or eight of them had arrived. They stood, chatting amiably – the rich and the poor, young and old – huddling close by the white china stove, holding their hands out to the warmth, stamping their feet, swiping sleeves across leaking noses, waiting impatiently for the enchanted number ten to be reached. Finally, the tenth man arrived, a stranger, guided by a footman.

Without delay, they began their cryptic ritual. Cloaked in their prayer shawls, each removed from his velvet drawstring pouch two small black-lacquered leather boxes – the *teffelin*, the phylactery – containing the anthem of their faith, which enjoined them:

> *These words, which I teach thee this day... shall*
> *be for frontlets between thine eyes, and thou*
> *shall write them as a sign upon thy hand.*

Fastened to the boxes were arm-length black leather thongs. Releasing their left arms from jacket sleeves, each person placed one box high up on the bicep near the heart, winding the thong round and down the forearm to their hand where, laced between their fingers, it formed the Hebrew letter *Shin*, emblematic of the name of God. They placed the other little square black box on their foreheads; it was held in place by a band of black leather that fit around their heads, terminating in two strands that hung down over their shoulders.

Their hats, some of fur, some with wide brims, others with tall crowns, perched precariously on the back of their heads, defiant of gravity, as in their fervor, chanting their prayers swiftly, they rocked back and forth and swayed from side to side.

To Herschel, a witness to this ceremony all his life, it was a medieval enigma. It was totally incomprehensible. It was unalloyed superstition.

•

It is much too early for the *Akademie* where he will spend his interminable day. But clutching his satchel, he stepped out toward the *Kleine Konditorie*, where he sipped steaming coffee and immersed himself in the pages of the *Arbeiter Zeitung*. He displayed the paper ostentatiously, hoping that the other patrons would take him to be a sophisticated observer of the affairs of the world.

The headline declared that Prussia was on the verge of a new era – *Eisen und Blut,* Iron and Blood – Bismarck's aphorism that was the dogma of Prussian *Kultur*. The Iron Chancellor, in his cavalry boots, high-collared tunic, and spiked helmet, was in Herschel's mind the very personification of the romantic, heroic warrior. Herschel took great pride in the superiority of Germanic culture and intellect, believing that he himself was German, though he knew full well that they would never accept him as one of them.

Groping his way through the early morning haze he started off on the journey to the Akademie. Until this year a succession of tutors had educated him at home. And of course he had attended religious school, as did his brothers before him. But Herschel abhorred his religious education, which he felt was narrow and constrained. He longed for a learning experience that would open up the wider world to him. About the wider world, he and his father, a devout Jew, disagreed bitterly.

But to Herschel, an argument with his father was unthinkable. His father was infallible. His father was sacrosanct. In fact, it was inconceivable that circumstances could possibly arise that might oblige Judah Hartenstein, the patriarch of the family, to impose his will. A word, a raised eyebrow, had always sufficed.

Herschel had stood before him apprehensively. He argued incoherently.

"Papa, my Jewishness is of no consequence, What does it matter that Jewish blood flows in my veins? I am a German in my heart. There isn't even a hint of Jewishness in my appearance. I could even pass for a gentile."

His father recoiled as though he had been physically assaulted. His face clouded over. His breath caught in his throat.

He burst out, "Have you gone mad?"

Herschel replied hastily, "Not that I want to. Not that I ever would."

Judah stared at his son in disbelief. He trembled.

"You must be in the grip of some fantasy!" He said. He thrust his finger at him. "Don't you know you will carry your Jewishness with you wherever you go? That is a fact. An inescapable fact. Everywhere in Germany – in hotels, theaters, restaurants, in business and society – it will always be with you."

"But why?" Herschel asked. "Why do we accept it as inevitable?"

He couldn't imagine himself ever being persecuted, excluded, ostracized, or driven from his home, in fear for his life.

"This is Prussia, Papa," Herschel said. "This is the nineteenth century. Those irrational prejudices are a thing of the past."

His father turned his back on him and stalked off.

•

Eventually, Herschel received support from an unexpected quarter. His brothers believed that they had been disadvantaged in the world of business by an education, however rigorous, that was so circumscribed that it deprived them of knowledge of the real world. By which they meant the gentile world. They finally convinced their father that Herschel, the youngest son, was sufficiently imbued with the principles and practices of his religion that exposure to gentile boys would put him at minimal risk of infection.

So Herschel joined the sons of other aristocrats and moguls at Professor Balthazar's Akademie.

•

The Akademie Balthazar occupied a small seventeenth-century edifice, set back from the street in a garden bordered by a high wrought-iron fence. On his first day at school Herschel passed through the iron-studded oak doors with a light heart and grand expectations. He entered the classroom with an amiable smile on his face.

As one, all heads turned toward him. Their faces expressed astonishment. They whispered behind their hands, the murmur traveling around the room: "Who is he? Who is he?"

Echoing through the room came the reply: "The Jew." He heard it being passed from desk to desk: "The Jew."

In that single moment, with those words ringing in his ears, all his hopes and dreams vanished, fleeing like mist. He stood stunned, helpless in his humiliation and dismay. When he found a seat he sat silently, listening to the whispered conversations all around him. He forced his lips into a smile that masked his dread.

Furtively, he looked around the sepulchral salon, examining his classmates. He observed their arrogance and studied their condescending scornful faces.

"So this is the elite of German youth," he thought.

He took refuge in the fact that not one of them – these sons of Prussian nobility, the cream of Berlin's social order – was his equal. Not one. Not in wealth. Not in influence. Certainly not in culture and tradition.

He had grown up in a world of bankers and nobles, physicians and lawyers, writers and musicians. It was an urbane, educated, open-minded world of intellectuals. He lived with his family in a grand villa in the *Charlottenburg* district, staffed by gardeners, chauffeurs, footmen, maids, and butlers. His parents gave him piano lessons and classes in painting and languages. His family traveled. They attended the opera, the great performances of the times. They dined at the finest establishments – coffee and pastries at the *Kaiserhof*, dinner at the *Kempinski*. As children he and his brothers and sister walked sedately with their parents along the *Unter den Linden* and in the *Tiergarten*, conforming to the good manners expected of German youth, speaking German without a hint of sing-song Yiddish. They even mixed with gentiles, naturally of the appropriate social standing. They took pride in their tolerance.

He studied his fellow students – all gentiles, all older than he. They fidgeted and squirmed on the fragile, faded Louis chairs. They lounged apathetically – bored, indifferent, assuming an attitude of insolence. By their comportment and careless mode of dress, they expressed their disdain for the Akademie and their contempt for the professor.

•

Later that day, when Herschel entered the dining salon for lunch, he was greeted by a raucous burst of laughter. It was forced and false with no genuine jollity.

"They laugh with mirthless faces," he thought. "Their teeth are bared in a joyless grimace. They look directly at me and cackle as if I am too ridiculous to believe."

He slipped into his place with a shy nod of greeting, which was returned not so smilingly. Even the one or two who acknowledged him did so with formal courtesy. His gaze traveled the room with an outward show of courage that masked his anxiety. He studied their unblinking malevolence, their hostile cunning. His innate fear of the unknown life of the *goyim* was intense and insidious.

He heard them speaking of him as if he were someone descended from another planet. They laughed as they talked of the compulsory swimming in which all the boys bathed naked. They speculated hilariously that he must have a "cap" on his penis.

Seated across from him was a tall young man who inhaled the Riesling in his glass approvingly. It was Count Szigmund von Hagendorf.

"Obviously he has superlative German breeding. He must be heroic and imperturbable," he thought.

Herschel glanced surreptitiously at the man's great head, placed squarely on broad shoulders. It was topped by a brush of dark hair that grew low upon his beetled forehead. He had chiseled features, a nose like a broad beak, and heavy-lidded eyes set deep in hollows above jutting cheekbones.

"He is completely, totally German, an authentic son of the mighty Teutonic race," Herschel mused. "He has the dignity of a dueling scar, a noble *Mensur*, perfectly situated on his cheekbone. The mark of a genuine German, a token of his superiority."

Herschel looked up as Munzenberg, the senior boy, entered.

"A haughty minor deity," Herschel thought.

Herschel believed that every aspect of Munzenberg's face – the skeletal head, the beady eyes that were close-set and sly, and the pointed nose with flaring nostrils over the rigid mouth–reflected his personality.

"A perfect archetype of utter, mind-numbing self-assurance," Herschel thought.

"*Gross Gott*," Herschel said, as Munzenberg took a seat some distance removed from him.

The boy looked past him with aloof dismissal. Herschel shrank back into the dim hidden passage of his psyche. He grieved. Anger boiled up in him. His temples throbbed. His face turned pale.

"I must control my breathing." He held himself with stern immobility.

Conversation drifted at the table: the Russian threat, the crisis in the cabinet, the market slump, the mark, the American war between the states, the Kaiser, the English, the Jews.

"The Jews. Always the Jews," Herschel lamented.

Munzenberg said, "Never will we achieve our national destiny if we can't find a way to drive all of them out of Prussia."

The room fell silent. They looked at Herschel. A spasm of fear surged through him. His mind churned.

"Jew," he thought. "It is as if the mere mention of the word distresses them. It creeps into every conversation. It is a mania."

Herschel felt himself dissolving. He would have to bear the loss of companionship and empathy, the isolation from the communal life of one's fellow creatures. He toiled and flayed himself.

But then he told himself, "I don't care what they think of me. Why should I? Why does it matter what they think?"

He had told his father angrily that he had resolved never to be just another persecuted Jew. His father had scoffed.

"All *Goyim* detest the Jews," his father had said. "And those who act as if they like us are the most evil. They are charlatans."

He now understood.

"It is true," Herschel thought. "Papa is right. I will always carry my Jewishness with me like some dishonorable secret. What a disgraceful way of life for one who is so determinedly German!"

He heard his classmate von Hitzig's voice: "They are mongrels, the scum of every nation. They run the newspapers, the schools, the theaters – everywhere contaminating German ideas. They are in banking, trading – always haggling, wheedling, cheating, manipulating. Their German is execrable. They speak in that deplorable Yiddish dialect."

Herschel watched in disgust as throughout his diatribe, von Hitzig went on systematically cleaning his plate, mopping it bare.

"He leaves not a scrap of anything," Herschel observed. "He is a rapacious bird thrusting its cavernous maw forward to devour whatever is placed before it. He guzzles and gorges and gnaws, all the time blathering with his brimful mouth. Now his eyes are searching the table. Is there not another morsel to be found?"

Herschel sat in unyielding serenity, occasionally moving food around his plate but not eating. His expression was inflexible and motionless.

Munzenberg looked across the table at him. Munzenberg saw, at much too intimate a distance, he thought, Herschel's smooth, unblemished face and his large, innocent blue eyes.

Munzenberg was furious as he observed him.

"This arrogant Jew remains quite poised," he thought. "He is sitting back at his ease with his chin in the air, gazing down his nose at me!"

Munzenberg's jaw puffed up over his collar. His eyes were bloodshot, and his cheeks turned crimson.

Herschel looked at the cold, hard face. He felt as if he were staring into the eyes of some genus of ferocious creature that was observing him from a cavern, ready to fly at him from a forest.

Herschel sat quietly, controlling his passion with great difficulty, forcing his mind to an unwavering void. He told himself that all he had to do was remain silent and not let them goad him into losing his equanimity, giving way to his anger, playing into their hands.

His brother Simon had cautioned him.

"Heed these principles!" Simon said. "They will ask, 'Are you a Jew?' 'I am a German,' you reply. Never dignify their hostility with a retort. Ignore them."

But Herschel was growing increasingly agitated. Perspiration formed on his brow. His breathing was labored, and a wave of nausea came over him. His eyes brimmed, and his lips trembled.

He felt himself dissolving, giving way. He had had enough. He stopped eating and pushed his plate away. He wiped his lips with his napkin, folded it with care, and laid it next to his plate. He placed both hands on the table and slowly raised himself up.

"Gentlemen, allow me to be excused if you please," He rose and left them.

•

Time seemed to be suspended. The days melded into weeks, but he was unaware of the passage of time. He tried in vain to get a grip on himself, but formless dread invaded his thoughts. Anxiety overwhelmed him. His heart pounded. He struggled to breathe. There was a festering in his mind and a silence in his soul. He felt as if he had been abandoned, that he was all alone in the world. Alone in his room, he sobbed and moaned to himself. Now, when he walked through the doors of the Akademie Balthazar, he felt that he was approaching a hostile frontier, where before crossing the border, he had to surrender at the customs shed his real persona, his fundamental self.

•

When his day at the Akademie finally drew to a close, Herschel departed for home, trodding the Berlin streets exhausted and disheartened. The faded facades of the houses and shops, the gray stone, and the grotesque Gothic of the ponderous public buildings closed in upon him. Overhead, the sky filmed over. The shadows deepened. In the light of the fast-fading day the lamplighter made his way slowly down the curving, cobbled streets. The necklace of street lamps flickered to life.

Herschel endured the tedium of the days, anticipating the moment when he would escape to the library at home. Ensconced in the window seat of the dark-paneled room, he would listen to the song of the wind outside the window, and he would gaze out at the gray lake rimmed by tall tents of cedars and pines. He found comfort among the heavy Baroque furnishings, surrounded by the faded tapestries in which nymphs gamboled in wooded glades, in the dim splendor of the leather-bound volumes on the looming shelves, and in the reflections of familiar bibelot behind the glass of ormolu vitrines. Here he was in his fortress. Cliffs of books reached up beyond the flickering candelabra. The aroma of leather and vellum blended with the musk of faded Turkey carpets and the vapors emanating from the white china stove.

Here he sought solace in his writers. His heart expanded. He was in the company of friends. His writers delivered him from despair. Goethe, who wrote so poignantly of the sensitive, ill-fated Werther. Blake, who depicted the exotic and the mysterious. Scott, Keats, Byron, Shelley. And of course, Wordsworth, who returned to the subject of the poor over and over again, insisting, as in *Michael*, Herschel's favorite, that a poor man, though lacking a formal education, could still be deeply sensitive and possessed of pride and dignity.

But the afternoon's gratification did not reside entirely in books, as welcome as they always were. Fulfillment lay in reaping the harvest of a prolific imagination, in the contemplation of grand deeds and feats of nobility. He heard the clamor of battle. He was in a sailing vessel, snug in his cabin against the pounding sea. Here he was secure in his cave in a mountain redoubt, lying close to his fire, sheltered from the fierce Alpine storm.

He banished from his mind the knowledge that this chamber, his sanctuary, was at the start of the day, a far less congenial place. But late in the day, in the fading light of an autumn afternoon, there was nary a hint in the library of that earlier presence of the morning prayer meeting.

Each day, when he left the Akademie and stepped out resolutely toward the *Klauberplatz*, he yearned for his mother's affectionate welcome and her amiable, anxious concern. Helena Hartenstein's face, her skin paper thin, was feverish when he rested his forehead against her cheek. She was pre-occupied, faraway, in a world he couldn't reach. The recollection of her that would always remain with him was of a meditative woman, quiet and shy, an invalid who passed her days in the tranquility of the bright conservatory, looking out on their sun-swept garden.

On those rare occasions when she felt well enough to venture outside, he would accompany her, walking with her in the garden, or riding with her in the carriage for a brief excursion into town. Sometimes, on cold gray days, she welcomed him home in her boudoir, where she lay on a chaise lounge, gazing solemnly into the fire.

"*Leibling!*" she would cry. She embraced him warmly, taking his face in her hands and saying, "I have been waiting for you all day."

She would inquire about his work at the Akademie. She wanted to know what he had eaten for lunch. No aspect of his world was too trivial for recital. This was the ascendant moment of her day: the reclamation of her son. Observing his somber demeanor with deep concern, she would entreat him to make new friends, pursue new interests, and to travel. She wanted him to be strong and independent. But as things were with him, she could not imagine how he could get on without her.

For his part, it was inconceivable to contemplate life without his mother. Yet he sometimes felt that he had to prove to himself that he could survive without her. He felt that he owed it to himself to do something bold, heroic, and adventurous. He worshipped Hegel, who saw man not only as young and pure, but also as dynamic, forceful, and capable of totally transforming the world.

"Why," Herschel wondered, "can't I be a young Siegfried, astride my steed, sword in hand, forging my way out of the forest primeval?"

• • • •

4

THE GARDEN PARTY

Joachim Malkovitz took in the sweep of the Hartenstein garden with deeply felt pleasure. He lolled in his white wicker chair, his eyes drifting down to the banks of the lake and the abundant hills beyond, to the vineyards and the summer house barely visible through the copse of trees. He was at his ease. He felt very much at home. He had been welcome at the Hartenstein's villa since he was a child.

But he was preoccupied. His mind was on tomorrow, which would be a special occasion. For the first time, he would visit Baron Hartenstein at the bank.

Malkovitz was a man whose imagination surpassed all limits and whose ambition knew no bounds. As he pondered the baron's summons Malkovitz felt that nothing was beyond the realm of possibility. A mission perhaps? An offer of a place at the bank? A business opportunity? He knew that the baron held him in affectionate esteem. And he believed that among business people he had a reputation as a man of great promise.

Now in his twentieth year, Joachim Malkovitz had been more or less on his own since he was sixteen. He lost both his parents in childhood, and he had been raised in the Lübeck home of his Uncle Jacob, the baron's life-long friend. As a young boy, he was clever, lively, good-natured. Less obvious was the fact that he was cunning. He was capable of effortlessly deceiving his uncle and aunt. He could look into their innocent faces, read their gentle eyes, and calculate precisely what it would take to win their approval.

He grew into a quick-witted, amiable highbrow. He was haughty and shrewd, and he lived his life according to the prevailing ethical principles, interpreting them, however, with a certain liberality. He was more inclined, in a phrase of Balzac's he savored, "to impart the morality of pleasure than to preach the pleasure of morality."

He worked in his uncle's business, in lace and linens. Business came easily to him. His clients admired his easygoing charm. He was an entertaining man who brought with him an aura of foreign climes, an intimation of adventure, a whiff of the spice of life. He was a man you could talk to and laugh with. In short, he did well. But, regrettably, he did not do well enough to satisfy himself.

His travels had brought him face to face with a world that was being remade. Trains were obliterating boundaries between countries, steamships were reaching out to faraway continents, and distances were evaporating. Newspapers and books were bringing the world within the grasp of more people, who were becoming aware of the possibilities that life held for them.

He foresaw that the great maritime cities of the Germanic states would become the crossroads of this new age. Even now they pulsed with vitality. He walked streets that swarmed with purveyors of vegetables and produce. Porters hefted great bales of merchandise on their shoulders, dogcarts carried bolts of fabrics, donkeys pulled wagons of fruit and poultry, and heavily laden barges, passing under innumerable bridges, sailed swiftly down narrow canals. Proud, prosperous businessmen thronged the markets.

Bitterly, Malkovitz felt that he was watching all this from a great distance. He would have liked to pursue other interests - the military perhaps. He pictured himself in uniform, straight, formal, elegant, with the knee-length tunic buttoned to the neck, the ruby sash bright against the somber serge. But he knew full well that he would never achieve social parity with the dashing Hussars he saw in the cafés and music halls. In his manner, in his speech and dress, he had always tried to emulate the young gentile *Herren* he saw on the boulevards in the company of fashionable and glamorous women. He envied the jovial students who swaggered about the streets in their brightly colored caps, greeting each other noisily with elaborate ceremonial bows, clattering into the *Schloss* gardens to swill vast quantities of beer and bellow *Volkslieder* at the top of their lungs. But he knew that he would never share their carefree lives.

Though the face that Malkovitz presented to the world was bright and confident, he felt that contemptible conditions surrounded him. They were uninspiring, disheartening situations from which there was no escape. But still he had unwavering faith in his substantial natural abilities. He was confident that he was somehow destined to rise to a position of authority and influence.

He looked back toward the villa, to the flagstoned terrace, where Rachel, the baron's young daughter, was surrounded by her carefree friends. As a child, Rachel had doted on Joachim Malkovitz.

"How smart he is, how handsome," she had thought.

At first she pretended that he was her older brother, then her lover. They played at being husband and wife. He amused her, showed her books of lithographs, held her in thrall with his tales of adventure. He still exhilarated her, even now that she was on the brink of adulthood. She adored him.

He was an exceptionally handsome man, tall and slender, with a trim waist and broad shoulders, which he emphasized with his meticulously tailored frock coats. He combed his fair hair in waves over his ears, and contrary to the fashion of the day, which decreed elaborate handlebar or stiletto-tipped mustaches and mutton-chop whiskers, he was clean-shaven.

Brazenly, Rachel gave herself up to the joy of gazing at him. Leaving her friends, she walked down the garden path, taking a circuitous route to come up behind him. The shadow of her straw bonnet fell upon his face. He looked up to see her silk parasol dancing lightly in her fingers, the gentle breeze caressing her satin scarf. Silently, she sat down beside him.

Looking at her now, he pictured her as she was as a child, in white ruffles and buckled shoes, with long golden tresses flowing down to her shoulders in tight curls. Today, in the spirit of the summer day, she was wearing a gown trimmed in pink, deep rose, and pure pearl white. It frilled and billowed, softly bending to the breeze, slyly embracing her body.

He took her hand and asked, "Where have you been? Why haven't I seen you in all these months?"

She laughed and said, "I have been here all the while. But obviously, with all your women at your beck and call you couldn't even spare a moment to think of me."

He looked deeply into her eyes.

"Not true," he protested.

But of course it was true. He ruled arrogantly in the world of femininity. He cavorted among his abundantly diverse women: a fresh-faced English lass, a dusky Sicilian, a tall and elegant Parisian. He was a connoisseur of bow-shaped scarlet mouths, of opalescent teeth, long graceful necks, alabaster breasts, and soft white arms. He delighted in silk and satin, lace and feathers, the gentle radiance of baubles arrayed on low-cut bodices, musky fragrances riding the current of fluttering fans, gentle murmurs, and bright strains of laughter.

Rachel noticed that from time to time his attention strayed to the terrace. She saw her cousin Klara look up from her sketching and observe Joachim furtively with her pale blue eyes.

"She is married, you know," Rachel said. "And she is all of twenty-one. Older than you are!"

"Who?" he said, feigning innocence.

"Come now! You know who," she said with a bitter laugh. "She has lost no opportunity to preen herself before you."

Of course, this was no unaccustomed circumstance for him. Malkovitz knew that everything about himself stirred womanly attention – admiration, curiosity, a passion to know him more intimately – appetites he was always inclined to appease.

Rachel looked at him adoringly, her face delicately flushed at the cheeks, her lips smiling, her dark eyes beaming mischievously.

"Regretfully," he thought. "She is not beautiful."

He subjected her to a painstaking appraisal.

"Her mouth is too wide. Her nose a bit too long. Also in the minus column, she is given to loud, uncontrolled laughter," which was a lack of refinement that he found disconcerting.

"Furthermore, she is hardly a model of sagacity. Her head harbors a host of childish ideas. However, she does have robust health. And money."

Of course, one could not overlook the money, and the preeminent position the Hartensteins occupied in a dazzling social world.

"All in all," he concluded, "She is not unattractive."

"You have missed me," he teased.

"No," she said. "I haven't."

He pulled her toward him and said, "You can't deny it."

She looked with anxiety back to the ladies on the terrace.

"They are watching us," she said.

"So what," he replied. "We are not children anymore."

Then it dawned on him: Rachel was seventeen. She had reached marriageable age.

"A man could do a lot worse," he mused. Then he drew himself up short.

"What am I thinking! Not by the most extravagant reach of dreams would I ever be the Hartensteins' choice for such a match."

But then he thought, "Why not? Aren't I gentlemanly, chivalrous? Don't I have untiring energy and a confidence of manner? Certainly, these are qualities that must be enticing to a girl's doting parents."

In a calmer mental state he came to the realization that it was impossible. Impossible! He knew full well that he didn't have the wealth, the rank, or the family connections that would render him acceptable to Baron Hartenstein.

So, in characteristic fashion, he devised a motive to rationalize his circumstances.

"Why", he asked himself, "would I want to give up my freedom?"

Still, he could not resist spinning dreams of the life as Rachel's husband – a life that ascended like a tower into the heavens, a life of opulence and grandeur. In the vision of this new life, myriad luxuries came into view. They were so enthralling that the realm of his true existence perished completely. He dreamed of a town house in the city and a villa in the country. Of course he would have a picture gallery, and a library like the baron's. He would ride a chestnut hunter, and in town he would have a brougham – bright blue – and yes, a servant in brown livery.

He saw himself standing at his mantelpiece, one foot on the fender, his guests – bankers, politicians and statesmen, writers and poets – would sit smoking their pipes and cigars as he held forth on the Customs Union, the Eastern Question, and corruption in the civil service. He would not be outdone in erudition.

And, of course, there was that one diminutive word: bank. A wee word, yet one that conjured up epochs of grandeur.

Such were the images that invaded his mind as he contemplated the summons from Baron Hartenstein.

•

The next afternoon, Malkovitz traversed the linden-lined boulevard, approaching the gray granite edifice of the Hartenstein Bank. Baron Hartenstein had asked him to call!

"Judah Hartenstein." As Malkovitz spoke it silently to himself, his lips caressed the name. "Judah Hartenstein, the confidante of princes, architect of governments, a central figure in the life and times of the Germanic principalities, an intimate of the Rothschilds, the Warburgs, and of Gerson Bleichroeder, the financial advisor to Bismarck himself."

The footman ushered him into a marble-columned foyer, where a liveried page guided him along, hushed corridors lined with gleaming mahogany doors. The halls, which reached for such a long way that he felt that in some supernatural manner he had passed a limitless procession of rooms, reaching perhaps to infinity, into an unattainable void.

What went on behind those doors? He pictured rank upon rank of men with black cuffs over their sleeves, in row upon row of desks. They were bookkeepers, copyists, and clerks who recorded transactions, filed documents, and counted money in diverse foreign currencies and in unimaginably colossal denominations.

He was nervous. He reproached himself for his apprehension. After all, had he not been on the most intimate terms with the Hartenstein family?

Soon, he stood before lofty double doors flanked by marble columns - a salon in which the parquet was covered by softly yielding Turkish carpets. A silent, inert, and incorporeal antechamber, this room guarded the temple altar, the tabernacle - Baron Hartenstein's sanctum. After whispering his name to a somberly attired secretary, with a bow, the page left him, and the secretary ushered him into the salon to await the baron.

He looked about the room with curiosity. It was dazzlingly bright, with light flooding in from large windows that looked down upon a garden. But it was rather smaller than he had expected. A large cluttered desk with an inlaid leather top dominated the room. Family photographs in silver frames marched across the desktop, sharing space with ancient artifacts in marble and crystal – relics of the baron's travels, bestowals from world leaders, and mementos of commercial triumphs.

Opposite the windows, over the mantle, hung an imposing portrait of Judah Hartenstein's father Moses. He was standing against a deep red velvet background with his right hand in his pocket. His wig was powdered, his face was round and glowing, and his eyes shining. Somberly dressed in the formal style of the early 1800s, he wore a white silk cravat, lace at his wrists, and decorations on his breast and at his neck.

Promptly at four o'clock, Baron Hartenstein entered. He came in jauntily, smiling, both hands extended in warm welcome. Though middle-aged, the hair over his ears and in his beard was still dark. His eyes, like the eyes in his father's portrait, were bright and sharp.

Although Malkovitz knew very well that there could be no question about it – this was most certainly Judah Hartenstein –nevertheless, it seemed to him that the man before him was not real, but merely the representation, an icon of the great man, who himself must always remain mysteriously hidden from view.

Without delay, Baron Hartenstein launched into the subject of their meeting.

"Joachim, I have watched you grow into manhood, and I have often thought how proud your father would have been if only he could be here to see you today. How pleased he would be to know of your business success, and especially the way you conduct yourself. Your high moral standards, your keen wit and intelligence."

He placed his hand on Malkovitz' shoulder and looked into his eyes. Joachim trembled inwardly.

"You are dear to us," the baron said. "You know we think of you as one of the family. The baroness and I could not fail to notice how attentive you have been to Rachel, and she, I'm sure you know, thinks the world of you."

Joachim's heart was racing.

"And you have always been amiable and obliging," the baron continued.

Thus, Baron Hartenstein had reached the conclusion that given his many fine qualities, his unimpeachable moral standards, his physical vitality – Joachim Malkovitz would be eminently acceptable as a companion for his son.

•   •   •   •

5

HERSCHEL AND JOACHIM

They left the boat in Lauterbourg, the French frontier town on the Bavarian border, where they dined at an inn that was an ancient structure of whitewashed stucco and exposed wooden beams. Herschel had never seen an inn like this. The old beams were blackened, and the plank floor was scarred. The small panes of the window cast diamonds, and stripes, and shadows on the paneled walls. The hearth was a forest of black iron stakes, hooks, hobs, cranes, and pots.

Herschel's eyes fixed on Malkovitz. For several months now he had accompanied Malkovitz on his travels as he pursued his business interests throughout the Continent. Now, sitting with their legs outstretched, their heads resting on the backs of their chairs, Herschel wondered how he could have ever judged him so harshly. His thoughts took him back to the bright spring day at his sister Rachel's garden party. The laughter from the circle of frolicking girls had floated up to him. He saw that at every opportunity they had glanced furtively at Joachim, admiring him as he strolled in the garden, down the flag-stoned path before settling into a chair. Joachim had gazed back across the lawn, touching his brow with a silk handkerchief, combing a lock of hair on his fore-head with long, thin fingers.

Malkovitz' airs had offended Herschel. He had mocked Malkovitz's fashionable manner of dress, scorned his sophistication, his facile wit. Herschel thought of him as a wastrel and a playboy.

But then he had asked himself, "Why am I so exasperated by this popinjay? He means nothing to me. In fact, I hardly know him. Why am I so irritated by him?"

He speculated that it might be because of Malkovitz's way with the girls, or the spell he cast over his mother, or his father's admiration of his business acumen and his delight in his humor.

Then, suddenly, looming over him, there Joachim had stood, asking earnestly, "So, young man, how has the world been treating you?"

Though Herschel's response had been perfunctory and dismissive, Malkovitz had not been put off. He went on to recite a flood of accounts of his recent travels – dazzling entertainments, cafés, music halls, concerts, and plays – and an enchanting itinerary: London, Paris, and Vienna.

"Diversion, amusement, gaiety," Herschel had thought. "Is that all this man lives for?"

Could it be that it had been only a half year ago? It would have been unthinkable then that the detested Malkovitz would now be his comrade, his confidant.

Herschel's first intimation of Malkovitz' dramatic transformation had come some months after the party, in the library of the Hartenstein villa. Joachim had taken a book from the shelves. Leafing through it, he paused, then read aloud.

> *"Cosette and Marius fell on their knees, overwhelmed, choked with tears, each grasping one of Jean Valjean's hands. Those august hands moved no more. He had fallen backwards, the light from the candlesticks fell upon him; his white face*

looked up towards heaven. Cosette and Marius covered his hands with kisses; he was dead. The night was starless and very dark. Without doubt, in the gloom some mighty angel was standing, with outstretched wings awaiting the soul."

Listening to those words, Herschel felt that he had been endowed with a new spirit. Nothing he had ever learned from his tutors at home, or from the masters at the Akademie, had prepared him for the sweeping vision of humanist culture enshrined in the works of Victor Hugo. Joachim spoke of Hugo's portrayal of injustice, of his depiction of corruption and poverty. He spoke of a world in which unjust governments were overthrown and greedy landlords were swept away.

Long into the night they had talked about their lives and their prospects.

"What have you been doing with your time?" Joachim had asked.

"The Akademie, the library," Herschel said.

"That's all? What about life? Learning is laudable. It's fine in it's place, but it's not a way of life, is it?"

Herschel laughed bitterly and said, "It's not? What else is there?"

Joachim scoffed. "For one thing, there is joy! Life doesn't have to be a desperate business. Before you abandon yourself to drudgery, don't you think you should apply yourself to something adventurous?"

Herschel smiled desolately. He knew that he was not destined to have a legendary life.

•

They left the inn after lunch and returned to the boat, which by mid-afternoon had plied its way downriver. Herschel sat on the deck, his back against the cabin bulkhead, braced against the motion of the river. Supporting his diary in his lap, he wrote:

"The reverie of our quiet sojourn at the tavern in *Lautenburg* was rudely interrupted when the door suddenly flew open. Two boisterous soldiers burst in. Austrians. One wore the badge of a *Feldwebel*. Each embraced a giggling buxom Rhine maiden. Flushed with excitement, they ran to a table at the far side of the room, shouting raucously for the innkeeper.

"Soon, one toast after another rang out, and after the custom of these country people, with every toast they all rose, and with much hilarity, they violently clashed their steins together, slopping beer on the table and on the floor, and on each other.

"Later, when the boat's siren signaled the time for departure, the soldiers raced from the tavern with the girls close behind them. The *Feldwebel*, who had been particularly attentive to the youngest of them, a farm girl of about sixteen or seventeen, lingered behind the others with his fair companion. She was a bright, blooming lass, as plump as a partridge. The approaching departure of her lover had somewhat clouded her joyful animation. With a pensive look and a lingering step, she accompanied him to the *coche d'eau*, and as the 'all aboard' was shouted, he threw his arms around her. After a long, lingering kiss, he finally raced up the gangplank just as it was being withdrawn.

"The lasses waved their handkerchiefs and shouted *'leben sie wohl,'* which was returned by the two soldiers in louder and louder voices as the boat breasted the current. The *Feldwebel* remained at the rail, stretching his neck to catch one more glimpse of his fair one. She ran along the shore, waving her handkerchief. She quickened her pace, attempting to catch another, and yet another, view of her admirer. And when the trees edging the river obscured the boat, she mounted a hillock where still she stood waving farewell. She remained fixed as a statue, spreading her handkerchief to the wind, calling her last *Ich liebe dich* as the boat sailed around the promontory."

•

Herschel had observed the scene with a strange melancholy. Lounging on deck next to him, Malkovitz perceived his longing. He saw that a circle of animated German women had engaged Herschel's attention. The wind molded their filmy dresses to their bodies. Malkovitz viewed them despairingly.

"The ladies of our native Germany are too large for grace and elegance," he said. "Not as well-formed as Frenchwomen. And their countenances are less expressive than French or northern Italian ladies."

He paused in earnest deliberation. "Their faces have more color than those of the ladies of Paris, but they are lacking in the expression that forms the most striking feature of French beauty," he said. "And in our *Mädchen* there is nothing of that light airy tread that makes the *Parisiennes* the most beautiful objects on a promenade."

Joachim took Herschel's silence as assent. He continued his appraisal.

"Our women lack the grace, the light, airy step, the sylph-like forms you so frequently meet in the *Tuileries* and on the boulevards," he said.

Gravely, he pondered the problem.

"Could it be the large feet of our German ladies that is the principal cause of their want of grace? Yes, the heavy German tread, the moping walk, must be the cause of the want of la mode."

Herschel remained engrossed in the swiftly passing countryside.

Failing to provoke a response, Joachim said, "You must agree, nothing is as charming as the soft-flowing conversation of an animated Parisienne."

Herschel shrugged, feigning indifference. But in truth, he was tortured by his youth. He had never learned anything about women. They were a complete mystery to him. On many mornings he would awake with his heart pounding. He lay tangled in the twisted sheets, his nightshirt damp with perspiration. He had fantasies about some of the maidservants. Sometimes in the evening, he found some pretext to lurk near the servants' quarters, waiting surreptitiously for the steps of the parlor maids on their way to the bath.

"How does one behave with a woman?" he wondered. "What does one say to them?"

He saw this as a crushing failing. He felt incompetent and graceless. What must he learn in order to deal with a girl? How could he explain all this to Joachim, a self-made man who lived a glamorous, exciting life? Malkovitz traveled, attended the theater, and frequented cafés. Herschel could not burden him with these childish sentiments.

But Malkovitz, who never failed to read his thoughts, perceived his longing. He prodded him in the ribs, and smiling knowingly, he said, "We must find you a woman."

•

Herschel's red leather-bound Baedeker guide was by now showing signs of wear. It had accompanied them through France, Italy, and the Tyrol. Now in Cologne, Herschel and Malkovitz stood at the bottom of the winding stone steps at the entrance to the Church of Saint Ursala. A musky odor of damp and age mingling with incense rose from the catacombs. Joachim read from the guidebook.

"Here lay the skeletons of eleven thousand virgins, more or less perfectly preserved," he said. "They refused to renounce their belief in Christianity."

Joachim mocked their martyrdom, as he did all contrivances of religion. Leaving the church, they walked in the shadow of the lofty towers of Cologne, wandering along dirty, narrow, cobble-stoned streets, arriving finally at the Jesuit's Church, the repository of the crania of eighty saints. The skulls grinning up at them were adorned with crowns, their lower parts enveloped in red satin bordered in gold.

Later, Herschel wrote in his journal.

"In the church of the Jesuits we gazed up at a statue depicting Michael destroying Satan. Satan has horns, and his ears are large in the shape of a satyr. He twists his long tail about his legs like a snake. His face, a union of satyr, dragon, and monkey, is thrown into an expression unlike anything on earth."

Standing before the statue, Herschel felt a chill. Malkovitz laughed and said, "The only emotion it excites is ridicule. Yet the church knows full well that vulgar depictions such as this produce not a little effect on the ignorant poor. They instill in them such dread of the horns of the devil that to escape them, they count their beads and rain their *grochen* upon the priests."

•

Back on board they saw that their boat had taken on more passengers. They had boarded that morning from a caravan of diligences and post horses, which had carried them from warmer climes. Russian, German, French and English, the passengers were part of the legion of tourists dashing through the passes of the Alps and spreading like a fan over the north of Europe. They were students, dandies, half-pay officers, mothers, spinsters, maidens, princes, dukes, and soldiers.

"*Johann Bull* and *Onkel Sam* are everywhere," Herschel wrote. "One can't escape them. One can't enter a carriage or a hotel without hearing them exclaim 'Humbug!' and 'Nonsense!'

"The French speak of politics with surprising freedom, whereas at home when one speaks of politics it is the custom to look about to see who may be near. And who speaks of religion in public? It is virtually excluded as a topic of conversation.

"Italians speak with their hands. To make the picture more distinct, their hands and arms are thrown into a great variety of gestures of grace and elegance. They speak of nothing but music! I find that though their operas have a melody and a lyricism that is very pleasing, they are not comparable to the passion of the operas of Mozart – *Don Juan* or *Magic Flute* or Beethoven's *Fidelio*."

The sun cast the shadow of their boat on the western hills across the river. A rich flood of golden light shined upon the feudal ruins, which they saw as the boat wound around a bluff. Three or four decaying castles were visible at the same time. And then others came into view, their deep red sandstone still retaining its color even after six centuries.

Gazing across the water, Herschel's imagination restored the towers and the battlements which time had leveled. He peopled the castle with its chieftain and his band, and he stocked its storerooms with helmets, swords, and bucklers. He conjured up legends of chivalry, of gallant knights drawing their swords in defense of helpless damsels. He was transported to the days of their glory. He was lost in admiration of the valor of the conqueror.

"But people don't seek adventures any more," he thought, "At least not outside the covers of a book."

He often imagined that was what he was - a character in a book.

Herschel looked up from the swiftly moving river toward mid-ships, where Joachim was now in animated conversation with a crowd of travelers who had just returned from Italy. Herschel observed him with admiration, and some envy, for his urbanity and wit, for the ease with which he charmed strangers.

Joachim was the very embodiment of the new generation of thoughtful intellectuals Herschel so admired. He was one of the modern earnest young men of the 1860s.

· · · ·

6

THE FACE OF THE WORLD

Summer was drawing to a close when they arrived in London. The days were getting shorter, and already a few of the trees in the parks were turning gold and rust, and leaves drifted lazily to the ground. Small birds with bright crimson feathers darted here and there, settling on branches tinted gold by the fading sun. It was unseasonably warm. The temperature had reached eighty degrees. The newspapers reported that farmers had collapsed in the harvest fields, and horses had fallen dead on the road. Even in the evening the city was sweltering. Yet, undaunted by the heat, throngs of men and women in evening clothes gathered at theaters and restaurants. The air was heavy with the aroma of perfume, cigars and whiskey.

As Herschel and Joachim walked through the heart of London, they passed streets swarming with carts, drays, and handbarrows. There was an ear-splitting din. They heard coarse laughter, raucous music, and the clatter of hansom cabs on the cobbles. A cacophony of sounds assailed them. There were musicians – one-man bands, drums, violins, and bugles – that clashed with coaching horns, the screaming of racing urchins, the frenzied barking of dogs, and the exhortations of men who blacked shoes, sharpened knives, or sold pots, pans, and furniture.

Boys held placards and signs aloft, some of them staggering under the weight of gigantic papier-mâché replicas of umbrellas, huge walking teakettles, colossal hats, and monstrous pipes. Giant sausages, cigars, and immense laughing shoes were pulled along in dogcarts. All manner of monstrosities – bearded ladies, tattooed men, fire-eaters, dwarfs and giants – hawked circuses, fairs, music halls, and other entertainments. And everywhere on all the street corners, in the doorways, spilling out of the alleys – the outstretched hands of beggars confronted them.

Eventually they came to streets lined with aging houses. They walked past awninged shops of chemists, drapers, milliners, and wine merchants. They passed booksellers' stalls and curiosity shops. And finally they stood at the railing of London Bridge, staring down into the river in silence.

The Thames, a coal-black, foul-smelling stream awash in debris and waste, flowed sluggishly below. Globules of vapor arose from the depths of a long string of green slime pools lining the bank. Hovering in a haze that welled up from the tanneries, bone mills, and gasworks, the immense city – five million souls - was spread out before them like a slumbering giant.

"The smoke mixes with the dust of the mills," Malkovitz said, "causing all sorts of respiratory diseases. Bronchitis, pneumonia, asthma. And no one knows how many die from typhoid, typhus, influenza, and cholera. You have never seen a victim of cholera, have you? It's a frightening spectacle. Something outlandish and monstrous. Their skin turns a sort of bluish-grey. They die of thirst and dehydration, in agonizing pain."

The color drained from Herschel's face.

They walked on, past Shoreditch Station, turning into Hackney Road, a dismal street of poor shopkeepers. As they moved toward Bethnal Green the streets became more desolate. The passed Loan Street, Long Meadow, and Cronk Hill – narrow, winding streets lined with ancient tumble-down houses leaning one upon the other, their roofs aslant at perilous angles.

"Jo, what on earth are we doing here?" Herschel asked.

"You wanted to see the sights, didn't you?"

Stepping over heaps of waste and filth, they tried to avoid stagnant pools of urine and excrement. They wandered from one court to another, turning innumerable corners, through a labyrinth of tunnel-like passageways.

Herschel stopped suddenly. "We are lost. We will never find our way out!"

But finally, at the end of a narrow alley they spied the rusting iron girders of the railroad bridge, and they were able to get their bearings. In the shadow of the bridge there was a court, the filth and dreadfulness of which exceeded the other yards by far. It was lined on three sides by two- and three-story houses – a jumble, one on top of the other, back-to-back. On the open side there was a pigpen into which several inhabitants of the court were throwing their garbage and offal. The air was unbreathable. In the yard there was a wash house, a water pump, and an uncovered privy that was a deep hole dug in the corner.

"A hundred people share this privy," Malkovitz said.

Herschel's stomach turned over. He shuddered with revulsion. Nearby, a dozen people stood at a pipe, holding pans and bottles for drinking water. A foul drain oozed into the yard from the neighboring court.

"That water," Malkovitz said, "water they drink and cook with, is mixed with ashes and filth. You can see the drainage is very bad here. Cesspools overflow on rainy days, spilling into the cellars where dozens of workers live. The soakage contaminates the wells. That's the cause of diarrhea and the main killer of children. At St. Mary's and St. Bart's they will tell you that in the last ten years over thirty-five thousand infants have died here. Decomposing filth from sewers and cesspools spreads smallpox, diphtheria, cholera, typhus, and what they call 'bowel fever' - typhoid, the most lethal and dreaded disease."

Herschel stared at the half-naked children playing listlessly near the overflowing garbage barrels. Their eyes were large in pale, pinched faces.

Taking Herschel by the arm, Malkovitz drew him into one of the tenements. The dark hallway gave off an overpowering odor of cabbage and rotting fish. Several doors stood open. One room was lit only by the end of a sputtering tallow candle and a feeble flame in the grate. Tattered laundry hung from a line strung across the room. A damp chill was in the air.

A large group of people gathered listlessly about the fire, waiting their turn to prepare their food: a bit of fish or scraps from a barrel. Several people – how many Herschel couldn't count – sat and slept on narrow benches that lined the walls. Some bedded down in the corners on heaps of rags. A few gaunt women and emaciated children sat at a table in the middle of the room, gluing matchboxes and putting buttons on cards. They looked up at Herschel without curiosity, no emotion at all registering on their faces.

Echoing down a steep staircase they heard wild shouting, cursing, and drunken laughter. Reluctantly, Herschel followed Malkovitz up perilously unstable steps. On the first landing there were two rooms.

"Ten or twelve people probably occupy each of these rooms," said Malkovitz. "The elderly, children, infants, men, women, all thrown together. They sleep in the one room, and they take in lodgers in order to gain an extra shilling or two a week. They rent a corner to three or four workingmen, perhaps a half-dozen, who share the beds, sleeping in shifts."

Roaches scurried as they made their way down a narrow, vermin-infested hallway. Herschel shrank from contact with the damp viscid walls, which were coated with fungus and mold. He pressed a kerchief to his mouth and nose. He was at the point of gagging.

In one of the rooms a tall, withered woman stood before a stained wooden table. She stared at them. But her face showed no fear or curiosity. Instead, she looked at them with a harsh, defiant glare. Herschel saw that a child, a girl, he believed, was sleeping on a cot against the wall. An older girl, perhaps eight or nine, wearing only a threadbare chemise, her shoulders and arms bare, ran to her mother and grasped her legs. Ignoring the woman, Malkovitz entered the room.

Herschel was astounded. "Jo, what in the world are you doing? Where are you going?"

Malkovitz beckoned to him. "Don't worry. They don't care."

Herschel paused apprehensively at the doorway. Ignoring the woman, Malkovitz lectured on, his voice flat, uninflected by emotion.

"This is probably home to a whole family," he said. "They are consumptive, many of them syphilitic. They are stunted by malnutrition and crippled by rickets."

He gestured toward a corner, to a pile of rags that vaguely, had a human form.

"They lay sick in the dark like wounded animals, and when they die they are swept out like so much litter."

He paused, then said, "The only way out of here is death. And it comes often."

Herschel wondered, when they die, what evidence there was that they had ever lived. He looked about him. He saw the pathetic possessions of a lifetime - a fragment of rag, a piece of string, stained newspapers, and a stale crust, which certainly was destined to be spirit away by the rats.

•

On the street, Herschel collapsed against a wall. His mind reeled. He was nauseated and exhausted. "Appalling!" he cried.

He could find no more words to express his revulsion.

"Now you have stared into the face of the world," Malkovitz said. "Now you see the brutish face behind society's mask of morality."

Herschel, his face wan and pinched, his nostrils still filled with the stench of the tenement, reflected on Joachim's words. He pondered what he had seen. Certainly he had known that poor people lived in slums, and of course he knew that they were dreadful places. But never before had he been brought face to face with naked, abject poverty.

Herschel followed Malkovitz along the street, oblivious of the jostling passersby. They walked out of the neighborhood to a tavern and found seats on a bench near the door. Malkovitz looked at Herschel's ashen face.

"Don't you wonder how people can slumber blithely in the comfort of their homes, insensible to the misery of others?"

Herschel was overwhelmed with shame. He knew that his own existence was utterly trivial. He sat silently for a time. Then he spoke quietly.

"I am concerned about people, about ordinary people, but is it wrong to think first about my family, about myself?"

Malkovitz smiled benevolently.

"I don't find fault with you. I don't judge you. I don't think I am superior to you. Only you can decide what is right for yourself."

But Herschel took Malkovitz' words as a rebuke, an unspoken challenge to look at the world in a way that is not at all agreeable or gentle.

"I know you must despise me. I admit that I may dwell too much on my own pleasures and not enough on the lives of others. But I am not cold-hearted."

"No, of course you aren't, but in order to have a true understanding of the world you have to see it as it really is, not as it is portrayed in romantic novels, not from the isolation of your sheltered existence."

Shadows crept into the corners of the room. The day was drawing to a close The barmaid replaced their tankards on the table. Malkovitz tapped Herschel on the knee.

"Do you see why I feel as strongly as I do, that life is worth living only if a man has some spark of sensitivity in him? Life is worth living only to the man who devotes himself to helping people in need."

Herschel had been listening intently. "Are you saying that you can't live honorably, decently, without giving up your life?"

"No," Malkovitz answered. "I don't intend to abandon my life to pursue some monastic existence. I don't intend to give up all worldly pleasures. God knows, I don't argue with any diversion that isn't sordid or brutal. But I refuse to participate in an indecent contest for cash and status. I should hate to continue living a life that is mawkish and insincere. I should hate to live, as I have been living, scrabbling for profit, pretending not to see duplicity, justifying chicanery. If I give up my life - what some people consider 'the good life,' - it is only because of my desire to be a man of my time."

•   •   •   •

7

A CHAMPION OF THE POOR

To Herschel it was a mystery. He was confounded. The
Malkovitz that Herschel knew was preoccupied with the
realm of the purse, with the world of great homes and fashionable clothes, and perhaps above all, with the right social
milieu. Herschel believed that Malkovitz' owed all his gentil-
ity and refinement to diligent observation of the thorough-
breds of society. He was inspired by their dress and attuned
to the nuances of their speech. Herschel was convinced that
life for Malkovitz was an ardent pursuit of personal advance-
ment. He was certain that politics and the plight of the disadvantaged had never even penetrated his consciousness.

But Malkovitz could point to the very moment when he
first became concerned with the condition of the oppressed
classes, which is what he now considered them to be.

A few months earlier, before he had begun his journey
with Herschel, he found himself in unaccustomed circumstances. He was ensconced in an elegant salon in the midst
of a political soiree. He sat perched uncomfortably on a
spindly gilt chair in the grand ballroom of a stately Viennese
mansion. He was ill at ease. He was restless. Speakers droned

on. He endured them impatiently, finally seeking diversion in carnal contemplation of a shapely, plainly dressed young woman.

His attendance at this gathering he owed to being a criminal. Wasn't he entitled to call himself a criminal? After all, he had been unceremoniously taken into custody by the *Polizei* during a brawl on the docks.

On that day, a brisk breeze swept the wharf of the Hanseatic Shipping Company. Mingled odors of tar, fish, oil, and coal drifted in the air.

Malkovitz had come to the warehouses on the landing stage to watch his goods being unloaded. As always, the respectful salute of the watchmen at the gate gratified him, and he took great pleasure in the formalities of the custom shed: the lists, the duty forms, manifests, shipping instructions, and bills of lading, all of which he perused punctiliously. He stood at the window, his thumbs thrust into waistcoat pockets, looking down at the long ranks of storehouses and quays, watching the dancing masts of the coastal schooners, the stacks of the side-wheelers belching black smoke, and the long-reaching cranes extending arms out over the water, arching into yawning holds. He enjoyed the commotion of the men of the docks shouting to one another in a babble of foreign tongues. With a proprietary eye, as if they were toiling exclusively in his service, he observed the swaggering, bearded, tattooed sailors, the wharfmen and haulers in their knee breeches, the brawny, tobacco-spitting stevedores, and the shippers and carters, whips in hand, standing by their sway-backed dray horses, which restlessly struck their hooves against the planks of the landings.

But on this day, because the tumult was out of the ordinary, he had descended to the wharf to stand at the verge of a milling crowd. He listened to a man who had climbed to the topmost of a stack of crates and bales. The man was small and thin, and he was dressed in a threadbare seaman's jacket. Some of the dockworkers were agitated with drink, but most of them were earnestly engrossed, and they pressed in closely to hear the speaker, whose reedy voice was barely audible above the clamor of the crowd. He was pale and pathetic. His arms jerked spasmodically as he railed against working conditions on the docks. Passion impelled him, and he exuded an enthusiasm that stirred the crowd.

"Obviously," thought Malkovitz, "he is a paid provocateur, a professional rabble-rouser."

The throng, growing restless, shouted and hooted. An occasional word was carried on the wind. "Socialist pimp!" someone cried.

"Capitalist whore!" came the rejoinder, followed by stomping, whistling, booing, and hissing.

Shouting and roaring followed, then curses and vile oaths. Inevitably, there came the howling and the sputtering, the jostling and the punching. Pushing and pulling led to scuffling, then wrestling. Solid blows sent men battered and lame from the docks and warehouse sheds.

Malkovitz shrank back from the melee and watched with disdain. He considered the demonstration to be senseless. He viewed the tumultuous crowd with contempt.

Then, above the sound of the crowd, shrill police whistles rent the air. A harsh cry went up. The horde retreated before the advancing *Polizei*, who lashed out with lead-weighted canes. The crowd, enraged, countered with crowbars and belaying pins. They kicked at the policemen with their heavy boots and struck out at them with barrel staves. But the police pushed forward. The howling mob retreated before them. Some stumbled, fell to the ground, and were trampled. Some were pursued through the length of the wharf to the end of the pier, where they tumbled into the oily river.

In the panic that ensued, Malkovitz was lifted from his feet by the howling crowd and was carried along the wharf toward the gate, which the police had barricaded.

Later, in the long line formed to facilitate the interrogation of those arrested in the demonstration, Malkovitz, sputtering with indignation, furiously surveyed the damage to his clothing. He found himself standing behind an exceedingly thin, long-limbed man of considerable years and obvious distinction. Turning to Malkovitz, he bowed from the waist. A smile glinted brightly on his face, which was flushed with excitement.

"von Escher," he proclaimed. "Baron Wolfgang von Escher."

Malkovitz, in return, brought his heels together and inclined his head smartly. "MalKOvitz" he replied, laying stress on the penultimate syllable in the Russian manner.

•

Malkovitz learned that Baron von Escher believed himself to be a gentleman of affairs, though the precise nature of his affairs defied definition. Over the years his opinions and loyalties ranged widely over the entire political spectrum, from left to right and back again. Perhaps in a confusion of objectives animated by his advanced years, he no longer had any fellow-feeling for the aristocracy or the mercenary capitalist. He now had an overabundance of compassion for human wretchedness. He had become an ardent, generous benefactor of liberal social causes. Thus, his ballroom, in which Malkovitz was seated, had become a magnet for faded aristocrats, Bohemian artists and poets, impoverished students, and freethinking professors, advocates all of causes lost and found.

Malkovitz' mind wandered restlessly. Finally, he rose and sauntered across the room to stand at the side of the tall, tawny girl he had been observing. She listened intently to a disheveled, bearded, bear-like man who lumbered before the tall, arched windows.

"Class warfare… the proletariat," the man cried out.

Searching for an appropriate conversational gambit, Malkovitz whispered, "Who is he?"

She looked at him, astonished.

"Marx," she said.

"Who?" Malkovitz asked.

"Karl Marx," she replied, her arched eyebrows revealing incredulity.

Then, to Malkovitz's amazement, the young woman, in a loud and clear voice, suddenly addressed the room. She spoke with great passion of the need for measures to benefit health and education, of the futility of trying to bring compassion or common sense into politics. With her glowing face and angry dark eyes, she looked fierce and indomitable. This was not at all the mild, shy, modest maiden Joachim Malkovitz had been taught to admire. She was, in fact, one of several educated, emancipated Englishwomen present that day in Vienna who had lately entered the arena of radical thought and revolutionary politics. Her name, he found out later, was Frieda Boté.

Taken aback by her boldness, Malkovitz drew away from her. He sank into a chair, lolling nonchalantly, hoping to convey to anyone who might be observing a general sense that no woman's opinions could possibly be worthy of his attention. But, in truth, he was intrigued.

"This one is courageous," he thought. "In some ways even ferocious. Obviously, she would be completely undaunted by any obstacle. Nothing would stand in her way."

He had never before been in the presence of such a woman as this Frieda Boté. Female innocence was Malkovitz' ideal. In fact, it was female ignorance. He joined ladies and children together as innocent and gullible beings. He, and male society in general, treated "the ladies" like children.

"Notwithstanding her plain, unfashionable, and somewhat careless mode of dress, she is a curiously attractive animal," he thought. "She moves with feline grace. A feral heat emanates from her. Beneath my station, no doubt of that, but if nothing else, she is a pleasant distraction from the incessant nattering of this boring afternoon."

Frieda had noticed him. She saw that he was a gentleman, several cuts above the other men present. She found him interesting.

•

That evening, Malkovitz lay in bed reflecting on the events of the day. This Frieda Boté, though she certainly exuded sensuality, reminded him not at all of the easy women of his acquaintance – the actresses he escorted to candlelit suppers in private rooms of restaurants, the women he met in his travels, in the cafés, or the *gasthausen*. He was perplexed. He had always considered himself to be an authority of the *metier de femme*. He categorized womankind with the same calculating diligence that he applied to his business. He measured women by their delicate nature. He judged them by their physical qualities, their poses, and their attitudes. He was inspired and enlivened by the sensitivities of the female – their delicacy, coquetry, and artfulness. He loved the complex maze of love – the flirtation, the tryst, the jealousy, and the elaborate mendacity. He believed that in the end, the labyrinth of feminine ways and wiles all led to the same place and accomplished the same end: the stimulation of the emotions of man. Woman's vocation, he held, is man's gratification.

"But this Frieda," he mused, "She puzzles me. Here is a female who does not fit the usual pattern. This is a girl, this Frieda Boté, who apparently even takes up a book!"

•

Later, when he reflected on the circumstances of his first meeting with Frieda, he cursed himself for a fool. He had entered into one of those conversations in which every subject he raised proved to be irrelevant to her. He talked about Bernhardt at the *Comedie Francaise*, Berlioz in Baden Baden, Verdi in St. Petersburg, and the International Exhibition in London. He conjured up vivid images of the nightlife of Berlin and Paris. He boasted of the banquets he had attended. He invented elaborate tales of his years in the Prussian cavalry. He hinted at the mistresses he had had and the duels he had fought.

She was silent and unresponsive. She took no pains to hide her disinterest from him. He cursed himself.

"Of the many things I could have told her that might have appealed to her intellectual inclinations – my scholarly attainments, my influential friends, my mercantile triumphs – what possessed me to boast to her, this serious girl, of my preoccupation with amusement?" he thought.

He was unfamiliar with rejection, and her indifference wounded him. Since it was impossible for him to draw the line between the real and the romantic, her reticence transformed her into an extraordinary being. He speculated about the gentle undulation of her body, unfettered by stays and corsets. He was overwhelmed with desire.

"*Gott in Himmel!*" he thought. "Those eyes really bore into you! And that dusky complexion!"

•

He saw Frieda often in the ensuing months on his frequent business trips to London. She subjected him to a hectic life of journeys, meetings, debates, and lectures. They visited factories, mills, and mines. They went to slum neighborhoods and the hovels of the poor. He met many of her comrades, who at first he thought were arrogant and treacherous. He believed that they would drag the world down about their ears. But in time he changed his mind. Gradually, he came to understand that many decent educated young people were being caught up in the great wave of social agitation that was washing over Europe. Even some of his old Lübeck gymnasium classmates, and many of his companions at the *Hofbräuhaus*, were railing against the harsh working conditions in the mines and factories.

"Does it make sense," Frieda asked him, "to persist in your old views when your companions are against them? Wouldn't it make more sense to be swept along with the tide rather than resist it?"

For Frieda's benefit, Malkovitz assumed what he solemnly believed was a benevolent attitude. Philanthropy was the solution to the plight of the poor; food and shelter was the answer.

"You are deceiving yourself," Frieda argued. "You want to believe that when you drop a few pence into the collection plate you have done your duty."

What he observed as the wretched ignorance of the poor, Frieda saw as brave, long-suffering endurance.

"I will not rest until our blighted political system that promotes harsh affliction is defeated." Frieda said.

When she cursed the capitalists, saying, "They are tyrants and oppressors, ruthless exploiters of the downtrodden masses,"

Malkovitz's mind instantly leaped to Judah Hartenstein.

•

Though several months had passed since his ignominious encounter with Hartenstein, every macabre detail, every moment of humiliation he suffered at that fateful meeting remained fixed in his thoughts. He couldn't cope with the fact that it had never even crossed Judah Hartenstein's mind to consider him as a suitor for Rachel's hand.

His mind recoiled from the memory of that day, and of his headlong dash from the ominous, cold, granite Hartenstein Bank, down the long avenue of trees, as far from the hostile edifice as his infirm legs would carry him. His memory took him repeatedly to the corner opposite the bank, where on that afternoon he had remained frozen, pale with shock and humiliation, as he attempted to quell the chaos of his mind, while the sound of the traffic in the street roared in his ears like waves pummeling the shore.

Whenever he thought of that dark day he cursed himself. He, a man who took such pride in his self-assurance, who took so much satisfaction in his facility with words, had been struck dumb! His face burned when he recalled that in response to Hartenstein's outrageous proposal, he had even forced a smile!

Later, of course, he thought of all the things he might have said or should have said. But upon calm reflection, he congratulated himself on his forbearance. Somehow, something deep within his psyche had taken control of his propensity to lash out in anger, and it warned him not to clash with Hartenstein.

And his innate sense of worth shielded him from the worst punishment of all: self-condemnation. He did not rebuke himself, though he could not deny that he wished he had never thought the thoughts or dreamed the dreams that had brought this ignominy down upon him. Still, he was unrepentant. He did not cringe, though a small inner voice may have whispered that he had been imprudent, perhaps even presumptuous, or that he may have overreached and possibly earned some measure of his humiliation.

But then his abundant ego helped him to retain his balance. His appetite for power had been whetted, and he was utterly convinced that he would achieve it. His prodigious imagination took over. Inspired by Frieda Boté, he began to imagine himself as a radical and a reformer.

"Why not? Why couldn't I be a benevolent champion of the poor? I would support 'the advancing self-affirmation of the proletariat,'" appropriating the language from one of Frieda's tracts.

To Malkovitz, the character of the deed mattered little. He could be equally satisfied with a munificent self-sacrifice, a noble act of heroism, or with an inspiring falsehood, even a brilliant crime, as long as it was an exploit with a thunderbolt of melodrama in it.

So, he began to sketch out a new existence. He would lead the secret life of the revolutionary!

• • • •

8

A GATHERING AT THE BOTÉ'S

The Boté's house was once red brick, but it had long since been blackened by soot and grime. Two small windows flanked the scarred door, which was reached by three cracked stone steps. In one window a forlorn yellow shade was drawn down to the sill. The other was missing a pane, replaced by a newspaper, which sun and rain had faded and stained. A few old men shuffled by in the fog, their shoulders hunched against the damp.

After a brief wait, Frieda Boté admitted Herschel and Joachim. When her eyes met Malkovitz's, she assumed an attitude of studied indifference.

They followed her into a shabbily furnished parlor, dimly lit by two hissing gas jets, which cast long shadows of the half-dozen occupants onto the walls. A gaunt, reedy, middle-aged man paced restlessly before a hearth in which a coal fire smoldered.

"The majority has the right of establishing its will by force," he lectured. "The individual must give way before the general welfare."

This was Alfons Boté, Frieda's father. He was a bookseller and author, a publisher of tracts, pamphlets, and leaflets that were poorly printed on soiled paper and delivered by a motley collection of comrades to schools, mill gates, and workingmen's drinking establishments, where most of them fell from indifferent hands into the gutter.

Alfons Boté, a peripatetic talker, was, he often said, tired of words. He longed for deeds. These were not, to be sure, to be performed personally. He knew, by virtue of his intellectual standing, that he was destined for a position of authority and influence. That fate had denied him his due, fueled his demonic aspirations and left him with a festering anger.

He and Frieda lived in three rooms on the ground floor of the house. A print shop occupied a shed attached to the kitchen at the rear. The upper-floor rooms were rented to transient travelers, most of whom found the location, a quiet narrow street near the rail station, convenient for their continued journeys north to the industrial cities. Like Joachim and Herschel, some of the Boté's lodgers came to London from the Continent, on what business they never said, appearing mysteriously without notice and disappearing as they came, wraithlike.

Tonight, Boté addressed his meager audience: a retired teacher whose bald dome reflected the light from the gas lamp, an artis t who dressed the part, in a flowing cravat and a commodious cloak, an artisan whose habit it was to puff out his cheeks as a preamble to expressing his opinion, a university student who observed the proceedings with hooded eyes, stifling an occasional yawn, and sitting apart from the others – not by choice - an unkempt laborer who, it appeared, was not on familiar terms with soap and water.

Professor Boté spoke with great passion of the rising laboring class, which would soon cast out kings, nobles, and priests.

"We will take back what has been stolen from us by the bourgeoisie," Boté preached. "The benefits of industry will for the first time raise living standards for everyone, not just the rich."

Even as he spoke, peasant riots were erupting across the
Continent. Disturbances had swept Russian universities, and
mysterious fires had broken out in St. Petersburg and in a
number of towns along the Volga. Leaflets urging revolution
had appeared in Russian cities. And now Poland was on the
verge of erupting in a rebellion against Russian rule.

"A boiling over is coming," Boté´ said. "And the new ruling class, the proletariat, will take charge. Most of the func-
tions of the state will disappear. The need for government
will be reduced to almost nothing."

Frieda interjected, "The government – all governments -
are frustrating the people's dreams, obstructing their efforts,
their struggles, and all their benevolent labors," she said.
"Corrupt governments have dragged all of human society
into corruption."

Observing Herschel's astonishment, Joachim smiled
broadly.

"Frieda Boté is certainly a new experience for Herschel."

She lectured on in a proud, incisive voice.

"Equal political and economic rights," she said. "An equal
moral standard, equal status for married women..."

Her temerity scandalized Herschel. He thought that she
must be one of those modern women, "feminists" he believed
they called them – women who assaulted society with their
bizarre attire and aggressive behavior.

"Why," he wondered, "do girls want to take on such tire-
some responsibilities?"

•

It was late. One by one the others had departed. Malkovitz
had gone to his room, and Herschel, fascination overcoming
his timidity, lingered to talk with Frieda.

"Here is a girl who is alien and exotic," he mused.

Certainly she bore not the remotest resemblance to
the gentle, overbred, frail flowers of femininity he knew.
He thought of his sister and her friends. They were pretty,

delicate maidens in trailing gowns, with froths of lace coyly revealing décolletage, hair elaborately coifed, and painted fans dancing in white-gloved hands.

Never before had he met an earthy, plain-speaking, strong-willed girl like Frieda Boté.

He and Frieda talked into the night. He learned that she was one of those women who questioned the traditional notion that a female's exclusive goal is wedlock.

"Marriage is of no importance to the main purpose of my life," she told him. "Marriage would stifle my ability to contribute anything of value to the community. As for childbearing, it serves no purpose to go on producing human beings merely in order that they would produce others in an endless process of procreation."

She shocked him with her language, using words like "pregnancy" and "prostitution," which women in society referred to only in genteel elusions. To his amazement and embarrassment, she discussed homosexuality and lesbianism quite openly. She weighed the advantages of various birth control devices, which were subjects of mystery and misinformation even to young men, certainly including himself. In her candor, she was unselfconsciously bold. She had never been taught to think of sex as indecent.

She paced the room restlessly as she talked, breathing rapidly. Furtively, he watched her breasts gently rising and falling. When she sought the warmth of the fireplace she boldly raised her skirt, extending a damp boot toward the hearth, revealing her ankle. In the flickering flames, her face was framed in a curve of dark hair that streamed over her cheek. By the glow of the fire, Herschel could make out the curve of her body through the folds of her dress. Each time she raised her arm, her dress gave an upward twist, and he followed the gradually paling shadow cast down her neck. He stared at her, bathing her in admiration.

Frieda, looking at Herschel, saw a serious, formal, bashful schoolboy. He was a slender boy of medium height, dressed neatly in a blue coat and vest and dark-blue trousers, a style that the Germans had copied from the English. His face was lean and his features soft. He expressed himself shyly but amiably. She thought he possessed everything that a young man should have, even, behind his spectacles, blue eyes that were appealing and expressive. He reminded her of old sepia photographs of somber young men engaged in artistic endeavors, or of those romantic etchings by Gessner and Goldsmith that depicted young lovers by a stream in some hidden glade. She was certain that he had never before even been alone in a room with a woman. Of course Frieda perceived his longing. She was amused.

•

Herschel sat on the edge of the bed in the garret bedroom of the Boté's humble house. He felt the chill from the plaster walls fall on his shoulders like the touch of a damp cloth. Pallid light from the street lamp entered through uncurtained windows. He looked down on the rain-polished roofs of the brick buildings opposite, and beyond them to the crooked streets disappearing in the mist that rose up in the moonlight. His thoughts lingered on Frieda. Just the sound of her voice, or the sight of her person, stirred the voluptuousness of his musings. His attraction to a sensual, sophisticated, worldly girl who was older than he, brought his heart to the breaking point.

Idle and dreamy, he wondered, "Could it be that I might find what I have missed in life in this girl?"

Finally, he slept, giving himself up to shadowy dreams, schemes, and fantasies of the future.

• • • •

9

THE REAL WORLD

Herschel followed Frieda into the tumult of a market square. Out of the night came a relentless pandemonium the shrill voices of hordes of hagglers mingling with the bawling of street vendors. On the south end of the square, a swarm of rowdy children was laughing and screaming and leaping in and out of a fountain from which a paltry stream of water issued.

As they walked into a neighborhood of narrow, mysterious streets that streamed in the night, fog began to obliterate the rising moon and the first early stars. A flickering streetlamp cast their shadows onto the walls of a red brick factory building that loomed up before them.

They entered and proceeded down a long, dark passageway, then up three flights of narrow, precarious stairs. Herschel breathed in a musky odor of rot, of unwashed bodies, and mouse droppings. He heard a strange, sharp thwacking sound reverberating in the distance.

The office they entered was oppressively hot and damp. It was crowded with old worktables and desks that were nicked, stained, and burned in spots. It was deserted; the managers and office workers had long since departed. Warily, Herschel followed Frieda to another room where two men sat at a table, awaiting them.

One of them Frieda knew well. He was a gaunt young man, Wadizlaw Franzos, a medical intern at St. Pancras Hospital. The other man, name of Silas Greenleaf, smiled ingratiatingly. He had an oily, pockmarked face, a sleek head of black, pomaded hair, and protuberant red-rimmed lips. The union had sent him to be their guide through the mill.

They followed Greenleaf down a long ochre-painted corridor. The mysterious sound followed them, growing louder, echoing off the walls. It was a loud, rapping noise – insistent and rhythmic – reminding Herschel of a stick striking the pickets of a fence. In the background there was a humming sound, a relentless drone, like the swarming of an enormous hive of bees.

When they opened the door at the end of the corridor the din burst upon them in a crescendo. The noise was deafening. They entered a long, dimly lit, high-ceilinged room that was suffused in a kind of hovering haze. The air was misted with minuscule specks of lint, the fine filaments floating eerily in the dim light, like snowflakes drifting lazily from the sky.

The windows in the room were closed; there was no visible source of ventilation of any kind. The air reeked of sweat, grease, and gas, which leaked out of the lamps hanging from the ceiling. In one corner an ink-stained sink was awash with foul water. Barrels lining the walls were filled to overflowing with scraps and rags.

In the middle of the room was the source of the mysterious sound. Reaching far into the gloom were row upon row of looms. Before the clattering machines, Herschel saw more than one hundred children. They were engaged in a grotesque ballet – bending and bowing, crouching and reaching, twisting and turning. They worked without pause, slaves to the relentless machines that clacked like the rattling of bones.

"Have you ever seen a more pathetic collection of boys and girls?" Frieda asked.

Herschel saw that their complexion was sallow and their hair was thin and straight. Many of them walked lamely. They stood before the looms in all the shapes of the letters of the alphabet. Herschel looked at the emaciated children sadly.

"You see how low their stature is?" Franzos said. "Their limbs are slender and ungraceful. Their backs are crooked, and they have a general bowing of the legs. You notice the peculiar flatness of their features? It's caused by the lack of adipose substance to cushion out the cheeks."

Tears formed in Herschel's eyes.

"They have an appearance that tells the world that they have been cheated of life," Frieda said.

Franzos spoke with a Slavic accent, Herschel thought – that was more pronounced in the angry rush of his words.

"This is the effect of prolonged toil on the tender frames of children at an early age," Dr. Franzos said. "A continuity of toil in a standing posture, in a poisonous environment, during thirteen hours a day or more."

Greenleaf, the union man, puffed up with self-importance and anxious to flaunt his expertise on matters such as these, spoke up.

"On the loom, at the top of the spindle, you see there is a fly that goes across? Note how the lad takes hold of the fly in his left hand."

The child, a boy of nine or ten, threw his left shoulder up and his right knee inward.

"He has the thread to get with the right hand, and he has to stoop his head down to see what he is doing."

Franzos said, "That's why all the children have a permanent bend in the right knee. The pelvis yields beneath the opposing downward pressure, the legs curve, and in consequence of this general yielding and bending of its parts, the whole body loses height."

A sad-eyed little boy, bent under the burden of an enormous load of bobbins, stopped to make a delivery to a nearby loom. He wore only a shirt and pants; he had no shoes or stockings. He looked at them curiously. Herschel walked over to him.

"How old are you?" Herschel asked.

"Nine, sir," the boy said.

"How much are you paid?"

"Penny an hour."

"At what hour do you start work?"

"At six."

Frieda said, "That is very early. Supposing you are not on time in the morning, what is the consequence?"

The boy frowned. He looked at Frieda quizzically.

"I mean, if you are late, what happens?" Frieda asked.

"We are quartered," the boy said.

"What do you mean, 'quartered'?"

"For every quarter of an hour we is late, they take off half an hour from our pay."

"Are you generally here on time?"

"Oh yes. My mother has been up since four o'clock. The colliers go to their work about three or four o'clock, and when she hears them stirring she has got up out of her bed and shook me. I have sometimes been at work at two o'clock in the morning, when it was streaming down with rain."

"When you get home at night," Herschel asked, "have you any time to be with your parents?"

"All that we do when we get home is to get the little bit of supper and go to bed. If the supper has not been ready directly, we have gone to sleep while it was cooking."

Franzos took hold of the boy's shoulder and gently turned him toward the others.

"You see the roundness of his back, the hunching of the shoulders? Remaining in one position for a series of hours, one set or system of muscles alone is called into activity. It cannot be wondered that the effects are injurious to the physical growth of a child."

He looked at the boy's wasted condition. "You see the consequences of malnutrition?"

"How much time is allowed for your meals?" Herschel asked.

"Fifteen minutes at noon," the boy said. "When the work is busy, we have no time to eat at all."

"What do you eat?"

"Onion porridge and oatcake."

A young girl tending the loom nearby listened to them as best she could over the hissing and clatter of the machines. She broke in, her voice raised over the din of the loom.

"The porridge being covered with dust, we often cannot eat it at all. When we don't eat it we are obliged to leave it for the overlooker. He takes it and gives it to his pigs."

Herschel saw that she was just a child, an adolescent.

"How old are you?" he asked.

"Thirteen," the girl said.

She was pretty in a delicate way. Immense eyes dominated her face. Her hair fell over her damp forehead. She wore only a dirty linen shift. She was barefoot. Her arms were thin, and her collarbones protruded. She had no sign of breasts.

"What do you do here?" Herschel asked.

"I'm a doffer," the girl said.

"What does a doffer do?"

"When the frames is full, you have to stop them and take the flyers off and take the full bobbins off, and carry them to the roller. And then put empty ones on and set the frame going again."

"You are constantly on your feet?"

"Yes."

Herschel marveled at the ease with which the girl conversed with him. She answered matter of factly, accepting his cross-questioning without apparent resentment.

"At what age did you first go to work?" Herschel asked.

"Eight or nine," the girl said.

Franzos looked at her closely. "This lass will in all likelihood have trouble in childbirth. Many of these girls do. Because they stand in an upright posture for long periods, the pelvis is prevented from being properly formed. Instead of developing an oval aperture, it forms a triangular one. In these circumstances sometimes there is not enough space for the exit of the baby."

"How long do you stand at the machine?" Herschel asked.

"From six in the morning to eight at night. When trade is brisk, from five in the morning to nine at night."

Herschel said, "It must be a very grievous hardship to be roused so early in the morning?"

"Yes. I is most generally lifted out of bed, sometimes asleep, by my ma."

"Do the rest of the children here have to rise at a similar time?" he asked.

"Yes, all of us. But they is not all of them so far from their work as I is."

"How far do you live from the mill?" he asked.

"About two miles."

"What happens if you are late?"

Herschel noticed that the girl glanced apprehensively at the union man standing with them.

"I is beaten," she said softly. "When I is got up in the morning the fear of that is so great, that I run and cry all the way."

"Suppose you flag a little in doffing?"

"They strap us."

"Are they in the habit of strapping those who are slow?"

"Yes."

"Constantly?"

"Yes. You can hardly be in the mill without all the time hearing crying."

Herschel observed her closely. He saw that thin fine lines radiated from her eyes to her cheeks. They were lines of fatigue that he had never seen in a girl so young. It seemed to him that somehow the child had aged even as they stood there.

"They strap girls as well as boys?" he asked.

"Oh yes, 'specially the girls. They pulls up the skirts of the big girls and throws them across their knee, and flogs them with their hands."

"Who straps them?"

"Him," she said. She pointed defiantly to the union man, Greenleaf, standing by their side.

The man shrank back. He seemed to wither before their eyes.

"What!" Frieda exclaimed. "You are the overseer here?"

"No!" he exclaimed. "No more. I were until a month or so ago. But circumstanced as the lads and lasses are here, I couldn't work here no more."

"And now you work for the union?"

"Yes, M'am. We must all do our bit for the workers against the owners."

Frieda said, "Oh, I can see that you are a humane person. But why do you think a naturally compassionate person would find it necessary to beat children?"

"Compassionate?" Greenleaf said.

He seemed perplexed. He was struggling to comprehend how compassion entered into it.

"You don't understand, M'am," he said defensively. "The overseer must keep the doffers up with the machines or be found fault with hisself. The overseer must spur 'em to keep up."

He mauled his cap between restless hands.

Herschel thought, "There is about this wretch the unmistakable air of one who has intimate knowledge of every form of distress of mankind."

"The machine turns out a regular quantity of cardings," Greenleaf said. "And of course the overseer must keep 'em regularly to their work the whole of the day."

"In this mill, are the children locked up?" Frieda asked.

"Yes," Greenleaf said.

"Do they ever attempt to run away?"

"Oh yes."

"Are they pursued and brought back again?"

"Yes, the overseer pursues 'em and brings 'em back."

Herschel asked, "Were you yourself a child working in the mills?"

"Yes," Greenleaf said.

"Did you ever attempt to run away?"

"Oh yes," he said proudly. "I ran away twice."

"And you were brought back?"

"Yes. I was sent up to the master's loft, and thrashed with a whip."

"So, when you were overseer here you inflicted the same punishment on the children that you yourself had suffered?"

"I had to."

He was now highly anxious. He cowered as he looked from one of them to the other. His words came in a rush.

"I was the overseer," Greenleaf said. "I had to beat 'em in order to get 'em to attend to their work, from their being overwrought."

"Overwrought?" Herschel asked. "You mean fatigued?"

"Yes, very fatigued. They sometimes has been brought to such condition that I had to go and fetched up the doctor to them."

"Yes," said Franzos. "And sometimes they are so fatigued that they fall into the shafts!"

"It has happened," the overseer mumbled uneasily.

"Only a month ago," Franzos said, "a doctor at St. Bartholomew's told me he was called here to see to a girl who had been whirled round and round with the horizontal shaft by which the frames are turned. As she was drawn tighter and tighter within the works, her arms, legs, and thighs were snapped asunder and crushed. Her head was dashed to pieces. He said her blood was spattered onto the frame and streamed onto the floor."

The smaller children who were employed as scavengers to pick up the loose cotton that fell on the floor appeared to be near exhaustion. Some of them, a bit older, were working as roving winders, running from loom to loom. Many were not tall enough to reach their work. They stood on boxes, leaning perilously into the machines. With the insufferable heat, the stench, the dust, and noise – with the whirling motion of the machinery, and their hunger and exhaustion – it was a wonder, Herschel thought, that more of the children didn't collapse into the looms.

Frieda asked Greenleaf, "What are the hours of labor in this mill?"

"The hours were at first fourteen," Greenleaf said. "But then I told the master I was not able to produce the quantity of yarn that was required in only fourteen hours. So he took the timepiece out of the mill so the workers would not be able to see the hour."

"Since the clock is now gone, how long do the hands work per day?"

"Nineteen hours," he said.

•

Herschel walked with Frieda toward her home through streets painted silver by a fine mist. They were silent. Herschel was tortured by the specter of the children.

"Nineteen hours!" he said. "How can this be? At a time of prosperity such as the world has never known, how can it be that children are clothed in dirty rags? That their bellies are empty? That they have never drawn a breath of uncontaminated air? How can it be that people are dwelling in alleys and eating out of dustbins? That women and children are dragging pain-wracked bodies to the pits and mills?"

The little lass at the mill told them she came from a family of ten. Her mother and several of her sisters made matchboxes; her brothers made paper bags. In three or four hours' labor, they made a gross of matchboxes, for about two pence. Together they didn't earn more than ten shillings a week. Solemnly, he contemplated the torment of their lives. The image of the children in the mill would not leave his mind.

•

Throughout the months that Herschel had accompanied Malkovitz on his business calls in cities and villages across the continent, Malkovitz had lectured and sermonized, preached and prodded. He had pressed books and treatises upon Herschel. They were books on the socialist movement and on utopian societies. Some were impenetrable, full of technical detail, but others recounted tales of death and deprivation in the mines and mills, which moved Herschel profoundly. Though he hadn't yet gathered all the strands of his reading, by degrees the mortification he felt at his ignorance fell away.

His travels with Joachim had now come to an end. As he prepared to depart for home, he struggled to assimilate what he had learned from Joachim and Frieda. His bourgeois upbringing had never allowed him to know that most people lived under barbarous conditions in a confused and suffering world. Though he had been raised to embrace ideas cautiously and prudently, in his heart he had begun to feel that however illogical and emotional, it would be more courageous, more laudable, to be impelled by passion.

He marveled at how easily Frieda adjusted to the sordid conditions of the outside world – the real world. That is how he thought of it – this world of pain.

• • • •

PART II

London and Warsaw – Winter 1864

10

JOURNEY INTO THE UNKNOWN

The blast of the whistle startled him. The stationmaster bellowed, "*Achtung! Achtung!*" and the crowd on the *bahnhof* platform surged forward. They pressed against him, jostled bundles and luggage against him. Herschel swore at them under his breath. Finally, he clambered up the steep steps of the carriage, struggling awkwardly with his suitcase. He cursed the heat, the damp, and the woolen coat that chafed him. He loathed the steamy compartment and the benches where they sat, crammed and cramped, six abreast.

After what seemed an interminable delay, the vast attenuated train tore itself loose from its bonds. The behemoth advanced resolutely along the long gray platform, gasping its way out of the station and through the rail yard into the dark. The lurching of the train and the shriek of the wheels grinding against the rails grated on his nerves.

From the smeared windows, people on the streets were no longer discernible as individuals. The villages appeared to be sliding backward in the autumn mist. The train passed several stations, crowds congregating expectantly on the platforms. It roared past long lines of freight trains that stood at silent terminals in anticipation of cargoes destined for who knows what exotic destinations. It passed piles of debris on the banks of the river and lines of mill houses grim in the rain. Onward, onward – past the first scanty crops and the women who paused in their crooked-backed labor to observe its passage with dull eyes, past the small child whose arm was extended in a clumsy wave. Onward. The passengers were propelled onward, reaching into the empty darkness. The train's whistle echoed mournfully as the dark maw of a tunnel swallowed it up.

Despite the oppressive warmth of the compartment, Herschel burrowed under his jacket. Things around him were vague and impalpable. He scarcely noticed the shimmering ribbon of track. He saw the faces of the other passengers reflected in the misted window, obscure and somnolent. Their countenances were blank and their eyes glassy; they were like people wandering in a dream. Some kept vigil at the hastening countryside; some receded into repose. Soon all conversation faded into an indistinct murmur. They drifted into sleep, their heads upon their chests, bobbing and nodding with the motion of the train. He felt that they were now to be sown haphazardly, like seed scattered over the fields.

A blinding blaze of light! A deafening concussion of air! Another train hammered its way in the opposite direction.

"It is going home," he thought. "while with each moment, each crack of the track, I am being carried farther away from home, deeper into the unknown."

He thought, how tenuous are the bonds that had bound him to his family. At home they would soon be aware of his absence; they would be anxious for him and imagine him to be in danger. He realized that he himself did not fully comprehend the perils that awaited him. Abstractly, he had embraced the romantic notion of overcoming misadventure, injury, or even doom. He had thought of himself as a warrior venturing abroad into a realm of uncertainty, girding for mortal combat. Yet, somehow, his imagination had never grasped the real circumstances under which calamities might actually befall him.

Last night at the villa, lying motionless in his room, he had dwelled in a kind of twilight, longing for the serenity of sleep. Keeping his eyes tightly closed, he had tried to banish all the objects in the room to the darkness, hoping to detach himself from the confusing world. He was harried and his mind was filled to bursting. His pulse throbbed; he could hear the cadence of his heart on the pillow. He felt that he was suffocating. He was like a lost child groping his way through a dream landscape in a ghostly world. He was filled with despair. He was afraid of loneliness, afraid of failure, and fearful of his destiny.

The rails uncoiled before him. The enormous, humming engines drove him on. He thought of the journey as infinite and endless. But then from nowhere an insight flowered in his mind. He felt that he had returned from a great distance. Wisdom that had been covert and buried had now emerged. Somehow he had forged the last link in a long chain of reasoning, like an intricate puzzle he had at last solved. He told himself that it was the righteousness of his goal that gave him the courage to continue. He heard the heartfelt whisper of the revolutionary. He would be liberated, born anew, and become powerful!

His hand passed over the smooth soft velvet of the seat, and finally, he took refuge in sleep.

•

Judah Hartenstein arose from his bed at dawn. Silently, he opened the door to the adjoining bedroom to look in at his sleeping wife. Then he slipped into his dressing room where his valet awaited him. Steam rose copiously from the vast marble tub. A sponge, a stiff-bristled brush, and a large, neatly folded, crisp white towel were arrayed on the stool at its side. The rotund and mournful valet, Weissenfels, stood by as the baron gingerly lowered himself into the steaming

water. Then, amidst much commotion and splashing, he surfaced, beet red, awaiting the contents of the icy bucket that
Weissenfels dashed upon him. Finally, he emerged. The valet
wrapped him in the voluminous bath sheet, and he seated
himself upon the barber chair – like Caesar Augustus, he
always thought.

Just as he finished dressing, a footman appeared with his
coffee and newspapers, and the first of the day's many folios
of business documents. He sat at a small, round table in the
dressing room, sipped scalding coffee, and glanced through
reports that had arrived from Constantinople, Hong Kong,
New York, London, Paris, and Vienna. Finally, reassured
that all was right with the Hartenstein world, he dressed, as
usual, in his black frock coat and striped trousers. Then he
descended the stairs to the breakfast room.

There, awaiting him as always, was Rudolph Hoffman,
his dear friend and intimate business associate. Hoffman -
a tall, spare, ascetic Alsatian – peered at him over his *pince
nez*. Before him lay the leather portfolio containing the day's
agenda: meetings with industrialists, briefings by diplomats,
conferences with foreign eminences. Baron Kronfeld would
be with him at ten o'clock to discuss the Tilsit-to-Insterburg
railway line in East Prussia. At eleven o'clock, Platt, the
Minister of Public Works, would pay a courtesy call with Lord
Trimble and Lord Pyenson, visitors from London.

Hoffman has brought with him memoranda of talking
points for these meetings, recommendations that Judah
Hartenstein would memorize at a glance. His reputation
for absorbing information was justifiably acclaimed, so
Hoffman's briefings for the meetings over which the baron
was to preside were prepared in meticulous detail.

The men discussed intelligence reports that anticipated
the crisis in Schleswig-Holstein, where Prussia was demanding the liberation of Prussians from Danish rule. They
were apprehensive about the tensions developing between

Prussia and Austria, which were centers of the Hartenstein Bank's interests. They knew there would be no place for the Habsburg Empire in the new Germany that Prussia was planning. In Poland, the struggle for national freedom from Russia had dragged on for many months, and to further complicate matters, Prussia was attempting to Germanize its Polish provinces in the East.

In the carriage, as they set out for the bank, the baron and Hoffman were preoccupied with the intricacies of a strategy for protecting and advancing the bank's interests, despite all the challenges that the events unfolding in Central Europe presented.

At his desk, Baron Hartenstein went page by page through an encyclopedic dossier, harvesting impressions, blending diverse insights, and making notations in the margins, which he etched in his minute, fastidious, and upstanding hand. He required elaboration, he needed further guidance, he approved, and he rejected. Whatever his decisions, they were made with absolute certitude and complete self-assurance.

But on this day, shortly before nine o'clock, his deliberations were suddenly interrupted. In the doorway stood Hoffman, a note in his hand. Behind him, in his greatcoat, stood Snyder, the major domo, who had obviously just come from the villa. Hoffman's face was ashen.

•

Helena Hartenstein awoke at nine o'clock as usual. Her maid assisted her from her bed and helped her into her bath. The doctor was expected at ten thirty. By then she would be dressed and, as always, exquisitely coiffed. In the sitting room adjacent to her bedroom, her daughter Rachel awaited her. Helena barely picked at the little that Rachel could press on her of the tea and brioche, her usual breakfast. Gazing at her mother, Rachel despaired. Her mother was ghostly pale, her skin transparent and stretched tautly over her high cheekbones. Her mother was fading before her eyes. Dr. Feingold's daily visits, his potions and diets, had not availed her. She was dying, Rachel knew.

Today, like all days in recent months, she would spend at her mother's side. Today she would read to her from George Eliot's recent novel, she would entertain her at the piano-forte with the Rumanian folk ballads she loved, and she would gossip with her about the gowns at last night's concert.

The knock at the door was not the discreet tap that customarily announced the doctor's arrival. It was loud and urgent. And in that flashing instant before the door burst open, Frau Hartenstein and Rachel both sensed that something had gone horribly wrong. In the doorway there stood, not the doctor, but the butler. In his hand a single sheet of paper trembled.

•

Rumors swept through the villa. In the scullery, they heard that something had happened to Baron Hartenstein at the bank. A stroke. A heart attack. He was dead!

At the bank, the fiacre was left at the curb, and the horse was not tethered. The major-domo's arrival, unprecedented in itself, and his disarrayed, distressed appearance, could mean only one thing. "*Die Baronin* is gravely ill," the tellers whispered. In the counting house, the news leapt from desk to desk. The clerks put aside their pens.

On the carpeted marble stairs leading to the upper reaches of the bank, managers paused and whispered, "She is dead. *Die Baronin* is dead!"

Agitation radiated from the bank and advanced across the broad boulevards of Berlin. Telegraph messengers carried coded messages to be transmitted to distant cities. By noon, the news had spread from the cafés to the brokerage houses. The monstrous mock Renaissance Berlin Bourse echoed with rumors that something had gone terribly wrong at the Hartenstein Bank.

It soon became apparent that neither the master nor the mistress was dead, though her condition was certainly grave; Dr. Feingold was constantly in attendance.

At the villa, at the bank, and throughout the far-flung outposts of the Hartenstein realm, consternation and confusion were rampant.

Herschel's brief farewell note, addressed to his mother and father, with tender references to his sister, gave no hint of his whereabouts.

•

From Frankfurt, Elias Hartenstein immediately departed for Berlin. Amelia Oppenheim, hurrying to her brother's side with her husband Sandor, boarded a train held for them at the Vienna Southern Railway Station. Judah's son Kurt, and Judah's nephew Moritz, had caught the channel steamer at Dover.

With the arrival of each member of the family, the inevitable questions were raised again and again. Had they visited the Akademie? Had they talked with Herschel's classmates? Was he unhappy at school? Were there any hints in his demeanor?

Suggestions - some of them preposterous - came tumbling forth. Simon Hartenstein's wife knew of a physician, a Dr. Braide, who had a patient who, when under the influence of hypnosis, had powers of clairvoyance.

Judah was exasperated.

"Mesmerism!" he said. "Quackery! Next we will resort to spiritualists, mind-readers, and psychics."

Soon enough, he thought, confidence tricksters, crackpots, and fortune hunters would pursue them.

Sandor Oppenheim suggested hiring a private detective. He knew of a retired Vienna police inspector. Moritz argued for Cook's Detective Agency in London.

"London is justifiably famous for the skill of its private detectives," Moritz said.

There would be no private detectives. Any sign of panic or desperation could have widespread consequences at the bank and on the stock exchanges. They had to proceed with circumspection.

Amelia Oppenheim said, "That Malkovitz must know something." She spat the name. "We should find Malkovitz. We should find out what he knows of this. You can be sure he put ideas into Herschel's head. What other explanation could there be?"

Judah abruptly rejected any suggestion of Malkovitz' involvement. But what sinister influence could have persuaded Herschel to abandon his home and family? It was unthinkable that he would contemplate such a thing on his own.

In the end, Judah felt that he had to resolve the situation into a proper scheme himself, bringing to the crisis an efficient business-like response. Whatever fear and guilt Judah Hartenstein might be feeling, he, of them all, had to maintain his perspective. It was up to him to direct the family's energies and provide organization for the search for his son. Certainly, he thought, the logical place to start would be with Joachim Malkovitz.

•

Malkovitz rushed to Berlin by train and coach from Basle, catching what little sleep he could and barely pausing to eat. He appeared before them weary and solemn, his lined brow evidence of his deep concern. Long before he had received the urgent call, which of course he knew would come, he had conscientiously prepared a plan of action and rehearsed it painstakingly. He had thought it all through with his customary calculation and thoroughness. His fundamental stratagem was simplicity. His story would be uncomplicated. He would guard against embellishment.

It was imperative that Hartenstein's confidence in him remain staunch; above all, he should harbor no suspicion that he had been complicit in Herschel's disappearance. He recognized that it was only natural that the Hartensteins would assume that he, with his long experience in the world, must have had some influence over his immature naïve charge. But Malkovitz was an expert in the fabrication of conviction.

He painted a picture for them of an impressionable, emotionally overwrought boy, who was motivated by a romantic notion and a passion for the mystical.

"Like many boys his age, he is fascinated by the violent, the curious, the foreign and the unknown," Malkovitz said. He is in thrall of mysterious inner beliefs, enchanted by the wild forces of nature – gales and torrents, the immensity of mountains, the wildness of the seas. He sees himself as a Goethe hero – Wilhelm Meister or young Werther – who, under a romantic spell, abandons their comfortable homes to journey into the unknown, wandering in their minds, through a fantastical maze. Like all boys his age, he is a 'Romantic.' He thinks of himself as lonely and misunderstood."

Amelia Oppenheim stared at Malkovitz in amazement. "Rubbish!" she thought. She was more convinced than ever that Malkovitz was involved in Hershel's disappearance.

In reassuring them, Malkovitz conveyed the attitude of a man trying mightily to set his friends' minds at rest, while he himself remained deeply concerned. "You will see," Malkovitz said. "He will be back soon enough when his money runs out."

Judah Hartenstein swept Malkovitz's optimism aside with a brusqueness that was uncharacteristic of him.

"All that may be true," the baron said. "But we can't wait to find out."

Naturally, Malkovitz would devote himself to the task of finding Herschel, traveling the length and breadth of Europe should it be necessary. He would revisit the cities that he and Herschel had traveled together; he would make inquires among the people they had met on their journeys. No call on his time and effort would be excessive.

"Enlist the aid of your friends," Hartenstein told him. "Offer rewards for information. You must find him before he comes to harm."

Judah Hartenstein valued Malkovitz for his presence of mind, for his steadfast behavior, and the clarity of his opinions. Malkovitz's diligence had always made a good impression on him.

Malkovitz told them, "Be assured that I will stop at nothing."

• • • •

11

A MEETING WITH BAKUNIN

Herschel left his room and walked down the stairs to the Boté's parlor. It was early. There were only a few people in the room standing about. He glanced diffidently at the group congregated in the far corner. He knew two of them: the tall, gaunt Englishman, Richman, and the painter, Marshall, a Frenchman. He didn't know how to approach them, but he knew he couldn't just stand there by himself. He walked to the window. A fine rain was falling. A damp earthy smell came up from the wet cobbles. He was chilled, though the room was warm and overheated.

Finally, to his great relief, Frieda entered. Halting at the door, she saw him standing alone. She smiled.

"You are rooted there like a tree," she said.

She took his arm and led him to join some of the others, but they were interrupted as she turned to greet someone who had just come in.

"I am so glad you could come," she said.

Herschel was amused, thinking of Frieda in the role of a hostess. He was left in the void in the center of the room.

"Be at ease," he told himself. "Pretend that you belong."

Frieda's father came in. He stopped in the doorway and surveyed the room. Seeing a look of concern on his face, Herschel gathered that he must be worried that attendance would be meager. After all, no more distinguished guest had ever entered his home.

The old comrade, Mikhail Aleksandrovich Bakunin, was a major force in the revolutionary movement and a prominent Russian revolutionary agitator. Unlike his rival, Marx, he was an activist of rebellion, not merely a theorist. He led a network of secret revolutionary societies with a following in Italy, Spain, Germany, and Great Britain. Even now he was preparing to embark with a shipload of volunteers to fight in the Polish rebellion against Russian rule.

The professor stopped to greet his guests, offering as he went oddments of the adventures of his "old friend" Bakunin.

"During the Dresden uprising he was imprisoned…three years in Peter-Paul Fortress. Three years in Schlisselburg. Exile in Siberia. Tonight, you will meet the man who, two years ago, made a dramatic escape from a Russian ship sailing down the Amur River, and began the voyage that made his name a legend among radical groups throughout Europe."

More people were coming in now. There came Adelaida Fillippovna, Dr. Pinsky, the Fufkovs, the Vershitskis, and Colonel Kavkaztev. Joachim Malkovitz also arrived. He waved to Herschel across the room. In the nearly six months that Herschel had been living in London with the Botés, he and Malkovitz had seen each other only occasionally.

Professor Boté hurried off to meet a new arrival, the gaunt old Scotsman, Jonathan Marr. Now a woman entered. Frail, her iron-gray hair pulled back severely into a bun, she darted about, birdlike, chatting up people as she went.

The room was now quite crowded. Frieda moved among the guests. She saw Malkovitz leaning against a bookcase, lounging with ostentatious nonchalance, an open book in his hand. In contrast to the well-worn attire of most of the other guests, Joachim's costume was, as usual, elegantly polished.

He wore striped trousers, highly shined nankeen boots, and a sparkling white batiste shirt flashing in the opening of his dark twill waistcoat.

"Look at him," she thought. "He holds his head with such bold assurance."

His cheeks, freshly shaven, were pale; they were not the reddish flush of the faces of workingmen she knew. And unlike them, his hands were soft, unblemished by manual labor, with his fingernails long and tapered. He spent a great deal of time caring for them.

Malkovitz appeared to be oblivious to the hubbub of the crowded room. He acted as if he was absorbed in his book, one of the slender volumes it was his custom to carry. He felt Frieda's gaze upon him. He looked up at her and reflected on his brief time with her.

"Frieda is the girl in this book," he imagined. "She is Goethe's Lotte, a young girl who is captivated by a handsome, cultured young man."

Glancing down at his book, he read:

"Lotte puts all her hopes in him. She forgets the world around her, hears nothing, sees nothing, feels naught but him, longs only for him. He is her all. Promises, repeated over and over again, seem to assure the fulfillment of her hopes; bold embraces increase her desire and make her soul captive. At last she stretches out her arms to grasp all she desires —and her lover leaves her."

He could not help but feel some measure of compassion for Frieda. She must feel Lotte's anguish, he thought, with a twinge of guilt. But it was only a momentary pang.

"How could she have ever taken it seriously?" he thought.

For his part, he had known how their story would end when his eyes first came to rest on her. The glow of enchantment would gradually fade; passion would give way to boredom.

He read, *"She jumps and drowns her torment in the embrace of death."*

Looking across the room at Malkovitz, Frieda breathed deeply of the air of liberation.

"This man of such vast experience has no idea that I am fed up with him," she thought. "He has no idea that I am tired of his cunning, weary of his churlishness and his small-mindedness."

Frieda, after all, was not of a delicate nature. She had seen her full of the turmoil and coarseness of life. She had ample experience of the world's poseurs and cads. She did have to admit, however, that she could not contemplate the early days with Malkovitz without pleasure. She remembered lying in her bed after their first meeting, watching the dim shadows cast by the flickering streetlights playing on the ceiling. Her thoughts had drifted lightly over him. He was so far removed from her own walk of life, so urbane and cosmopolitan. But now, standing in the whirl of the noisy room, she reproached herself.

"Though the face he presents to the world is calm, dignified, and affable, it is merely a façade It conceals an arrogance that comes from having one's every whim satisfied, every blow softened, and from having one's vanity constantly soothed. He is fatuous; obsessed with the thought that one might mistake him to be bourgeois."

She had known all along that there could never be a real bond between them.

The room filled up. Voices rose. More strangers arrived.

Herschel's thoughts took him back to the early meetings he had attended at the Botés' house, when he had been too self-conscious to participate. For the first time he had met the men and women of the revolution – people from all over Europe – émigrés, factory workers, miners, and teachers. All were fervent, vehement, and impatiently yearning to do something. They spoke of their ambitions, of their failures and disappointments.

When at last, after several weeks, when he finally had summoned the courage to speak, he couldn't seem to bring his insubstantial thoughts to completion. The ideas that roiled his mind had confused him. Stammering, his voice trailing off, he left his words drifting in the air. The others in the room had exchanged amused glances. They hadn't even tried to conceal their contempt. Some of their remarks behind their hands had carried across the room to him. He hung his head in humiliation.

The monographs on politics and the economics that Professor Boté had pressed on him overwhelmed him. Frieda had urged books on him that extolled utopian communes and portrayed the suffering of the working class. Letters from his newly found friend, Dr. Franzos, who had been traveling abroad, described the mortal illnesses of the laborers in the mills and mines. Eventually, he felt that he had achieved a rational grasp of the anarchist tracts that described the rampant depredations of the ruling class and the cold indifference of the bourgeoisie.

With the passing of time, resentment against the tyrant flooded his soul. But his heart was still sorely burdened. Though his heritage mortified him, and though he longed impatiently for the ascendancy of the downtrodden masses, he could not overcome his revulsion at the violence and bloodshed that his comrades espoused. Of course, he could not admit this to the newly found friends whose acceptance he yearned for. They must never know that he found some of their ideas repugnant. Moreover, some inner sense told him that the outrageous acts of terrorism these comrades spoke of with such fierce passion was merely bluster.

Yet here tonight, standing before him in the circle of yellow light cast by the flickering lamps, was Frieda, who was strong, clever, and totally dedicated to the doctrines of anarchism. Here was Joachim who, though Herschel now suspected his sincerity and doubted his commitment, still remained in his eyes a dashing, romantic figure. And here also was Wadizlaw Franzos, whose words, though always so softly spoken, were strangely incongruous with his fanatical conviction that the objectives of socialism could be achieved only through the violent destruction of the status quo.

Suddenly, as if conjured up out of his thoughts, Franzos appeared beside him. His eyes were red. Exhausted from a long tour on the wards, his smile was forced as he glanced around the room. He slumped back into a chair. He looked at the people congregating animatedly in small groups, astonished as always at the infinite variety of the human form. Richman's face was lacquered in perspiration, two deep furrows running down from a sharp nose to a thin-lipped mouth; Marshall's face was all hummocks and hollows. Their countenances changed as their bodies shifted in the pale sickly light cast by the streetlamps, entering the window.

"Who are all these people!" Herschel asked Franzos.

Looking at Herschel's doleful face, Franzos thought, "What a strange young man! Thin and pale. Inhibited. Pathologically shy. Deeply troubled."

He knew that Herschel was hopelessly confused about their objectives and their means of achieving them. In this room a few weeks ago Herschel had voiced his bewilderment. Leaning forward in his seat, obviously in fear of being overheard, Herschel had spoken to him barely above a whisper.

"What I fail to understand is that you, with all your concern for humanity and the sanctity of life, how you can justify wanton murder."

"Murder? You speak of murder?" Franzos had replied. "Haven't you learned anything at all? Didn't you learn anything at the mill? Didn't you see starved and beaten children, their bodies broken by their toil? Every day their corpses are carried out of the mills. And you speak of murder?"

Slowly, Franzos had recited the history of the persecuted multitudes, which were crushed by mine owners and suffered a lifetime of backbreaking labor.

"An entire generation – not just men, but women and children as well – choking and dying below ground in the pits."

Methodically, he had listed, one by one, the horrors to which he had been witness: asphyxiation from asthma, black lung disease, crippling rheumatism, anemia, rickets, and starvation.

"Every day, in a funeral procession that never ends, the miners' crushed bodies are hauled out of the pits."

Herschel had replied diffidently, struggling to organize thoughts that were half-formed. He spoke bitterly, his distress apparent.

"And you are going to set the world right by rage and pillage and arson?"

Franzos, leaning forward in his chair, said quietly, "Yes. By acts of terrorism that will cripple the government."

"But what could you possibly hope to accomplish?" Herschel had asked. "What kind of a world would we be left with?

"With a simple, austere, new world, an undefiled society," Franzos had replied. "Some lives must be forfeited so that the world can be redeemed, so that we can achieve a new innocence. The world must become utterly barren, if that is what it takes, so that we can begin at the beginning."

"But murder and slaughter!" Herschel had cried.

A memory out of his childhood had been stirred. Blood pooling on the sidewalk. A man's body on the cobbles lying in an impossibly awkward position. His skull was crushed. His sightless eyes stared skyward. Their coachman frantically tried to detour their carriage around the overturned wagon. The horses balked. They reared up in their traces. His mother violently pulled his head down into her lap. But it is too late. He has seen. What he has seen he can never forget.

There were only ten or twelve of them in the room that night a month ago. Listening to Franzos talking to Herschel, they had been swept along on a current of vicarious emotion.

Joachim Malkovitz had been there. Franzos had seen a look of ill-concealed derision on his face.

•

Rain had started in earnest now; it beat against the windows. The hats and shoulders of late arrivals were dark and wet. The room was very stuffy. People shuffled furniture against the walls, making room for more chairs. Across the room, Frieda spoke animatedly to Marr and to an untidy, florid woman whose face was fixed in a smile.

There was a commotion at the door. The focus of the room shifted to a disheveled old man who was being greeted with exorbitant geniality by Professor Boté and several of his acolytes.

"So that is Bakunin," Herschel said.

"Yes," said Franzos.

Herschel heard the tone of reverence in Franzos' utterance of that single word. He knew that Franzos thought of Bakunin as the indefatigable conspirator, the ceaseless revolutionist, the seer, the romantic.

Looking at him, Franzos saw that his health was in ruins. Judging from his appearance, he was obviously destitute. In fact, Bakunin was living day to day on meager funds that his devoted disciples contributed to him: Russian, Polish, Serb, and Romanian émigrés, and British and German intellectuals. Some present this night were would-be assassins, anarchists bent on perpetrating a series of outrageous acts. They spoke of attacks against royalty, against religion, against the state, all calculated to electrify what they called "the complacent bourgeoisie." Others were volunteers who had enlisted to accompany Bakunin to Poland to join the guerrilla war against Russian rule.

•

It was late. The crowd had departed. Only the Botés' inner circle remained behind. Bakunin motioned Herschel over.

"So, you are from Berlin, comrade. Please permit me to condole with you. In Prussia you breathe the atmosphere of an immense political slavery. In all her international relations, Prussia, from the beginning of her existence, has been slowly, systematically invading and conquering. And when finally Prussia establishes in Germany a single unified power, it will become a greater menace, a danger to the liberty of entire Europe."

Staring at Bakunin, old before his time, it was difficult for Herschel to think of him as a revolutionary leader. The old man asked, "You are, what, sixteen or seventeen years old?"

"Sixteen, comrade." Herschel replied.

"And you are educated - or so you think?" Bakunin smiled. "But you would not be here if your mind had not been liberated from the irrational beliefs that your teachers have without doubt thrust upon you."

Peering intently into Herschel's face, Bakunin spoke quietly. He affected a jocular tone.

"And I take for granted that you don't heed the ranting of parsons and priests. And you are not a rake who has a penchant for pleasure at any price. On the contrary, I believe you to be a warm, compassionate human being. Why else would you be here?"

He leaned forward slightly, extending a knotted finger.

"You ask yourself, 'What am I to do with this life of mine?' One must be depraved indeed if, after having acquired a trade or science, he applies his learning and skill toward self-enrichment, when the opportunity before him is to proffer his intellect, his aptitudes, and his enlightenment in the service of those who grovel in wretchedness. It matters little in what rank you were born. Perhaps you were meant to be a doctor, a lawyer, a man of letters, or a man of business. Perhaps you began life with extensive knowledge, with a trained intelligence. What matters is that you have the vision, do you not?"

Lurching to his left, Bakunin glanced at the ragged youth named Agate, who smiled shyly and tugged nervously at a shapeless cap.

"Perhaps you are only an artisan, with little education," Bakunin said.

The boy, embarrassed, was in fact a printer's devil.

"But you have the advantage of first-hand knowledge that a life of exhausting toil is the lot of a worker of our time," Bakunin said.

He turned to address the small group that remained.

"Imagine yourselves in the midst of a triumphant revolution. The state, and with it all sociopolitical systems, is demolished. The filth that has accumulated in immense quantities rises to the surface and is cleared away. It seems to be terrible and hopeless. But a violent revolution, sweeping away all existing institutions, is the necessary prelude to the construction of a free society."

Bakunin's rheumy eyes took on a passionate glow. His face flushed furiously as he was propelled along his rhetorical track, overcoming inertia and lurching forward in fits and starts. His arms jerked like pistons beneath his well-worn coat, which had long since given up any pretense of shape and form. His beard was unkempt, and his hair curled over his ears onto a frayed collar.

"Imagine in the midst of this universal anarchy there is a secret organization that has dispersed its members in small groups over the whole expanse of the empire."

His words sloughed over empty gums, his teeth having taken up permanent residence in the dungeons of his native Russia.

"These small groups, unknown by anybody, are ardent in their ideas, which express the very essence of the people's instincts, desires, and demands. This, comrades, is the collective dictatorship of the secret organization."

Herschel saw that Bakunin was exhausted. Perspiring profusely, he sank back into his chair at the side of the stove, his voice barely a whisper.

"Our enemies," he gasped, "are the tormentors, the oppressors, the exploiters of humanity - priests, monarchs, statesmen, soldiers, policemen, gendarmes, jailers, executioners."

His audience strained to hear him.

"Monopolists, economists, financiers, and politicians of all shades," he was gasping now. "Down to the smallest vendor of sweetmeats!"

In Herschel's mind, he saw the specter of the long rows of clerks, cashiers, and bursars, all behind the highly polished doors of his family's counting house. Rank upon rank of them, blackbirds perched on stools before slanted desks, pecking, scratching, and laboring in the cause of holding the workers in servitude.

"If only I could burst in to grasp my uncaring family by their throats," Herschel thought. "If only I could compel them to see that they are drenched in gore and that their shameful ledgers are written in the blood of afflicted and dying workers."

Bakunin lay back in his chair his eyes closed

In the presence of Bakunin Herschel believed himself to be in the vanguard of a vast social revolutionary army of fearless brigands awaiting the order to attack. He saw himself as a member of a secret underground organization, a military machine, ready to follow Comrade Bakunin anywhere. His thoughts turned to Shelly:

> *"The loathsome mask has fallen, the man remains*
> *Sceptreless, free, uncircumscribed, but man*
> *Equal, unclassed, tribeless, and nationless,*
> *Exempt from awe, worship, decree, the king*
> *Over himself."*

• • • •

12

MARIUS

The riverboat was a specter, barely visible through the mist, its looming stacks and massive paddlewheels shrouded in the gloom. The voices of the sailors on deck and the sounds of freight being shifted were muffled as they were carried across the quay, and from over the water came the mournful peal of a distant bell. A weather-worn sign on the wharf read Vistula Steam Navigation Company.

Herschel clambered up the shifting gangway. Dodging plumes of steam rising from below decks, he made his way between teetering stacks of luggage and towering bales and crates. He stood some distance apart from the knot of people gathered on deck. Many of them warmed themselves near the grating over the engine, which throbbed like a pulse below the vibrating iron plates of the deck.

Finally, after much delay, the ship's siren blared, and the crew jostled about in a brief fever of activity. The paddlewheels bit the water, and the boat slipped from its mooring. It seemed to Herschel that the boat remained stationary and that the houses, mills, and church spires on shore glided by.

With the coming of dawn the mantle of mist had blown away, and he saw that the river swarmed with small fishing boats, dinghies, rafts, and barges, quivering in the wake of the steamer. The boat passed a broad fenced meadow and a large red barn. Then a hamlet slipped by, and then a small town, the cross on its church steeple flashing in the sunlight. Along the left bank, carts rumbled by on a dirt road barely wide enough for carriages. Canals, rocky passages, and shallows impossible to navigate ran parallel to rapids along the shoreline. On the starboard side there was a lovely valley, from the center of which a conical rock rose sixty meters or more, crowned by the ruins of a Romanesque church.

By midday most of the people had found seats on their luggage or on deck cargo. They sought vantage points from which they could observe the shifting landscape and the novelty of the river traffic. Most of them – working men and women, shopkeepers and clerks – were dressed in their old clothes, which was the custom for traveling. They wore threadbare calico dresses, tattered frock coats, and old, scuffed, cracked leather boots. Eventually, their sausage and cold chicken consumed, their linen and cutlery returned to their hampers, they were lulled by the warmth of the sun and the motion of the boat. Laughter subsided, and conversation faded away to a murmur. Looking down on them from the first-class section near the bridge was a small group of travelers. The women were wrapped in furs and gripped broad-brimmed plumed hats, ribbons flying in the breeze like pennants. The men, smoking cigars, wore heavy cloaks and dark trousers.

"How blissful they are in their ignorance," Herschel thought. "They are completely unaware of the agitation that is mounting all over Europe. They are blind to the birth of a new way of life. They are heedless of the masses."

The ship's whistle sounded a prolonged blast. There was a flurry of activity on deck. The crew wrestled with lines, and bumpers went over the side. Passengers shifted luggage and hampers. The progress of the boat had slowed, and now the current carried them along. Herschel struggled to read the name on the sign mounted on a battered shack on the quay. It was unpronounceable: *Kedzierzyn*. This was his destination, a village in Poland close to the Prussian border, where he had been instructed to wait for orders.

•

The sky darkened as he trudged up a steep, rutted road from the quay. A chill came off the river, and a fine snow drifted down. Along the road, he passed rag-clad farmers with carts laden with hay, brewery wagons, and butchers' drays. He passed orchards, a granary, and a timber yard. At the road crossing he had to make way for a herd of sheep driven by two gaunt peasant women wearing shawls wrapped around their heads and shoulders. He walked past the village schoolhouse and the remnants of a church fortified with watchtowers, then through the village, which was surrounded by the remains of a wall that once was a defense against the incursions of the Tartars and Turks.

Finally, he came to a ramshackle stucco house. Skirting a black pool of stagnant water, he reached a gate that opened to a muddy yard littered with refuse. He looked about apprehensively. He saw no one. He called out. No one answered. He climbed stairs no wider than a stepladder to a gallery. Several battered doors opened onto dark rooms. Looking back down to the courtyard, he saw the large man who had been described to him.

He called down to him, "I am Marius."

After all, a true revolutionary must have a *nom de guerre*.

•

Wacek Siemanowski couldn't be bothered with the melodrama of an alias. He was a huge man, broad-shouldered, with lank blonde hair and a wide, flat nose that Herschel thought looked more like a snout. Despite that, he was blessed with a benevolent countenance. He exuded an amiable strength and wholesomeness.

They discovered that they could communicate in German.

While awaiting their instructions to arrive, they spent their time exploring the deserted house, which judging by the hand looms they found in many of the rooms off the gallery, was at one time a small family-owned mill for weaving fabrics. Now, with the coming of steam-powered knitting machines, it appeared to be abandoned. Evidently, other travelers had used the house before them; wood was piled high near the stove, and barrels of potatoes and other vegetables were stored in the corner.

They had been told that they should guard their identities from each other and that the strictest secrecy be observed, but Seimanowski had no qualms about talking freely about himself. Like the radicals Herschel had come to know, Seimanowski could not stop talking. Sitting at the table in the circle of pale light cast by the kerosene lamp, he talked long into the night.

Seimanowski had come late to the revolution, or as he told it, the revolution had been late coming to him. He had been a worker in a mill in Wroclaw, where he had labored unceasingly, without complaint, in blissful complacency, until one day he found himself in the midst of a workers' revolt. Prior to that he had never heard of the emancipation movement, let alone the revolution. But once he had, it could not come quickly enough for him. For a passionate revolutionary, it was ironic that Seimanowski had a cynical, almost melancholy view of the movement.

"The gentry who are handling the money," he grumbled. "They are greedy and crooked! No one knows where the money meant for the fighters is going."

He fulminated against the leadership, whom he accused of treachery.

"They are driving the masses into this reckless rebellion," he said. "And you'll see, they will abandon us at the first sign of resistance."

Herschel was dismayed. He was not the ideal of a terrorist that Herschel had in his mind, and he certainly was not one he would have chosen as a companion.

By the third night of their sojourn they had exhausted their meager store of conversation. They sat in the center of the room as close to the stove as they could, until the heat drove them back. Then the cold forced them closer again. Seimanowski produced a bottle of vodka.

"Drink?" he asked.

"Thank you, no," Herschel said.

Seimanowski shrugged. He poured a prodigious quaff into a chipped enamel cup. Eventually, as the evening wore on, he lost his aim and the vodka sloshed onto the table. Then he abandoned the cup and drank from the bottle. Herschel tried to read from the flickering light of the paraffin lamp, but Seimanowski, who sat opposite him staring, discomfited him.

Finally, Herschel broke the silence. "You said you have been to Russia."

"To Siberia," Seimanowski said.

"Siberia!" Herschel said with astonishment. "Why?"

"An assassination plot," Seimanowski replied casually. "It did not come off as we expected."

Seimanowski laughed. He had no interest in talking about the failed assassination, as if it was of no importance, but he took great pride in his sentence of imprisonment.

"Siberia!" Herschel said with awe.

"There were about forty of us," Seimanowski said. "We had no names. Just numbers. There were some among us who deserved punishment. Some were criminals. Some even murderers. But many of us were guilty only of dissent."

Seimanowski smiled grimly and said, "I was an assassin."

Herschel looked at him in amazement.

"We went part of the way by train," Seimanowski said. "Several thousand miles. In cattle cars. Packed in like animals. Several weeks in cold you could never imagine. When we reached Western Siberia, they took us off the train and marched us through the snow. Many days on foot. In temperatures below freezing."

He paused to take a deep pull at the bottle. His gaze fixed on some point in the distance.

"We wore heavy chains on our ankles" Seimanowski said. "Iron balls the size of canon shot were attached to the chains. We walked four in a row, the first and last in the row dragging the iron balls through the snow, sometimes in drifts up to our knees. They were afraid we would escape."

"Escape?" Herschel asked. "Was escape possible?"

"Of course not. Who would be fool enough to try? It was a land of endless snow. Snow as far as you could see. And wolves. Wolves. You could hear them baying at night. No, we carried the ball and chain just so we wouldn't forget who we were: the scum of the earth, helpless and hopeless. The shackles wore our skin down to the bone."

Herschel's hand involuntarily went to his ankle. He imagined that he could hear the ring of the chain, and the incessant shuffle of feet in the snow. He could hear the relentless wind in the trees and the labored breathing of the marchers.

"We walked for twelve hours a day or more," Seimanowski said. "The cold was killing. Every step was marked in blood. We were exhausted. Many fell by the way, left for the wolves.

The guards," Seimanowski sneered, his teeth bared in loathing, "Barbarians! They treated us with the same cruelty they themselves received from their officers. They walked beside us, constantly waving the knout."

"The knout?" Herschel asked. "What is a knout?"

"A whip," Seimanowski said. "Strips of rawhide woven with heavy wire. Every blow from the knout drew blood and raised great welts on our flesh. Blows came down on us for any reason, and sometimes for no reason at all, but simply out of cruelty and pleasure in torture. In the beginning, some of us raved and cursed, but the knout soon kept us quiet. We were starving. They fed us a small loaf of bread each day and two *taran*, dried fish. The weakest of the prisoners marched in the first row. When they stumbled and fell we had to hold them up and drag them along. If, after being beaten, they were still unable to stagger along, they were put into the carts that carried the bundles and the provisions and the women."

Herschel was incredulous. "Women?"

"Oh yes, women, Seimanowski said. "There were eight of them. Six were thieves and murderers; two were political prisoners. One of them a woman of high rank, a noblewoman from top to bottom, accustomed to every luxury. They let the women ride in the wagons for part of the day, but every day they were driven out of the wagons and forced to walk for hours."

Herschel could see them falling heavily on each other, pressing on each other. They stumbled in their chains. Their clothes were in tatters. Their feet were bound in rags. Their breath, gray in the glacial air, streamed from their mouths and nostrils. He could smell the stale odor that rose from them. He could see the entire gamut of human passion written in deep lines upon each countenance.

"The only thing that kept us from sinking to the level of our keepers was sometimes little human touches," Seimanowski said. "We would pick up a fainting and bleeding comrade and carry him a long distance. We put our own bodies in the way of the knout to shield the sick and injured. We often shared our miserable meal, our scanty ration of bread and water, with those who were weakest."

"How long did you walk?" Herschel asked.

"How long?" Seimanowski said. "Who knows? Many, many days. The roads were buried in snow, the chains grew heavier, the food was not fit for a dog, and we trudged onward in snow and ice. At night they stopped us at the side of the road, usually near a forest. They removed the chains and permitted us to make a fire."

Herschel saw them – huddled, rolled up in their blankets, sharing the heat of their bodies, left to their sorrows and regrets. Their faces, peering out beneath the blankets over their heads, were lifeless, and their features were frozen in a rigid grimace. Fear and confusion weighed them down. Herschel saw them drawing close to each other, as near to the fire as they could get.

"They must have suffered deep remorse." he thought. "They must have wondered why they had put themselves at risk.

"Why have I put *myself* at risk?" he asked himself. "Could this be the way my own life is to end?"

Siemanowski said, "In the heart of every one of us lived the dream of escape. We were so tired and exhausted that sometimes we could forget the cold, the hunger, the knout, and the wolves. But we knew it would be madness to try. No one could fight off the wolves without weapons. No one could survive the Siberian winter." He smiled grimly, and said proudly, "But I did."

He paused to savor Herschel's amazement.

"One night we ran into a blizzard. For twenty-four hours it blew. We couldn't move. The procession halted in a forest where we found what shelter we could under the trees. When it let up a bit I just got up and walked away. Just like that. I walked away."

He laughed and said, "I didn't know where I was going. I didn't care. I don't know how long I walked. I had saved part of each day's ration, so I had a little food. But soon it started to run out. I thought it was all over for me. Then I heard the voices. I knew that I was finished. They were coming after me. Out of the blowing snow they appeared: the Ostyaks."

"The what?" Herschel asked.

"The Ostyaks," Siemanowski said. "Little brown men, barely five feet tall, with smooth Mongol faces. Nomads. Ostyaks are primitive herdsmen of the Siberian steppes. They were driving sleds pulled by reindeer. And they had food! And warm fur clothing!"

"Could this be true?" Herschel wondered. "Things like this don't happen in real life."

But something within him whispered that it was true. Wacek Siemanowski, the assassin, the convict, was real. He was here in the room with him. And incredibly, he, Herschel Hartenstein, was really here too. He looked long at Seimanowski. He stared at him as if his gaze could penetrate his skull, as if he could look deeply into his mind to discover what was at work inside. He was a strange species to Herschel, something entirely new in his experience.

Seimanowski studied Herschel.

"Is this what they call a 'young gentleman'? The boy is silent. He doesn't speak of himself. He speaks no Polish. Only German. From the way he talks, and the way he looks, I can tell he isn't of the working class. So, what can this boy know of the pain of the worker? What can this boy know of the plight of the poor? Did he ever have typhus? Has he ever gone to bed without a meal? What can he know of poverty and hunger?"

Seimanowski was reminded of the children of the rich he would see riding by in his village. They perched on the seats of their coaches, wrapped to their noses in furs, or they rolled hoops in the park. Their laughter, as it came to his ears, was like the babbling of a brook. Growing up in the slums, how rarely had he heard the laughter of children.

He sneered, "This boy probably even went to school!"

•

Herschel slept fitfully. The cot was narrow, and the straw-filled pallet was damp and smelled of mildew. He wondered what filthy vermin crept about inside. His sleep was filled with strange vivid dreams that, when he recalled them upon waking, defied his ability to probe their meaning. He had dreamt of his childhood friend – why, he could not imagine – a boy he knew when he was ten or eleven. He was wearing a sailor suit. They played together in the ballroom of the villa. The tall windows were streaming with cold winter rain. They bounced the ball to each other. Back and forth. Back and forth. It made a hollow, clapping sound when it struck the floor. It reverberated off the walls in a faint echo.

"Whatever became of Karl-Emil?" Herschel wondered.

He had a dream about his brother Simon. He was wearing his heavy British tweed suit. When he wore it their father would laugh and call him, "M'Lord." They were playing whist. Simon laughed and slapped his cards on the table triumphantly when he scored. When Herschel scored, Simon scowled dramatically.

Herschel awoke with those dreams lingering in his mind, wondering what they meant and why they came to him now, at this time.

•

It grew colder, and the days were shorter now. The trees had shed just about all their leaves, and when Herschel got up in the morning he could hear them skittering about in the courtyard. Seimanowski was always first to awaken. Herschel heard him prowling about like a bear – big, clumsy, and lumbering. He would hear Seimanowski banging pots, stoking the stove, and placing a pot of water on the lid for coffee.

Seimanowski didn't seem to mind the waiting. But for Herschel, time was heavy. For Herschel, there was too much time to think. While the prospect of a heroic deed was distant he had been able to keep his spirits up. Now, he had to confront the possibility that in the mission to come, someone's life could possibly be forfeited. Perhaps, for all he knew, it would be his own.

All his life he had been schooled to keep his emotions under control. How could he now have allowed passion to overwhelm his judgment? He berated himself. He had been imprudent; he had not been circumspect, as he always believed it behooved a man to be.

On the fourth morning, he awoke to a fresh autumn day that filled his window with a bright, transparent light. Suddenly he was elated. It was as if the splendor of the day had driven away his fears. He was joyful and eager.

He passed the time ambling aimlessly along the river, wandering down lanes that bordered fields and meadows, observing farmers at their labor and women and children herding livestock. Walking the twisting cobbled streets of a neighboring town, he saw in the distance, on top of a tall hill, what appeared to be the remains of a great structure. As he drew closer, he realized that it was ruins of the church he had seen from the deck of the steamer.

When he reached the hill he saw that it was steep; the path to the top had crumbled in many places. It was a long uphill climb. But soon after starting out he found that the exertion exhilarated him. His breathing was labored, and he trudged upwards to its rhythm. It seemed that there would be no end to the slow ascent. At the top, the hill flattened out into a treeless plateau. He stood, catching his breath, his hat in his hand, enjoying the breeze against his brow. He looked out to the horizon, to the river snaking through the town. The houses below looked like toys jumbled together, and the people resembled tiny bugs rushing hither and yon. The clamor of the town carried up to him on the top of the hill. There were voices, the whack of wood being chopped, the reverberation of hammers striking anvils, the whinnying of horses, and the crowing of fowl.

On the plateau were the remains of the ancient church, which over the years had been reduced to little more than rubble. The walls had fallen to pieces, tumbling into what must have been a vast nave, from the floor of which splintered columns rose like shattered bones. Birds startled him, rising in a sudden flurry from the remains of soaring arches. He wandered, clambering over thick, heavy beams and massive stone blocks that lay haphazardly on the steps of the chancel. Standing on a pile of rubble, he looked out at the sweeping views of the surrounding valleys.

Then he saw the old man. He was wearing a black cassock. He emerged from a small decrepit hut. Herschel took him to be a warder, the custodian of the remains of the church.

He surprised Herschel by greeting him in German, apparently assuming from the cut of his clothes that he could not be Polish. They stood in the weak sunlight looking out over the valley, chatting amiably. The elderly man pointed a trembling finger toward a small space cleared on the flagstones where a quantity of curious large, round stones was neatly piled.

"Do you know what those stones are?" he asked. "In the twelfth century they were used as shot for the cannons that defended this citadel."

Herschel expressed the awe that the old man obviously anticipated.

"There was a custom here in the old times," said the custodian, "that no young man should be allowed to take unto himself a wife until he had carried one such stone from the bed of the river to the summit within the church walls."

He encouraged Herschel to lift a stone. He heaved it off the ground only with great effort. He could hardly walk two steps. The old man laughed.

"It was a test of strength that barred a weakling from marrying, lest he should spoil the hardy race."

•

As he followed the path back to the village Herschel felt the chill of winter fast approaching. The light was fading.

Candles were being lit, and windows glowed. Dogs were barking in the distance. He heard the protesting hinges of a barn door being closed. A woman was calling a child in to the evening meal.

Thoughts of home suddenly flooded his mind. He was separated from his family by a vast forbidding chasm. He yearned for his mother. Once again, he was beset by a sense of inadequacy and desolation. Wandering in the rapidly darkening streets of the village, he pondered why the transformation of the world, the regeneration of humanity, could not be accomplished without violence, without bloodshed, without pain. Above all, he had always craved order. He had always seen the world in neat, tidy terms - structured, organized and logical. And now, all around him was disorder. Here, order was a chimera. Madness ruled the world.

His thoughts turned to his comrades at the Botés. Their contorted faces had the appearance of madness. Their faces bathed in sweat and their teeth bared in anger, they had the fierce eyes of a lunatic religious cult. They were drunk with bloodlust, and their faces were bright with images of an inferno. They were like feral animals, raging through the world, attacking all that came in their way, creating chaos in the name of justice. He despised their ignorance and their aimless brutality.

"They are castoffs," he thought. "The dregs of society, disillusioned misfits, envious, rejected."

He told himself that he was looking in the wrong place for noble virtuous heroes.

"These are criminals," he thought. "Animals."

Yet, there was Franzos, who praised the nobility of anarchism, whose exalted aim, he fervently believed, was the liberation of the workers. And, of course, there was Frieda.

•

Beyond the trees, the rays of the setting sun glinted off the autumn leaves, glowing a gentle amber and crimson. He wandered aimlessly down the twisting lanes of the village, impatiently awaiting his orders and wondering what lay in wait for him. He stopped from time to time in some meadow mantled in golden leaves. The soft rays of the sun fell gently on the field, creating a shimmer of light, tempting him to lie down on the rustling leaves.

• • • •

13

THE CELL

It was bitterly cold in Warsaw that November. Rooftops, balconies, and streetlamps were draped in snow. Drivers cursed and cracked their whips as their sleighs careened on ice-slicked boulevards.

Following the instructions he had received, Herschel walked through the snow-covered streets, past banks, theaters, and restaurants. He passed colorful shop windows displaying gowns and furs. Uniformed school children, bundled in coats and scarves, rushed homeward. Elegantly attired gentlemen had trouble keeping their footing on the icy streets as they hurried along, one hand to their hats, the other wielding their canes. Their long shadows were cast onto the walls of the buildings as the streetlamps flickered to life. Women swathed in furs, burdened with gaily wrapped bundles, were assisted through the drifts by doormen from the fashionable shops, which remained crowded despite the cold. He heard the sounds of the trolleys as they scuttled through the streets, their bells ringing, mingling with the other bright sounds of the city.

He walked from boulevards of luxurious homes and shops, whose walls and windows glowed brightly, into narrow alleys and dark streets of market stalls where peddlers and carters bustled about. Pushcarts, haphazardly lining the roads, were laden with cottons, silks, woolen goods, thread, and buttons. He passed a slaughterhouse where the pavement was piled high with cages of chickens, ducks, and geese. A sickening smell permeated a street where troughs of fish, their bellies slit and their eyes glassy, were laid out on ice. Peddlers tried to sell him used clothes. Beggars plucked at his sleeve. Horses shivered in their traces, manure steaming in the frigid air. Wagons laden with coal and firewood juddered over rutted roads.

He crossed Iron Street to Leshno Street, then he turned left at Cecil Street, where finally he found the derelict four-story tenement. The number 254 hung drunkenly from the doorpost.

He unlatched the iron gate and entered the courtyard. The snow was stained and littered with refuse, garbage overflowed barrels, and slop accumulated beneath the windows. He trudged through the snow along a path compacted by the boots of others, past a stable where a team of miserable dray horses steamed, coming at last to the doorway. He stepped into a long, dark hallway lined with doors. Finally, at the end of the hall, he came to the door he was looking for. He knocked tentatively. An eye appeared.

"I am Marius," Herschel said.

The door opened barely wide enough to admit him. He entered a noisy, densely packed room. People sat on all manner of chairs. Five of them had crowded onto a well-worn sofa. Some sat on the floor, one of them on a teetering pile of books. The floor was bare and littered with cigar butts and cigarette mouthpieces. No one spoke to him. No one noticed him. He wandered aimlessly about the room, expecting his unknown contact to greet him. Passionate hand-waving and violent gesturing punctuated shouted conversations in a babble of Russian, Polish, and Yiddish. A large pale man with a bright red beard and flashing eyes shouted into the face of a disheveled teenage boy he held by the lapel. A middle-aged man, his high forehead glazed in sweat, smiled seductively, striving to impress a young girl whose wild curly hair tumbled into her eyes.

The room was filled with what Herschel thought must be the flotsam and jetsam of Europe. Some appeared to be mere school children, boys from the gymnasium. Others, who wore remnants of uniforms, may have been deserters. One was a German, judging from his accent, another a Frenchman. At the center of the room, cigarette smoke rose from a circle of a half-dozen people who, gesticulating wildly, talked all at once. In their midst, Herschel came face to face with Wladizlaw Franzos.

·

By day Wladizlaw Franzos was a physician in the clinic of the Children's Hospital on Alexander Street. His evenings were devoted to organizing the insurrection. Looking at him, Herschel thought that everything about him – his physical appearance, his bearing, his quiet dignity – marked him as a leader. He was tall and thin. His eyes were dark and passionate. He had the high cheek-boned face and the chiseled features that marked him as a Slav.

He was a tireless recruiter, enlisting members of his cell from among the business and professional class. They were physicians like him, or lawyers and teachers, as well as working people. His personality was irresistible, as is frequently the case with fanatics. He had a unique ability to fire the imagination of deserters, embittered pacifists, and revolutionaries alike.

Many of his recruits came from student fraternities, others from socialist youth movements. They were the radical left of the Polish independence movement, which had ignited armed risings in every generation since Napoleonic times. They were anti-Russian Marxists, anarchists, socialists, and nihilists. Franzos himself rejected labels. He was a revolutionist, and if they liked to think of him as an anarchist or a Marxist, so be it.

In 1855, he had been dragged from his school in the provinces and drafted to soldier in the Crimea.

"A Russian war," he would say with great bitterness.

Taken prisoner by the Turks, he was beaten, starved, finally released, and thrown back like a floundering fish to his village. He found that his father, a schoolteacher whose politics had been unpopular with the authorities, had been torn from his home and taken to a gulag. Shortly thereafter, his mother received word that he was dead.

Franzos had inherited his politics from his father, but his rampant revolutionary ardor was all his own. He organized the peasants in Ciechanow, fomented food riots in Lodz, resisted Russian army levies in Bialystok. Later, he led partisans in plundering army supplies. He ransacked the barracks of Russian Cossacks who were absent putting down student riots in Vilnia. And then, finally realizing the futility of this line of work, he applied to medical school in Warsaw under the sponsorship of an uncle. Despite the burden of his studies, and his ceaseless labor in the clinic with the poor, he maintained his contacts with underground cells of the revolutionary movement.

In this winter of 1863, Poland was rife with conspiratorial societies committed to overthrowing Russian rule. The inner circle of Franzos' cell, the Revolutionary Committee, was planning acts of sabotage and assassination. They were arming the peasants and preparing for the uprising. Several nights a week the comrades met to study politics and history. Tirelessly, they spoke of the condition of the peasants, the predicament of the Jews, and the plight of women. They railed against police persecution, mass arrests, and political trials. They argued tirelessly about religion. They quarreled furiously about the existence of God. They debated endlessly about Darwin's doctrines. The names of socialist writers – Marx, Lassalle, and Bakunin – were bandied about. They hectored each other in Polish, in Russian, or in a mixture of both. It seemed to Herschel that each of them had his own agenda.

Miriam Liebman – a girl he took to be in her early twenties– her long, narrow face tense in anger, railed against the apathy of the Poles.

"The world is changing," she said. "Everywhere, all over the world, people are advancing, but in Poland people remain servile and steeped in ignorance."

She was the daughter of the rabbi in the village of Vadzilovo. The *Hassids* reviled her father as a "modern." Nevertheless, when she left her home, he mourned her for dead, in the strict orthodox tradition. Her mother and sisters never mentioned her name in his presence.

A quiet, slender, dark-eyed girl, Miriam looked forlorn in her shabby brown plaid skirt and worn white blouse. She worked as a volunteer with Wladizlaw Franzos in the Children's Hospital, an undertaking that had dominated her life. Now with the revolution imminent, she eagerly ran each evening to her fervent comrades and their boisterous meetings.

One of the most outspoken was Anton Lipksy, a student of law at Warsaw University.

"The bourgeoisie have woven a web that is so impenetrable," he said, "that the people have come to believe that there is something mystical at the bottom of their misery. Something or other that is inevitable. Something that can't be explained or changed."

He was a small, thin, pasty-faced man. He had a clubfoot that he dragged painfully.

From across the room came the deep bass of the wild-eyed Russian Jew, Moses Borokhov – they called him Misha

– an émigré from Marshinov, where he had been a member of a group of about two hundred Jewish revolutionists, who were mostly Russian and Polish immigrants. An avid reader, he loved Turgenev for his affectionate portraits of the Russian peasant; he admired Tolstoy, who had established a school for peasant children.

"Poland's salvation," he said, "depends on getting down to the real issue of developing industry, of modernizing herself."

A tall blonde, Justine Malewska, her keen eyes blazing as she spoke, mocked the leaders of the world, the church, the military, and the landed gentry. Herschel thought she was a strong, handsome girl. At the university, where she was a student, they said that she was the daughter of a nobleman, that she had known writers and aristocrats, and that she had been received in Paris salons.

"The essential, preeminent element of the revolution is the law of love," said Justine.

"Love?" spat Miriam. "Love in its carnal form is sordid. It is nothing more than physical possession. It is a distraction. In the end, it only divides the fellowship and divests it of its meaning."

Their most vital undertaking, Franzos said, was the liberation of the peasantry from the Russian oppressor.

"By its policy of looting, torture, and murder, the Russian regime is bound to open the eyes of the peasants. The Russians are hostile, not only to the working class, but in fact, to the whole of the toiling peasantry. We must bring them to understand that only in alliance with the city proletariat ..."

"No!" Lipsky interrupted. "The liberation of the peasantry is a mistake. We have created a mob, an angry mob. And soon they will turn on us. First must come the education of the proletariat! The most important task is the education of the proletariat! Only when the people are educated will they no longer be docile and subservient."

Borokhov, though he tried mightily, found that it was impossible to abandon the Jewish world entirely.

"It is not so easy for a Jew to make a revolution among the gentiles," Borokhov said. "A Jew cannot simply put on a mask of racial anonymity. The *Hassids* still clung to their ancient ways. They still wear those long capotes and their hats perched on top of their skull caps, with their curled ear-locks hanging down."

The non-*Hassids*, known as "moderns" or assimilationists, walked about in European clothes. They wore hats, trousers, and shoes with buttons or laces.

"You can don the dress and affect the speech of a *muzhik*," Borokhov said. "But when you approach gentile workers you are always asked point blank, 'Are you not a *Zhid?*'"

It was painful to some of the radical Jews in the group that many of their gentile comrades in the insurrection, members of Polish socialist groups, supported anti-Semitic attacks by peasants who claimed that Jewish business-owners exploited them. After all, Jews were among the leaders of the rebellion. In Warsaw, a group of wealthy Jewish businessmen, and several doctors, lawyers, artists, and booksellers, were taking an active part in the uprising.

One night, the discussion turned to slavery in America and the progress of the War Between the States. They were appalled that Lincoln had welcomed the support of the Tsar and had approved a visit of the Russian fleet to the United States. Justine Malewska passed around a cartoon from a tattered issue of *Punch* her cousin had sent from London. Lincoln was depicted addressing the Tsar. Justine translated into Polish.

> "*Imperial son of Nicholas the Great,*
> *We are in the same fix, I calculate.*
> *You with your Poles, and with Southern rebels I,*
> *Who spurn my rule and my revenge defy.*"

The laughter was desultory. To Lipsky, Malewska epitomized the kind of woman who was happy only when she was ruled with a firm hand.

Herschel glanced from one to the other across the smoke-filled room. In the weeks that he had been with them their arguments had never ceased. They debated the merits of the new political movements that seemed to sprout like cabbages. Some of them thought of themselves as Narodniks, others as Marxists, and others as anarchists. They believed that they were disrupters of the entrenched establishment and defenders of progressive thought. There was talk of abandoning Polish socialism entirely and merging with the world proletariat. At every meeting the room echoed with shouts of "Criminal elements!" accusations of slackness, chauvinism, profiteering, and most damning, of being "Bourgeois!"

The conversations dragged on. They continued to argue with strident passion about things of which Herschel knew little or nil. On occasion their anger boiled over into physical skirmishing. Fortunately, their bulky fur coats protected them from serious injury, but the old, broken folding chairs were another story. However, the lack of space required to swing a chair properly limited the damage.

Nevertheless, the squealing, shouting and screaming, the insults and oaths, were sufficient to hold Herschel's interest. On most other occasions Herschel listened with impatience. He had only a cursory knowledge of the circumstances of Russia's domination of Poland. He knew almost nothing of the *Hassids*, of whom they spoke with such disdain. They were as exotic to him as, say, a Chinaman.

For that matter, the Poles, and the few Russians in their cell, were Slavic people, who were barely civilized, he believed. They sprang from exotic cultures, eccentric religious movements, and curious ethnic traditions. In their passionate character, violent mannerisms, and naked enthusiasms, they were so vastly different from his erstwhile comrades in London.

In London, they too were devoted to advancing the cause of the masses, but they were single-mindedly focused on anarchism as their means and their end.

"These comrades are more feverish and more restless," he thought. "In each of them there is persistent discontent. Their unfulfilled longings, petty jealousies and frustrations, their reckless drinking, aimless flirting and lusting, seems to arise from a melancholy belief that all is hopeless and life must end tragically."

It was surely nothing more than a romantic melodramatic pose, he believed. At times they seemed to be violently opposed to one another. He thought that perhaps they were torn by conflicting ideas and objectives, because in the heat and actuality of a revolution, in the rising proletariat of Warsaw, their polemics were bound to be more fierce. Yet, somehow they shared common values and aims. The power of the purpose that bound them together was obviously more consequential than the political partisanship that drove them apart.

At the end of each meeting the circle of comrades would sit quietly. They were exhausted. Cigarette butts floated in coffee cups, and tables were littered with the remnants of sandwiches. The air was blue with smoke from cigarettes, cigars, pipes, and the perpetually leaking stove. Their eyes watered, and they coughed. It was too cold to open the windows, and anyway, the curtains had to remain tightly drawn. Any gathering of young people was bound to attract the attention of the police.

Finally, quietly, one by one, they slipped past the janitor, who couldn't be trusted not to report their gathering to the Comissariat.

• • • •

14

THE INSURRECTION

The Insurrection arrived at Wadizlaw Franzos' flat at dawn. Herschel was awakened by the sounds of a melee in the street below. He ran to the window. A cavalry officer was furiously spurring his mount onto the sidewalk. A young man fled before him, running a frantic zigzag course, skidding and stumbling on the icy pavement. He gaped over his shoulder in panic as he ran, scampering and scuttling crablike, his arms flaying the air. The rider leaned low out of the saddle, his arm reached out, the sword swinging in a wide arc. The man rolled his body into a ball, desperately attempting to ward off the blow with his hands and arms. The wildly charging horse ran him down.

Herschel swung away from the window. His eyes were wide in horror.

"My God, Wadizlaw, what is happening?" Herschel asked.

Franzos stood behind him. His jaw was set in anger.

"Stay back from the window," Franzos said. "The last thing we need is for them to come asking questions about you."

Herschel had no papers. As it turned out, papers would have been to no avail.

The Russian puppet, the Polish Count Wielopowski, had
ordered the militia to comb the streets of Warsaw for its
young men. He intended to deprive the demonstrations
of their most ardent supporters by forcibly conscripting
the radicals into the Russian army. But the dragnet had
the opposite effect. The leaders of the Insurrection had
organized a demonstration in the center of the city.

•

Herschel found himself in the midst of a large, unruly
crowd. He stood in amazement as a deluge of outraged
people spilled out onto Smolensky Boulevard from the side
streets. Their faces were bright red, and they were bundled
in all manner of bulky winter coats, sheepskin hats pulled
down over their ears. He was surprised to see women in the
crowd alongside the men. He also saw university students,
girls and boys in school uniforms, and factory workers in
boots and leather jackets. They lifted their faces to the heavens and lustily, with great fervor, sang the *Marseillaise*. He
joined them as they marched under the somber sky, bellowing workers' songs, their footsteps echoing on the cobbles.
A few snow flurries drifted down, spiraling slowly and tim-
idly like fine gray particles before alighting on his shoulders
and the heads of the marchers. Then, as if on some signal,
the singing suddenly broke off, and the shouted slogans subsided to a whisper. Rumors swept through the crowd.

"The Cossacks are assembling in Saxon Park," someone
said. "They are waiting in the side streets."

His eyes wide in fear, Herschel searched in vain for refuge, as from all directions a torrent of screaming horsemen –
Cossacks, Bashkirs, and Caucasians – poured into the boulevard. They galloped their horses through the throng, their
sabers swinging. People shrieked in terror all around him.

"My God, they are cutting down the women, children,
and old people."

Herschel fell to his knees as the desperate crowd scurried to escape being trampled by the charging horses. People ran frantically into the alleys and side streets. It took only minutes. The marchers dispersed, disappearing behind a veil of snow. Herschel, bewildered and in shock, looked about him. Only the dead and wounded remained. Blood ran in the snow.

•

On Sunday, the governor-general ordered the city sealed off. The army was out in force looking for conscripts. Officers galloped to and fro importantly. A sergeant-major bellowed orders. Cavalry horses patrolling the streets tossed their heads and pawed nervously at the snow, breath pluming from their nostrils. Hundreds were arrested in the churches and synagogues. Men who resisted were shot where they stood. The hospitals overflowed with wounded. Terrorized young men scurried into hiding, many of them seeking refuge in the nearby woodlands. The Russians arrested the leaders of the Insurrection wherever they could find them. They dealt with them by flogging them as they ran them through a gantlet of soldiers. Herschel heard alarming reports coming into the headquarters of the Insurrection. There were all manner of rumors about arrests and abortive street demonstrations. The violence spread. Peasant rioting broke out in the countryside. Businesses were brought to a halt. Fortunately for the banks the outbreak began on a Saturday, giving the financial community time to assess the situation. But inevitably there came menacing financial panic.

By four o'clock on Sunday, telegraphic service was interrupted. There were rumors that the Cossack garrison on the outskirts of the city was on the move; rumors that there had been an explosion at *Novtny Polska*, forcing the suspension of publication; rumors that there would be a shortage of coal because a locomotive had been derailed, blocking the main rail junction outside of Lodz.

And then it began to snow in earnest.

In the hush of that dreary Sunday, with the city in the fist of a punishing snow storm, the people of Warsaw huddled around their stoves to contemplate something ominous and grim. The railroads weren't able to haul coal and the river overflowed its banks, disrupting transportation. Soon the people would be without coal, without heat, and possibly without food.

By late afternoon, though the snow and freezing rain was driven before a fierce north wind, some people emerged from their homes. Dressed in fur coats and long boots, some with their feet wrapped in newspapers and wearing all manner of outlandish headgear, they braved the gale to seek food and coal. In vain.

The homeless stood freezing in long lines at the soup kitchens of churches and synagogues, begging and crying for food. The dead remained in their homes. There were no coffins, and the frozen ground would not yield to the gravediggers.

At the Children's Hospital on Alexander Street, Herschel did what he could to assist Wadizlaw Franzos and the other doctors, who worked frantically to keep up with a seemingly endless stream of children who had developed respiratory infections. They now filled the wards. The homeless, the indigent and the aged, crowded the corridors. Many who were exhausted, frozen, and hungry slept on gurneys, on makeshift beds, and even on the floor in the hallways.

Herschel was surprised to find that several old Jews were there too. They were paupers who had always been fed and cared for at the Community House of the Great Synagogue. They had been turned away because of overcrowding and lack of food. And there were also some young people who had been wounded in attacks on "Jewish revolutionaries," who were accused of inciting the riots and bringing down upon "decent Poles" the beatings, the repression, and the famine. "And why not the storm?" asked an aged *rebbe* of Franzos, who was removing a shard of glass from his forehead. "Why should we not be blamed for the storm as well?"

•

Later that evening, Miriam and Herschel, returning from a meeting, trudged through the snow toward her home. It was colder than ever now. The windows of the hovels they passed were opaque with frost. They took a circuitous path through the gloomy alleys, avoiding the main boulevards where troops were manning barricades and stopping people to check their papers. The snow was so deep that sidewalks had disappeared, and in many places the snow had drifted to the height of the first-floor windows. And once again snow was falling, and the wind was picking up. The streets were all but deserted. The few people who had ventured out moved silently and slowly, some dragging their belongings behind them on makeshift sleds.

Occasionally, Herschel and Miriam were startled by the sound of gunfire.

"Pistols," thought Herschel. "That means Insurrectionists."

Then came the answer from the Russians: the thunder of Mausers. The shots echoed through the clear crisp air. Sometimes they would see a solitary figure darting into a doorway from the alleyway. Horse-drawn sleighs carrying troops knifed through the streets, bells on their harnesses ringing merrily in the night.

It was bitterly cold. Miriam wore only a threadbare coat and a woolen shawl over her head. Herschel wore an old, ratty fur coat he had borrowed from Franzos.

They stopped at the pump in the courtyard at the end of a street of stables for a can of water. An optimistic whore, huddled in her shawl, stamped her feet in the alley. Overflowing barrels awaited the garbage wagon.

Though it was late at night, children scampered amidst the laundry, which hung frozen on cords strung from door to door in the hallway of Miriam's rooming house.

Herschel and Miriam climbed four flights of stairs to her small room in the attic. Herschel smelled the musty odor of putrid straw and the stench of rotting cabbage. Miriam lit the wick of her lamp, placed one stick of wood in the smoking stove, and set the water to boil for tea. She sliced an onion and put potatoes on the stove to accompany a bit of herring.

"This must be her unchanging routine," Herschel thought.

He looked around the attic room. He saw one window, the narrow cot on which he sat, an old wooden chair, and the table where she was working. A long, jagged crack ran like a scar the length of one wall, the edges of stained wallpaper peeling away from it. He smelled a strong odor of lye and soap in the room. In the corner he noticed a large tub. On a table there was a heavy black iron. He realized then that she took in laundry.

He had learned that there were tormenting contradictions in Miriam's life. She had a ferocious devotion to her parents and even, sentimentally, to the miserable *shtetl* where she grew up. She still romanticized what she called "the ancient Jewish faith," though she rebelled against the *Hassidic* rabbis whom she thought hobbled Jews with superstitious ritual and iron-fisted regulation.

He watched her as she prepared their meal. Her lips were tight with bitterness, turned downward at the corners, disappearing into deep little furrows.

"A sad mouth. An angry mouth," thought Herschel.

Yet she was, Herschel had discovered, a synthesis of serenity, frailty, and compassion that was strangely at odds with the fierce anger and ardent passion that poured forth from her. She was only a few years older than he, but her youth had been annihilated. Her comrades in the cell thought of her as a genuine hero of the revolution. She was, they thought, the very embodiment of the principles of the true revolutionist, as laid down in the *Little Red Book*:

*"The revolutionist is a self-immolated person.
He has no common interests, feelings or inclinations, no property, not even a name. Everything in his life is
devoured by a single, exclusive interest, a single
thought, a single passion – the revolution."*

It was whispered that she had put her life at risk many
times and that she had even taken part in an assassination. Herschel had asked her about it, but she had always
remained silent. Finally, that night, in the seclusion of
her poor room, she relented. She turned toward him,
and drawing in a deep breath, she told her story, simply, without emotion, in a preternaturally calm, steady
voice.

"I went to Cracow by train," Miriam said. "I carried the
bomb in an old, battered leather portmanteau. They wanted
me to carry it because they didn't think the militia would
suspect a woman."

"Weren't you afraid?" Herschel asked. "Didn't you think
that your nervousness might betray you?"

"Of course I was afraid," she said. "But my fears were
groundless. I had no problems. The militiamen at the station didn't even give me a glance. When I got there I took a
droshky directly to the address I had been given. The land-
lady had a room waiting for me in the name of Landowska.

"In my room I removed the tube from the suitcase. Then
the powder. I let the powder dry in the air, then I loaded the
tube. It weighed about two kilos. I wrapped the tube in a box
and tied it with red ribbon. And then I went to bed."

Sprawled on her cot, his back against the wall, Herschel
saw that her dark eyes smoldered and that the skin of her
cheeks was taut.

"How could you possibly have slept?" he asked.

"I was exhausted," she said. "The strain, the tension, had
drained me. All I know is, I slept deeply until a knock at the

door roused me. When I opened my eyes, at first I didn't know where I was. I saw sunlight under the window shade. Then, the realization of what was going to happen that day surged back into my mind. There was another knock at the door. Louder. My heart beat faster. When I opened the door a crack, a group of children leapt out at me screaming. I almost fainted. They were all wearing gaily colored masks. Then I remembered it was the eve of the New Year. They had come to throw millet seeds at me."

Herschel was puzzled. A melancholy smile came to her lips.

"That is the custom, you know, in that part of Poland,"

The sharp rap at the door and the laughing screaming children were real to him. His pulse was pounding. He sat up. His hand caught in a tear in the blanket. He could hear Miriam breathing.

"The children were laughing uproariously, and just for that moment I was able to put out of my mind what was going to happen in a few hours. I gave them a few kopecks. They continued to laugh and caper. I shooed them away. They made the sign of the cross, wished me a happy New Year, and went on their way down the hallway.

"At noon, when the church bells pealed, I went down into the street. The day was bright and cold. A Cossack galloped past. The street was almost deserted. I walked toward the bridge. The governor's residence was across the bridge. His carriage was drawn up at the curb. Two mounted Cossacks stood by. When I passed them, one of them bowed from the saddle and wished me a happy New Year. Then I saw the comrade who had been described to me. He was walking slowly toward me. He tipped his hat. We stopped as if to chat. I handed him the package. He smiled and went on his way."

Herschel shifted restlessly on the cot. He imagined for a moment that he could see, reflected in Miriam's eyes, the stone pediment of the bridge, the soldiers' yellow-gray greatcoats, and the dark cloaked figure of the man carrying the package.

"I followed him with my eyes," Miriam said. "I didn't dare turn my head. The street was clear. The door of the governor's house opened. The governor came out and entered the carriage. It began to move slowly down the street, followed by the Cossacks on horseback. Then the man stepped down from the curb. He raised his arm and threw the package. Though it was heavy, it seemed to me that it was floating slowly on a current of air. The coachman saw it. He whipped the horses and veered at a full gallop straight in my direction. I ran the best I could to get out of the way. One Cossack wheeled his horse and sprang at the man. I heard the report of a pistol. And then a terrific force lifted me off my feet into the air."

A shudder surged through Herschel's body. He saw the man's blood-drenched body sprawled on the cobbles. The shattered carriage was tilted at an impossible angle. The horses were wild-eyed, rearing up in their traces. He saw the fierce Cossack in his fur-collared greatcoat, dismounting in a leap, standing astride the supine man. Herschel's body sagged. He sank back against the wall.

"I must have lost consciousness," Miriam said. "When I came to myself, I saw the man lying in the street. Blood streamed down his face. In the confusion, I drifted into the small crowd that had gathered."

Herschel's eyes were wide with wonder. He was in awe of her, lost in admiration. She sat close to him on the cot. His eyes searched her face. Hesitantly, his hand sought hers. And then she was in his arms.

•

On Monday, both the storm and the rebellion persisted. The snow continued to fall. The Vistula froze, but not before it overflowed its banks. The secret revolutionary government, having concluded an alliance with the large contingent of

Polish refugees in London, issued a manifesto calling for a national uprising. The leadership quickly gained support among artisans, workers, the lower gentry, and government official classes in the cities. They fomented peasant revolts against the landlords in rural areas.

On Tuesday, the Insurrection spread beyond Poland into Lithuania and Belorussia. It attracted volunteers from Prussian and Austrian Poland. In Warsaw, the roundups continued, as did the violence. All traffic came to a standstill. Barricades cut off the streets. Bullets flew down the streets, ricocheting off walls of the buildings. Random gunfire struck people who were still on the streets. Bombs were thrown. Store windows were boarded up. Banks, commercial houses, shipping interests, and transportation were disrupted. Manufacturers and wholesalers, retail merchants, and even farmers were thrown into panic. The smashing of store windows, the lootings, the arrests, and the beatings continued. The underground government in Warsaw was now waging a guerrilla war, fielding small units against a Russian army of three hundred thousand men. Patriotic demonstrations were answered by military repression, which was followed by a series of violent incidents. As he watched the ominous developments, Herschel came to the inescapable conclusion that his time was drawing near. Franzos and the other comrades were not overtly participating in the uprising, but they met more frequently, and if possible, more furtively. They burned scores of brochures, pamphlets, and piles of clandestine newspapers in the stove. Herschel suspected that their surreptitious comings and goings, and their whisperings, signified that an "action" was imminent. He speculated about what was expected of him. He was left with a feeling of deep weariness. He tried desperately, but without success, to free himself from it. He simply grew more disconsolate. Finally, emotionally drained, he took refuge in the conviction that in the end they would never carry out an assassination. It was too melodramatic; it was outrageous. And even if by some chance it did come to pass, he would refuse to participate. But he knew it was not going to happen. He knew it would never happen.

But of course it did.

•   •   •   •

15

MARSHALKOVSKY SQUARE

It is said that Marshalkovsky Square is so vast that if one stood at its center and gazed out toward its perimeter, it would be impossible to shake off the effects of vertigo. Herschel looked toward the eastern edge of the square, at the ominous, gray granite bulk of the Interior Ministry. Pummeled by the tumultuous throng, he struggled his way to the center, where an immense obelisk reached toward the sky like an admonishing finger.

The motley crowd, in spite of the angry cold and the biting, wind-blown snow, stirred and shifted, filling every square meter of the huge plaza. Their breath, redolent of garlic, onions, and schnapps, rose in a vapor above their heads until it was swept away by the brisk wind.

Lavishly appointed sleighs, sumptuous troikas, and elegant open carriages were crowded two or three deep, side by side with the primitive carts and wagons of the peasants. Men and women stood on the seats and the boxes of their conveyances. The well-to-do were swathed sleekly in mink and ermine. The poor, resembling animals of the forest, were dressed in layer upon layer of rags and patchwork skins of beaver, fox, wolf, deer, and moose. On their heads they wore turbans of towels, pieces of quilt, sheepskin hats, and uniform caps – souvenirs of bygone wars. One old peasant looked down from the seat of his rustic troika. He wore a greasy buckskin coat, a ragged old fur cap, and felt boots. His three horses were appallingly filthy, uncombed and brutish-looking, with beards of ice hanging from their muzzles. Their heads hung low, biting at the snow.

An alarming din – shouted greetings, curses, laughter, and insults rose from the square. Women bellowed to children who huddled under their skirts, scuttled between their legs, and raced away to be swallowed up in the crowd. Peddlers, shouting their wares, were immobilized in the crush, their carts billowing smoke that rose from samovars and black-crusted potatoes roasting in charcoal beds.

Herschel stood in his appointed place close to the obelisk. He was trembling. His teeth chattered, though he no longer felt the cold. He struggled mightily to bring himself under control. His heavy greatcoat sagged under the weight in his pocket. The bulge must be noticeable, he thought, glancing furtively at the tall blonde militiaman standing on guard duty at the edge of the monument not three feet away.

An hour earlier Franzos had thrust the immense revolver at him, holding it by the barrel. As the dead weight fell into his hand, Herschel's arm dropped under the unexpected heft of it. It weighed over four pounds. It was almost sixteen inches long. The metal of the barrel was pitted and scarred, the brass trigger guard tarnished green. Had he examined it carefully he would have seen that the grip was engraved with a scene depicting the Texas Rangers fighting off an Indian war party. It was a mystery how such a weapon, a relic of the American war with Mexico, one of only a thousand manufactured by the Colt Firearms Company, had made its way seventeen years later across the seas and into his hands.

"A macabre birthday present," Herschel thought.

Today he was seventeen.

At the center of the immense square, generals and the high functionaries of the civil service, accompanied by sumptuously attired ladies, arranged themselves in a long reception line. They chatted merrily until the moment arrived for putting on their masks of solemnity. Herschel wondered at their arrogance.

"How can they be preoccupied with pageantry while the uprising is erupting all around them?"

He turned to search the faces of the crowd, wondering who among them were his comrades. How many others were standing as he was, armed, poised to act, but also, like him, terrified? Of course he would not be able to recognize them. They looked like everyone else in the crowd, as he hoped he himself did

•

The shots, coming from several directions, were fired as planned, precisely on the twelfth stroke of the church bell. The Count Wielopowski, wearing a gold-embroidered uniform, in a carriage drawn by eight horses, preceded by a dozen brilliantly dressed pages, had entered the square promptly as the bells signaled the noon hour.

At first, the crowd seemed unaware of what had happened. Even those closest to the obelisk hadn't seen him fall from his carriage. Or if they had, they couldn't believe what their eyes told them.

The frenzied surge didn't begin until moments later, when a deafening explosion shook the flagstones under their feet. On the far side of the square, glass shards rained down upon the crowd. Smoke rose from the Ministry of the Interior.

The stampede toward the gates began like a wave approaching the shore – an immense roller, mountainous, leaping forward and upward, gathering speed and building strength. It swept everything before it - women, children, the elderly. A wall of humanity impelled by an inexorable force had thrust their bodies forward, bent them as one, and irresistibly propelled them along. All at once thousands threw up their arms in a great frenzy and tore at the air, their mouths cleaving their faces, all crying the same irrational screams.

They were all driven forward by the same chaotic power. Wailing, convulsed, and entangled, they swayed under the same devastating, driving force. Those in front were dashed to the ground. Those behind them were carried forward and forced upon the prostrate bodies of those who had fallen. Still others rose up on their backs. They disappeared beneath the thundering engine.

As Herschel looked at them they ceased to be individuals, as if their vital fluids, their sinews and flesh had fused into a single being. It was as if their very lungs had expanded and contracted in their chests in the same breath. In a single moment, joy, sorrow, rage, dread, and loathing, lust, and fulfillment – the entire range of human emotion – plunged though them. Until, at last, the wave crested, folded in upon itself, and finally subsided.

Now all Herschel could hear were the faint pathetic cries of the fallen, lamentations like the bleating of wounded animals. Dazed, in shock, he could not bring his mind to accept the enormity of the horror that he and his comrades had inflicted upon the multitude. He was on his knees in his own vomit. He rose to his feet and slowly picked his way through the dead and the wounded.

Fire raged in the stone and brick buildings along the lane at the rear of the Ministry. As Herschel stumbled into Leshno Street, brimstone, oil and turpentine stored in the buildings exploded. Immense tongues of fire lashed out at him. A whirlwind of smoke and flame leaped across the narrow lane separating the rear of the Ministry from the street, which was crowded with lean-tos and shacks where secondhand goods were sold.

The windows and pilasters of the Ministry smoldered. Pages and guards frantically pumped water from a small fire engine that had been dragged to the conflagration. Four lines of hose were pulled toward the fire, but three of them were found to be slit. The one useful hose received a scant supply of water, pumped from barrels that three desperate militiamen were trying to fill from buckets. From the rooftop, a couple of firemen shouted desperately, "Water! Water!"

Herschel walked through the smoke. He was choking. His eyes were burning. The fire was raging in all directions. Suddenly it rose in a huge column, a black plume writhing skyward like an immense snake. The fire now reached several blocks, and branching off from them in every direction were other shops, many not more than makeshift hovels, from which were sold or bartered old hats, dresses, suits, used and discarded furniture and bedding. Books and merchandise were stored in the stalls and in the narrow passages between them. Now, pages from burning books danced in the air and feathers from bedding were swept about. Roughly a half-mile away stood a large timber warehouse that was in imminent danger of being enveloped by the flames that spread from the labyrinth of shanties.

The crowd cleared what goods they could from the shops and threw them into Sadovaya Street, where they lay in smoldering heaps. Despite the unbearable heat, people tried to stamp out the fire with their feet. At the Ministry, clerks carried files of papers out of the building and loaded them into cabs. Occasionally, a bundle fell into the street, where the wind took its leaves and strewed them about the square.

Soon the lumberyard was afire. Through the smoke, Herschel saw the flames raging. Flaming barrels and wooden boxes littered the streets. Russian soldiers had emptied them of their contents and were filling their pockets with coffee and concealing conical lumps of sugar in their *képis*. They were enjoying the excitement and luxuriating in the warmth of the blaze. The merchants, exhausted, their faces black, their hair and eyebrows singed, looked at the scene with swollen and inflamed eyes, despairingly.

Herschel staggered, loose-limbed and catatonic, through twisting streets and down dark alleys where crowds milled and shouted. The ground quaked and shifted beneath his feet. Long lines of houses and shops loomed before him, their doors blank and their windows flashing in the sun. His face was pockmarked with splinters of bone and speckled with blood. He walked to Hendler Street, then Lenard Street, and turned at last into Alexander Street, to the gate of the red brick hospital.

Dazed and feverish, he wandered down corridors lined with patients, past wards and examining rooms. And finally, somehow, he reached the pediatric ward and threw open the door.

Franzos looked up at him from behind a stretcher on which a young boy lay. Franzos gaped at Herschel in disbelief. Herschel had been under strict instructions to go directly to the safe house that had been prepared. Franzos stumbled away from the stretcher. His eyes were wide with fear. He shrank to the wall, his hands outstretched as if to ward off a blow.

Herschel stared vacantly at him. At Herschel's side, in his right hand, hung the huge grotesque cavalry pistol.

• • • •

16

FUGITIVE

He plodded along on frozen paths under skies that were perpetually dark. His skin was chafed raw, and his clothing was encrusted in mud and stiffened by repeated soaking and drying. But soon the blistered heels, the running sores, the lice-infested shirt, became as nothing in his thoughts. But something mysterious tormented him. He was beleaguered by questions that never left his mind.

Marching on, on deserted roads, avoiding villages and hamlets, he marked time to the beat of a blacksmith's hammer echoing from a village down the road, maintaining a marching cadence to preserve order in his mind, to hold chaos at bay.

He had no shelter at night. He would spurn the opportunity of a hot meal. Even when he came to a town he didn't dare ask for a place to sleep. He didn't want to answer questions; he couldn't show papers. Better, he thought, to take refuge in a haystack. But every night when he lay down he was afraid that he would never rise again. In some farmer's field, in the middle of the night, alarmed by the barking of a dog nearby, he dashed out, grabbing his belongings as he ran, shivering in the cold.

He sometimes encountered long processions of peasants - farmers trudging their way to the fields, woodsmen shouldering axes and saws, beggars displaying crippled limbs, and women taking chickens and ducks to market, carrying jugs and pans, or leading goats. One day he saw a group of derelicts squatting by the roadside. He stayed far away from them, afraid that they would curse him as a *Zhid*, attack him, and steal his few meager possessions.

Emerging, as if from a grave, came the distant voice of a peasant woman singing a sad lament. He stood listening. Chance reminiscences tormented him. Kindled by what? A sight? A sound? A distant harmonica or an innocent ballad emerging from the evening stirred fragments of memories of blazing summers, dappled meadows, the hum of insects – sinuous dreams flowing and merging, like images reflected in a stream. Some wayward stimulus brought to light memories of his early childhood. He saw himself as he appeared in faded sepia photographs - a slender child with large dark eyes and long blonde tresses. He recalled parlor maids and governesses primping and fussing, and smothering him in kisses. A peasant girl seen in the distance, the arc of her arm reaching up to steady the basket balanced on her shoulder, called forth his first adolescent knowledge of love - a willowy schoolgirl, her dewy lips like petals. He saw himself as he was on his way to the opera - a young man ascending a marble staircase, white silk waistcoat, flowing cravat, posy in his buttonhole, striving to make an impression on some plump youthful person.

He had visions so distinct and crystalline – of his home, of the murmur of family voices, the melodies of the holidays, the fragrance of the Sabbath table - flickering candles, glittering silver, ruby wine in crystal glasses.

He thought of his mother. Whenever her face appeared before him, wherever he was, he would suddenly stop, and he would call out to her. "Mama! Mama!" And he wept. He longed for her embrace. He sobbed.

"I know she is dead. I killed her," he would cry.

Certain mannerisms of his father came to him – the way he carried himself, the tilt of his head when he listened, the tracery of blue veins on the back of his hand.

Melancholy often gave way to frustration and fury. His mind shrieked.

"They are hunting me, pursuing me like a pack of hounds. Come and get me!" he cried. "Get it over with!" he begged.

But then, after a time, he wondered, "Is it possible that they are really not after me? What if I am mistaken? What if it is all in my mind?"

Exhausted, starving, in desperation, he walked toward a village he could see in the distance.

"*Tomawiecke*," the signpost read. He stood in the bright village square and watched the peasants trundling carts and barrows through the snow. Across the market an elderly woman, swathed in shawls, used a straw broom to sweep the snow from the street in front of a thatch-roofed hut. Ruddy-faced children raced through the streets, slipping and sliding, shouting and laughing. Shopkeepers bustled about, shoveling snow from before their stores and stalls. A constant din rose from the town, but it was a clamor that spoke of happiness and contentment. It filled him with longing.

"What would it be like to live a simple, carefree, unhurried life in a town like this?"

Then he saw the militiaman. He trembled violently. He drew a deep breath and shrank back into an alley. The soldier was making his way through the snow toward the silent frozen fountain in the middle of the square. He wore a snow-covered fur cap. His legs were wrapped in strips of cloth up to his knees. A long musket was slung over his shoulder. Herschel knew that the soldier would see that he was pale and anxious. It was time to move on. He took refuge in a huddle of farmers who were leading a horse and wagon through town.

He was feverish, close to delirium.

"I am ill, but I must keep moving."

He was worried about his boots, which were worn thin. Two days earlier he had patched the hole in the sole of his left boot with the cover of a discarded Bible he had found in the rubbish outside a church. He was concerned that his money would run out. In an alleyway, he looked warily over his shoulder and removed the drawstring pouch from his waistband. He counted the little that was left of his money, yet again.

•

He stood at the side of a large broad-sided barn and peered through a smoke-stained window. A drunk stood half-naked in a stall, singing a bawdy ballad. As he entered, two others made their way unsteadily toward the door. They clung to each other and stumbled, jostling him as they passed. The barn stank of beer and manure. It was dimly lit by guttering oil lamps hanging from the beams. In one corner there was a pile of junk and discarded tools. An old two-wheeled cart, its shafts tipped to the floor, leaned against the wall next to a wagon lying on its side. Everywhere he looked there were barrels with rusted hoops and splayed staves and stacks of old buckets nesting one inside the other.

When his eyes adjusted to the gloom, he saw that the barn was swarming with people. There were dozens of men, all of whom, it seemed to him, were scuttling about, weaving and wandering, swaying to and fro, and shouting at the top of their lungs, attempting to be heard over a wheezing concertina in the far corner. He supposed that they, like him, had rented a place to sleep for a few *groschen* from the old blacksmith.

Their tattered clothes hung like shrouds from nails hammered into the posts; their packs and bundles lay in the straw. Some of the men were stretched out in spaces they had claimed for themselves; a few sat cross-legged, eating greedily with greasy fingers from paper sacks in their laps. A powerful odor assailed him – vomit, smoke, sweat, and cow dung. His stomach turned over.

He lowered his bundle to the ground in an unoccupied space between the wall and a tall haggard man with a ragged beard who was engaged in earnest conversation with himself. He sank to the floor into the damp hay and sat for a while, looking around the barn, furtively examining his fellow lodgers. Hands reached out, bodies whirled, eyes peered at him out of bright red pockmarked faces.

"They are looking at me. They think I don't see them, but I do. They know who I am. They know what I have done. They all know."

A moment later he forgot what he had been thinking. He held his head in his hands, his elbows resting on his knees. He looked around in confusion, not fully comprehending what he was doing there. The concertina played on. He heard the scratching of a violin. The din pounded his head. He moaned as he lay down in the straw and inhaled its fragrance. Somehow he was comforted by it.

He covered himself with his blanket and immediately fell into a deep sleep. But he dreamed incoherent dreams. He awoke in the middle of the night, wet through with sweat. His limbs were numb. He didn't know whether it was night or day, or what day it was. Once again he was terrified. I must escape! I must run! I must keep moving!"

Quickly, he gathered his blanket, and with trembling fingers he tied his roll together. Then he slipped quietly away.

• • • •

17

THE FOREST

Herschel sat sprawled in the mud on the side of the road, the aroma of the wet earth filling his nostrils. Freezing rain fell in a steady downpour, but he felt no cold. His thoughts no longer tormented him. Nothing mattered any more. Even fear, dread and anxiety had receded. He no longer felt the weariness in his legs, the spasms in his arms, and the hollowness in his gut. Day after day his body had staggered on.

Struggling to his feet, he looked out upon a desolate land. The woods were sparse and the ground was soft and boggy. He breathed the pungent odor of rotting trees and leaves rising from the ground in a damp mist. The land plunged into a dark and dismal abyss.

Gray vapors rose languidly from a vast somber swampland. Gray. Everything was gray - the swamp, the mountains with cliffs of slate, and the boiling clouds touching the tops of the trees.

Staggering from one patch of sandbar to another, he skirted fetid pools, some as large as ponds. But often he landed knee-deep in putrid black slime. From time to time he found himself lost in tall yellow cane and cat's tail, which rose high above his head. He was startled by the frantic beating of wings - ducks rising in his path. Bullfrogs leapt. Hares darted out of the brush. The sky, reflected in the dark pools, was vast and gray.

•

One day toward dusk he saw a dim outline of dark mountains overgrown with mighty firs, tufts of clouds catching in their tops. He lay down on a patch of dry sand and drifted off into a fitful, dream-tormented sleep.

When he awoke he was frozen to the bone. He sat heavily, his hand on his brow. He couldn't feel his hands and feet. His body trembled uncontrollably. How long had he slept? Was it now the next day? Had he slept through the night or dozed off just for a moment?

Translucent ice had filmed over the dark pools of the swamp. The trees gleamed. A rain driving from the north was mixed with snow. Soon it turned entirely to snow, which fell silently, ceaselessly.

He was afraid of losing the use of words, so he spoke to himself, reciting aloud all that he observed.

"Soon the swamp will be covered with snow, and it will be hard enough to walk on."

But then, in caution, he reconsidered.

"Footprints in the snow can be tracked," he murmured.

"I need a fire," he thought. But then he paused. "But the rising smoke will be visible."

He tramped through snow-covered thickets of thorns. He tripped over a buried tree stump, falling heavily into a crevasse. His face was lacerated, and his body was bruised. The snow floated down lazily, falling in large thick flakes. Silence. There was nothing but silence, except for the moaning of the wind in the trees.

From time to time a dreaded question found a fissure in his consciousness, into which it would seep unbidden:

"What have I done? Could it really be that I have blood on my hands?"

Shifting shadows spread over the plains of his mind, and he wrapped insensibility around himself like a cloak.

•

There was a village ahead. Through the gloom he saw flickering candles in windows. The streets were empty and silent. The air was thick with sleet, which soon turned to rain. Before long it was pouring with a fierce intensity. As he entered a large open square, rivulets of rain were cutting ragged paths through the snow.

On the far side, in the faint glow of a forge in the dark mass of a blacksmith's stables, he saw a place where he might rest. He approached warily. He was tempted to rush across the square, but he realized that it would be safer to shelter in the shadows, taking the long way around.

Then, above the drumming of the rain on the cobbles, he heard the sound of a footfall. His heart raced. A long, sinister shadow advanced across the square. The fog parted and from out of an alleyway a man emerged before him. He was a huge hulking man wrapped in what appeared to be several layers of clothing, a blanket pulled over his head.

Herschel trembled with fear. The man had seen him. He had stopped and peered into the darkness at him.

Then, in a hoarse whisper, the man called out, "Marius?"

Wacek Seimanowski stepped out of the night.

•

They collapsed onto the damp straw in the stable and lay with their backs against a stall. The blacksmith had gone, but the damped-down fire at the forge was still glowing. They stretched their muddy boots toward the fire, their heads drawn down into their cloaks, their hands thrust deeply into their pockets. They were both exhausted and famished.

Seimanowski's eyes betrayed his fatigue, yet somehow, as Herschel looked at him, he still seemed to exuded an aura of aggressiveness and strength. Seimanowski was massive, formidable and resourceful. Herschel was overjoyed to have his company, relieved to have someone with whom he could share the burden of his fears.

The assassination lay silently between them, unexplored, though it was obvious to each that the other had played a part in it. It cemented a macabre bond, a comradeship that required no comment or explanation.

Seimanowski's face, which Herschel had once found beatific, now appeared to him to be sly, malevolent, even terrifying. He was all the more frightening because Herschel knew that he could be cunning. He was extraordinarily intelligent. Herschel believed that if Seimanowski had been educated he would have made something of himself. As it was, he was the ideal revolutionary – solitary, isolated from other men, and utterly alone. He never had a friend. His whole life was an absurd, desperate struggle to gain by violence some recognition of his worth. And now he saw the failure of the Insurrection as a personal defeat.

He cursed the capitalists. "The goddamn swine!" He raved constantly about the traitorous leaders of the Insurrection. "They drove Poland into this hopeless uprising. The thieves! They stole the money that was meant for the guerrillas!"

Herschel knew that much of what Seimanowski ranted was true. As he thought about his comrades in Warsaw, he knew now that to them, the Insurrection was merely an adventure.

"They feed off schoolboy escapades and immature fantasies. Their egos are satiated only by chaos and turmoil."

He now knew that they were incompetent and ineffectual. He wondered, "Where are they now, my erstwhile comrades?"

Seimanowski said that some had been arrested. Very few had escaped. He heard that a few had committed suicide.

For several days pogroms had swept through Warsaw. There were beatings of Jews, smashing of Jewish store windows, and looting. A small group had fled to Palestine.

"Once our comrades had been inspired by glittering goals - enlightenment, culture, progress," Herschel reflected. "Once, the dream of a magnificent new future had smoldered within them. They would cast off the chains of oppression and struggle for the greater good. Lofty thoughts. Glorious ambitions."

Now Herschel knew there was no end to disorder, violence, and depravity.

"What have we accomplished? The bourgeoisie still torments the worker. The peasant still starves, and dissidents languish in Siberia."

He felt that their lives had been placed at risk unnecessarily, merely to appease the egos of the leaders of the committee. Racism – the hate of brother for brother had contaminated the ranks of their cell. There had been endless conflict over leadership. Divisions between the landed nobility and the radical bourgeoisie had sundered the insurrection.

Herschel had observed the disputes within his cell with growing dismay and disillusionment.

"How could I have allowed myself to be seduced by a rabble of opportunists, louts, and blowhards?"

He believed that the principles of the Warsaw cell were drowned in a flood of words that were pointless, utterly insincere, and foreign to life itself.

•

They wandered on. Occasionally they found work. Seimanowski would do a day's work as a woodsman. Herschel would carry bundles of wood from the forest to the mill, or to the market where the townswomen bought it for kindling. He sometimes worked as a shepherd. For a few weeks they labored wretchedly in a salt mine outside Wieliczka, but they left hurriedly when they saw the foreman eyeing them suspiciously.

They would take their few *groschen* and buy a simple meal. Seimanowski would have a garlicky pork sausage, and Herschel would have hot soup with beans and mushrooms. He would have a beer, and Seimanowski would have a glass of vodka. But more often they went without. It was not easy to find work in winter. They walked on, wandering on deserted roads from one village to another.

In the market squares, peasant women sat beside cans of milk and baskets of shriveled vegetables. They wore thick shawls and long skirts hitched up to their knees to avoid the mud. Seimanowski cursed them.

"Bitches!" he swore.

As a child, an orphan, he had never stayed anywhere for long. In the orphanage they fed him scraps. He stole food, and they beat him. He ran off. Everywhere the world conspired against him.

Sometimes they entered a town and Seimanowski would disappear. Herschel never knew where he went. But he always returned drunk, reeking of schnapps. Where did he get the money? They had no money even for food.

•

It was late. The night was cold. There was no moon. In his stupor, after wandering listlessly from inn to inn, Seimanowski, his head lolling on hunched shoulders and his deep-set dark eyes brooding, groped his way along stone walls that seemed to undulate before him. Despite the cold there were beads of sweat on his forehead. He turned into a dark street. It was quiet at the edge of town. He circled back and crossed the quivering wooden bridge in long, loose-limbed strides. He broke into a shambling trot across the open meadow. Shadows moved. There was rustling in the bushes. He was wary, but in the blackness he could see nothing at which to launch his immense strength.

Finally, he reached the haystack where Herschel slept. He sat down heavily. He looked long at Herschel through bleary eyes. He lay down beside him. Herschel smelled of the woods. A warmth radiated from him. Seimanowski burrowed his head into Herschel's shoulder. Feeling Herschel stirring, Seimanowski pretended to be asleep. And then, when Herschel's breathing resumed its rhythm, Seimanowski embraced him tenderly, cradling him in his arms.

Herschel awoke in horror. Seimanowski's contorted face swam before him in the dim light of dawn. He shrank back. He tried desperately to free himself from Seimanowski's grasp. Wildly, Seimanowski stood and lashed out at him. Herschel felt a blow that nearly cracked his skull. His knees buckled. But Seimanowski didn't let him fall. He continued to rain blows upon him.

Then, in slowly revolving circles, Herschel descended into unconsciousness.

•

When he awoke, he lay sprawled on his back in his own blood, dazed and helpless, in the stubble of a mist-shrouded cornfield. He moaned and swayed, cradling his arm against his chest, feeling pain that told him ribs were broken. He was soaked to the skin, buffeted by the wind. Fragments of sound collided in his head, and ghostly images emerged from the vapor of the forest, rising and shifting and disappearing. The golden orb of the setting sun sent beams of amber light into the crowns of the trees.

By the light of the first stars he rose and followed a well-worn path through the woods. Avoiding roads, he crossed the countryside, taking long-abandoned trails. He skirted villages and farms, bypassing inhabited places and making long detours around farmers in the fields. He passed fallow farmlands and vineyards, pastures and meadows. Exhausted, he took shelter in a hayrick.

The next day, he followed a road into a shallow valley watered by a rushing torrent that eventually petered into a meandering stream. He rested on the bank, pausing to remove his sodden boots. Slowly, gravely, he unwound the long strips of cloth in which he had bound his bruised and bloody feet. He rubbed his swollen ankles, studied the cracks between his toes, and held his feet up to the pale sickly sun.

Everyday minutiae, like finding a fistful of grain for porridge or shelter for the night, assumed a gravity, imposed a burden of such consequence, that it obliterated more exalted thoughts from his consciousness. His concern for humanity had long ago shriveled into a small, hard kernel that, though he could not dislodge it from his mind, was no longer a passion.

Again he fell into a deep troubled sleep. When he awoke the dawn was struggling to pierce the fog. A web of mist lay low upon the field, and a watery sun was beginning to tint the snowy fields gold. He had dreamed of home. Tears filled his eyes. Slowly he rose.

For several days he had trudged through drifts so deep that he frequently had to struggle to free himself. Now, the snow was hurled by a wind so strong that it drove the breath from his lungs. It was a blinding bedlam. There was no longer a horizon. He lost his sense of direction.

"I don't know where I am going. But what does it matter?"

He was lost in a white abyss. He was afraid that he might drop into a steep chasm, falling away into the mist onto the jagged rocks below.

At dusk of his fifth day in the wilderness he entered a deep forest. The snow fell into a vast void, obliterating the distant mountains. He fought his way up ridges and down into valleys. There was no trace of life and no glimmer of reality.

The wind sang through the trees, sending white clouds of snow into the air. He leaned into the wind, stumbling though the snow. The privations of his journey, his hunger and weakness, and the pain of his exertions were nothing compared to the loneliness, powerlessness, mental anguish, and fear that now seized him as he forged ahead against the full fury of the storm. He hoped to find a hollow tree or some other burrow into which he could crawl. But he knew that sleep was an enticement that he must resist at all costs.

Then, a gust of wind whipped the snow away. He thought he could make out vague, shadowy images in the distance. Then he saw that a group of men – slow-moving, plodding, and leaning at an impossible angle against the wind – were advancing through the driving snow. They seemed to be struggling to reach a shelter that he could barely see silhouetted against the gray sky. They were weighed down under their packs. One man led two unruly horses. As Herschel drew closer, he saw that some of the men were laboring mightily, trying to repair a crude shed with loose timber. Others worked on a dilapidated paling that surrounded a hut. Several struggling with a wagon. Two others were trying to keep a small herd of uneasy sheep together.

He would have to approach them. He had no choice. He had to chance it. Otherwise he would perish.

He stumbled toward the hut. They didn't appear to notice the solitary figure rising out of the billowing snow. Without addressing any of them, he began to pry loose timber from a snow-covered pile. They were able to work together using hand signals. Words were useless, torn from their mouths and carried away on the wind. Finally, breathless and frozen, they collapsed onto their bundles on the frozen mud floor of the hut, huddling close to the sputtering fire they had hastily thrown together. Their breath was thrust from heaving chests, issuing from their mouths in gray clouds. Their eyes swam with tears.

There were nine of them, most unknown to each other, strangers thrown together in the storm. There was a long-faced butcher and his young helper from Tchernowitz - the owners of the herd of sheep. Two burly caravan drivers with packs of wool were on their way to Jassy. A tall, fierce-looking Croatian foot soldier returning from leave to rejoin his regiment. A coachman and his passenger - an elderly merchant from Crakow who huddled in his furs, sitting as far removed from the others as possible. And a thickset, rugged-looking horse-trader.

It seemed to Herschel that far from being intimidated by their circumstances, they were inclined to joviality. They spoke in a confusion of Polish, Russian, and German. Herschel spoke not a word. He shrank into the shadows.

Later, when the wind died down and the snow diminished to flurries, the sky appeared clear and bright, studded with stars. The moon, a pale golden sphere, hung above the forest, bathing the long expanse of snow in blue. It was still biting cold.

They huddled in the hut, heads buried in hoods of horse blankets. Moving about, they were bulky, ungainly, bear-like. Their beards were frozen, icicles hung like visors on their glowing red faces. The butcher offered a bag of hardtack and dried smoked meat wrapped in newspaper. Herschel ate greedily. Some of them passed around a Turkish *chibouque.*

In the far distance they could hear the baying of wolves. Before falling off to sleep they mounted guard, each taking a turn replenishing the bonfire in the center of the makeshift corral they had thrown up to contain the sheep and horses.

•

They had just descended into an exhausted sleep when an explosion shattered the silence of the night. Herschel rose in terror. The hut was in confusion. The horse trader was angrily berating one of the caravan drivers. He had fired at a wolf.

"I wounded him!" the driver shouted proudly.

But the horse trader was incensed.

"Fool!" he shouted. "The other wolves will track his blood back to us. The whole pack will be down on us in less than half an hour!"

He organized them swiftly, sending some to strengthen the enclosure, barricading it with what additional wood they could find. Then he placed them in positions around the palings. Herschel's eyes widened. They were actually going to drive off a pack of wolves? The herdsman had only a pistol and the long knife he carried in his belt. The butcher had a light hatchet. But the caravan drivers and the coachman were armed to the teeth. The others found stout clubs. The sheep were bleating and the horses were jerking at their halters and whinnying nervously.

The first one then appeared in the distance - a large and powerful gray wolf, undoubtedly the leader. They waited in the cold. A half-hour passed. There was no sign of the pack. But then they saw them. They were standing in a line abreast at the edge of the forest, five or six of them, their elongated shadows sprawling across the pale blue snow. Soon, silently, they were joined by others. The pack was now assembled. They howled and barked, communicating among themselves, at least twenty-five or thirty of them. The leader, they could see, was enormous. He looked to be at least two meters long.

He must weigh thirty-five or thirty-six kilos!" the sheepherder exclaimed.

Boldly, the leader led the pack forward.

Don't use firearms unless you are sure you can kill them," the horseman warned. "The wounded will escape back into the forest to bring others."

With long and loping strides, the pack, moving as one, bounded across the snow field toward the enclosure. Their eyes, shining in the moonlight, were yellow. Their teeth were bared. Most of them pulled up at the fence, the weight of their bodies pushing it inward. The scent of the sheep was driving them into a frenzy. A few of the pack leaped recklessly, attempting to clear the palings.

Desperately, with all their strength, the men swung their clubs. Though he was sickened by the dull thud of the blows landing against the skulls and bodies of the wolves, to Herschel's wonder he was able to wield his club with as much passion and force as the others. He was exhilarated.

The wolves, yelping in pain and growling in frustration, were driven back. Several of them lay sprawled on the ground. But soon the pack rallied, attacking once again, this time from several directions. Three of what appeared to be the largest succeeded in breaching the fence. The Croatian and the caravan driver fired. Two wolves lay bleeding where they fell. The remainder of the pack devoured its wounded and fled.

•

Herschel awoke from a deep sleep. At first he could not separate his dreams from reality. His limbs were stiff. His hands and feet were frozen. He looked out to see the first rays of the sun casting long pink fingers over the surface of the vast snow field. He found that he was covered by an old faded Persian rug of the type that the horseman used as a saddle blanket for his mounts. He stirred himself. The others were just awakening. Outside the hut, the bloody remains of eight wolves lay at the foot of the palings. The butcher and his helper were busy skinning them. The travelers arose and packed their belongings, each to go his separate way.

The garrulous horse trader approached Herschel.

"Where do you come from, boy?" he asked, first in Polish, then in German.

"From far away," Herschel muttered.

"Where are you bound for?"

Herschel shrugged his shoulders.

"There is a village a few *versts* away," the horse trader gestured over his shoulder.

Herschel had been warned about Polish villages. The peasants were ignorant and brutal. There was no law. They settled their disputes with fists and cudgels. His eyes betrayed his fear.

"No need to be afraid," said the horse trader. "There is a settlement of Jews there."

"Jews," Herschel said. "What has that to do with me?"

"I just wanted you to know there is nothing to fear from them."

The horse trader walked away.

• • • •

PART III

Wladno, Poland — 1864 - 1865

18

THE VILLAGE

The sun swam in the cloudless sky. Birds shrieked as they wheeled overhead. Herschel trudged down a narrow road bisecting a field. As he rounded the next bend in the road he heard voices. He drew back in fear. Then, cautiously, he drew closer. He could make out a number of voices - young, pure, childish voices.

He saw a thatched-roof house and, soon, several other houses. Then he saw a Catholic Church, and beyond the church a square surrounded by ragged trees, boughs bent mournfully under their burden of snow. The square was a warren of wretched shops where all manner of goods were being peddled. One shop displayed brooms and pots, another sold textiles and leather. And then to his great joy, he saw a stall in which were displayed prayer shawls and prayer books, *yarmulkes* and *mezuzahs*.

Some of the shops were little more than booths in which strings of orange onions and bunches of herbs hung from the rafters. They were tended by small, bent, bearded men who huddled around fires burning in braziers. The square was crowded with Jews, some wearing gabardines down to their knees and wide fur hats, and women who wore shawls over their heads. Above the shops and stalls, dwellings perched precariously, one story piled haphazardly on top of another. They appeared to be too fragile to support their burden of snow.

An old stooped man was selling charred baked potatoes on the corner of the square. A feather of smoke emerged from the chimney of a small stove set up in his pushcart A small knot of elderly men gathered about the peddler's cart, holding knotted fingers toward the fire. A young boy came lurching around the corner, shouldering an immense load of firewood.

It started to snow in earnest again. An ancient *Hassid*, his beard flecked with snow, lifted the skirts of his long black coat as he forged his way through the windblown snow.

Dusk was rapidly descending. Dark, snow-laden clouds hung low over the rooftops.

Herschel slogged on. The snow formed a cape on his shoulders; it drifted into his collar. He passed a row of stores. The tailor was shuttering his shop. So were the butcher and the shoemaker. He turned a corner and found shelter from the wind under a fishmonger's wagon in an alley.

•

Now the shops were closed. The market rested. It must be the Sabbath, Herschel realized. Soon he saw several Jews hurrying through the market place. He followed them at a distance, through the market square, down a narrow road – "Warsaw Street" was painted on the wall of a building – past a *Talmud Torah* and a ritual bath house, before finally coming to Synagogue Street. There stood an ancient wooden *shul*, its tall, peaked roof resting upon six faded white columns. Four worn stone steps led to a pair of lofty wooden doors. Above them was a pediment that had in its center an octagonal window adorned with a Star of David.

He saw the men walking toward the synagogue, their wives and children in groups behind them. The men wore their best caftans, their shoulders draped with prayer shawls. Some of the older women wore long silk or velvet dresses, with trains embroidered with beads, and bonnets adorned with bows and silk ribbons. Many of the younger women wore small earrings and carried prayer books with silver or gold-trimmed covers.

For almost three hours, Herschel hid in a doorway across the street. He was weak and famished. Thoughts revolved and weaved inside his head.

"Would they give me shelter?" he wondered. "Perhaps they would be afraid to harbor a fugitive. Who could blame them?"

He was confused and harried. It was cold. Yet he felt warm.

"Am I ill? He wondered if typhus had migrated from the cities to the countryside.

Then he saw the children bursting boisterously from the synagogue, followed by the adults, chattering, hands fluttering like the wings of birds. They congregated noisily on the steps, the women kissing and the men shaking hands. Finally, they dispersed and went off to their homes, where he thought a Sabbath meal must await them.

When the street had emptied, Herschel crossed and paused before the steps, and finally, hesitatingly, he entered the synagogue.

He looked into a long, narrow, dimly lit room. It's walls were painted a faded dark red and blue, pierced at intervals by tall, slender windows. All the walls were inscribed with quotations from the scriptures. Paintings of animals and fish ornamented the vaulted ceiling, from which three brass chandeliers were suspended. Standing at the rear of the sanctuary he looked out on a sea of chairs of every description, scattered in disordered rows around a raised platform in the center of the room, on which stood a high table with a slanted top and a few high-backed chairs. At the far end of the sanctuary was the ark containing the Torah scrolls, over which hung a flickering oil lamp. Cautiously, he climbed the wooden stairway to the balcony, where the women worshipped. He walked toward a door that was outlined in pale light.

He stood in the shadows, peering into a room at the end of a corridor. A man was perched on a stool at a high desk piled with books. A pair of spectacles was perched on his long, noble nose. His eyes darted from one book to another. Licking his thumb, he rapidly turned pages. Though he was hunched over the table, Herschel could tell that he was very tall. He was thin. His cheeks were sunken. His beard was fair. Herschel looked at him and believed that he saw kindliness and compassion in his face. He suddenly felt an overwhelming urge to seize his hand. It was only with great effort that he was able to restrain himself.

The man looked up.

"Who is that?" he asked.

"I need the rabbi," Herschel said in German.

I am the rabbi."

"Rabbi," Herschel pleaded, "help me, please. They are after me."

The rabbi's eyes widened.

"The boy is running from conscription," he thought. "Maybe he is a provocateur. Perhaps an assassin even. He will bring the *Polacks* down on us."

"I am Herschel Hartenstein. From Berlin. I am from Berlin. I don't speak Yiddish. Do you understand me? I must find my way home. I can't go on like this."

The rabbi's fingers fluttered over the papers on his desk. He closed a book and carefully turned another one face down. As he gathered his thoughts, his fingers nervously went to his beard. Finally, he took the oil lamp from the table and brought it close to Herschel's face.

"The boy is feverish," the rabbi thought. "He looks half-starved."

Clutching Herschel by the sleeve, he led him toward the kitchen.

"Tova," he called.

A young woman looked up to see the boy, dressed in rags, unkempt and wan.

"He is ill," she said.

He wore a cap that was too large, and on his back he carried a makeshift knapsack, constructed somehow of a blanket and some cord. His clothes, steaming in the warmth of the kitchen, gave off a strong odor of the stable and the hayloft.

"What do you want?" the rabbi asked.

Herschel stood mute.

"They are after you, you said. You said, 'They.' Who is 'they'?"

"I can't endure any more," Herschel sobbed. "Please forgive me."

The rabbi and his wife stood silently. They were confounded.

"Please forgive me." Herschel said again, as he wiped the tears from his face with his sleeve. "I must stop running. I can't run anymore."

•

Rabbi Yonathan Mordoviscz put Herschel in mind of pictures he had seen of the American president, Abraham Lincoln. He was long-limbed and lanky. His beard was sparse, and his eyes were deep in his face above prominent cheekbones. When people spoke to him he stooped to listen as though from a great height. Indeed, he was over six feet tall. The villagers often said he must be the tallest Jew in the world. Though still in his thirties, by his appearance and demeanor he gave the impression of a man of many years. He conducted himself with shy restraint, which those who didn't know him well took to be haughtiness. In truth, it was just that he was usually preoccupied. He was immersed in Torah. If he had his way he would have secluded himself in his room among his teetering stacks of books, where alone with Maimonides or Spinoza, he was not of this world. His thirst for knowledge filled his entire being; it was his whole life.

Barely one year ago, much against his will, he yielded to the entreaties of his congregation and agreed to replace his dear departed father as their rabbi. But he was obsessed with the belief that he could never live up to his father's standards of wisdom and piety. A month after the death of his father, tragedy struck again. The rabbi's wife died giving birth to a stillborn child. The women of Wladno saw a star twinkling in the distant sky as mother and child ascended to heaven together. In accordance with tradition, the rabbi soon took another wife, Tova, the fifth daughter of the rabbi of the neighboring village. She was seventeen.

They said in the village that the rabbi and Tova were perfectly matched. Like her husband, she was tall and slender; she walked with her shoulders slightly hunched as if she were trying to hide her tallness. Her mouth was delicately curved, and her eyes were bright and large, almost too large for her face. Her hair was burnished gold, long and silken. A serious girl, her brow was almost always furrowed in a frown of concentration.

•

Through the weeks in which Herschel lay racked with fever, through his spasms of weakness and vertigo, Tova was his nurse. She heaped blankets on him when he shivered with cold; she supervised the Yeshiva boys, who changed his sweated nightshirt and tangled sheets. He coughed incessantly, struggling for air, and he constantly vomited the broth she spooned into his mouth.

Of that time, he had only vague, confused memories of a dark room, where the walls and ceiling drifted and shifted around his bed. There were days and nights when he had no sense of who he was. He turned and twisted in a bed drenched with sweat, crying out in his sleep - heart-rending cries, all the while struggling for breath.

He was lost in menacing shadows. His memories were pale obscure recollections of his early childhood, of a nursemaid whose name he made a vain effort to recall, of the gleaming glass eye of a hobbyhorse in his nursery, and of gentle breezes and soft blue skies. They came to him fragmented, like shards of broken mirror. He descended the course of his being, observing as from a great distance, scenes from his life. He saw himself ambling down a path of spring flowers in the park of the villa, watching from a misted window as a gentle snow drifted down, standing on the shore of the lake as evening came on, the last rays of the sun disappearing behind the hill.

Through it all he had a persistent sense of imminent danger. Confused incoherent images – grotesque faces, terrifying places, endless shadowy corridors – emerged from dark, hidden corners of his imagination. Spinning circles of distorted colors whirled around him. His mind drifted in dreams. He was entombed in a steel container flashing along at impossible speed. He saw rows of skulls grinning up at him from the ruins of an ancient church, and a cavern of sparkling crystals in a wilderness of shafts, galleries, and chambers. He dreamed of an elusive girl in a perfumed garden.

In moments of clarity, he heard sounds from the village street below. He heard a woman calling to her child and the sweet voices of children echoing from far away.

From time to time he called out softly, a sad, tormented lament, "Mama. Mama, where are you?"

He slept. And he wept. And he drifted off again. From time to time he saw a young girl leaning over his bed, speaking urgently in whispers with an old woman and with a man who was perhaps a doctor. He had moments of consciousness when he struggled with the damp tangle of his blankets, trying to rise from his bed. But then, exhausted, he again descended into delirium. He had lost all sense of time. He had no awareness of where he was. Yet somehow an inner voice told him that he shouldn't be there.

As one day followed another, Herschel's confusion deepened. He knew there were matters, urgent matters, he had to deal with, but he couldn't seem to bring them to mind. He struggled to sort through his memories, but he wasn't able to separate reality from events that existed only in his mind. He felt as if he had somehow been trying to flee, but he didn't know from what. He believed that he had committed a crime, an appalling crime. But what exactly had he done? He didn't know. He couldn't remember. At such times he was assailed by a terrifying anxiety. He had a sense that his guilt would always torment him. At night in bed, he gazed around the small tidy room, trying to recall how he came to be there.

•

Tova stood before her husband; her brow was lined, and her mouth was a taut line.

"The boy is very ill," she said. "Not just his body - in his mind. His mind wanders, he speaks in a language no one understands, and he talks to the shadows on the wall, and to people who aren't even in the room. Mattes Cohen has examined him, and he agrees. His mind is troubled. The potions he has given him haven't helped." The rabbi looked at her and he was dumbfounded. Here was this girl, just a slip of a girl, whose mind had never been burdened by a serious thought, standing before him in appalling bewilderment, over a boy who was a complete stranger to them.

•

One morning, when Herschel awoke, the room was filled with the light of a golden day. He saw shifting shadows of the curtains moving on the wall. He heard a dog barking in the distance. He breathed the aroma of freshly mown hay. He felt the renewed life of the burgeoning fields, fresh and verdant, flowing through the room. The patch of sky he could see through his window was pale blue and glowing. He felt the first faint glimmer of life.

When he was able to leave his bed, he was very weak. Every breath was difficult. Every step he took exhausted him. From time to time he was overtaken by a dreadful weariness. He would be apathetic, self-absorbed, and defeated. He felt as though he had been drifting in a miasma, a bleak loneliness, from which there was no escape.

But with the coming of spring, as life returned to the streets of Wladno, Herschel was reborn. He could feel the flow of richer, warmer blood. The fever was gone, and color had returned to his cheeks. All around him everything was more distinct, brighter and clearer, than they had been before. Hidden strands of his consciousness began to stir.

He watched with fascination as the birds, wheeling in the sky, flew back and forth, darting into the branches of the trees. The sky was filled with white billowing clouds, and the thawing snow, warm and sweet smelling, rose up in a low-hanging mist. Water streaked though the woods and formed pools in streets that glowed with the radiance of spring. The sounds of the village came to him so clearly. He heard the bell-like laughter of children playing in the streets, the droning of the scholars at their lessons, and the creaking of the limbs of trees coming into flower.

In the first weeks of his recovery, he wandered the streets of the village on unsteady legs, rejoicing in his newly found freedom, feeling for the first time in months that he was actually safe. These feelings didn't materialize all at once, and he didn't pause to analyze them; he simply felt that he was being shown the way by destiny.

•

The village of Wladno lies on the edge of a pine forest, twenty-one *versts* southeast of the Polish border with Prussia. This was about as near to Prussia as a Polish Jew could get. Jews were prohibited from living closer to the border than twenty *versts*. The town measured four square kilometers, all of it owned including its 202 houses by the Polish Count Stanislaw Roskowski, whose family had ruled since 1455. But it did not matter; the Russians ruled now. Thirty-four hundred people lived in Wladno. About eleven hundred were Jews, and the rest were Polish and a few Russians.

According to the records in the old synagogue, which was built in 1721, the first Jews came to the town in 1610; many of them settled there because they were attracted to the market square, which offered opportunities for selling boots, leather goods and clothing to the farmers in the vicinity. Eventually, they built mills to grind the farmers' grain, presses to make oil, and in recent years, factories to spin cloth. Many of the Jews of Wladno were craftsmen – cobblers, carpenters, tailors, weavers, tanners, and butchers. There was also an innkeeper who ran his own small brewery. And there were ordinary laborers - haulers and axmen who worked in the forest, loading and driving wagons piled high with massive logs. At the edge of the dark forest outside of town, in the damp fields shrouded by mist, were the thatched-roof huts of the Polish peasants, *muzhiks*.

In the market square in the center of the village, rising above the fog that often invaded the town from the river, stood a three-story stone building. It was the symbol of the iron fist of Russian authority – the headquarters of the Hussar squadron and the office of the *Starostwo*, the Polish district administrators who ruled for the Russians. The *Starostwo* building was grand, an imposing monument that was surrounded, incongruously, by ramshackle market stalls and shops, and the modest wooden and stone houses of the more prosperous families of Wladno. Reaching out to the sky from the roof was a tall tower housing the town clock. The oldest inhabitant of Wladno had never seen the hands of the clock move. A fitting metaphor, Herschel thought, for a village that had progressed very little since the seventeenth century.

Above the second floor windows of the *Starostwo* building, a Latin inscription was etched into the stone: "Here justice is to be found for all who enter these halls." Approaching this building, a Jewish soul was filled with dread.

The Jews and the gentiles lived on opposite sides of the *Starostwo* headquarters. On the west side of the market all the shops and houses belonged to the Jews - the families Boorda, Perla, Markewitz, Zaleska, and the Bialiks, Shapiros, Lichtenegers and Kovskys.

Hanging from Bialik's house was a large sign on which was painted the figure of a Russian officer. Bialik was the army tailor.

There was a long succession of stores in the square – the pharmacy, the distillery, and shops filled with hardware, groceries, leather, fabrics, and clothing - each tumbling one on top of the other.

Down a long alley there was a courtyard lined with wooden barrels. Jews with long thick beards, wearing dirty leather aprons, stirred hides in the barrels with long poles, while others removed the hair from the hides with sharp scrapers. Farther out of town was the granary, where millers, always covered head to toe in white flour, ground the wheat and filled the sacks. They were hefted into wagons by red-faced burly carters who wore stout ropes around their waists.

On the east side of the square were the houses of the Poles. In most of the Polish yards there was a fierce dog tethered with a chain.

In some of the streets of the Jewish neighborhoods there were small modest places of worship frequented by the adherents of various long-bearded *Hassidic* rabbis, who kept themselves apart from the less rigidly orthodox Jews - the "moderns" of Rabbi Mordoviscz' congregation. Many of them trimmed their beards, or worse, were clean-shaven and wore stiff collars and pressed trousers. It was whispered that they read "worldly" books.

Scattered throughout the Polish neighborhoods were *zajazdy*, inns that the Poles owned and frequented. They were the wellspring of the pogroms that were frequent occurrences. Looming over the square to the east was the Catholic Church. Around the corner, on Priest's Lane, lived the old priest, in a house that had in its front window a picture that depicted a well-fed gentile about to kick an ugly, long-nosed, cowering Jew. The caption on the picture read, "Don't buy from the Jews. Buy from your own kind." It was there, on Priest's Lane, that plans were laid for violent attacks on Jews and Jewish stores. From here the embers of hatred and loathing ignited and burst into flame.

From all sides of the market square, long and narrow cobble-stoned streets spread out like the web of a spider. And from the streets there extended a network of alleys, which connected to yet other streets, all of them occupied by small wooden houses, sheds, huts, warehouses, and workshops. Many of the streets ended in roads that led to other towns and villages. Warsaw Street led to Lodz, Wroclaw, Poznan, Bydgoszcz, and Kutno, before finally reaching all the way to Warsaw. Nieborg Street ended in the road that wound through the pine forest, across the river, to the forbidden place where Russian Poland ended and Prussia began.

Across the square, two blocks away toward the west, was the largest of the village's Jewish houses of worship, the synagogue of Rabbi Yonathan Mordoviscz, the Wladno Rabbi.

•

All day long people entered and left the rabbi's rooms, where Herschel slept and took his meals. Often during the night, his sleep was disturbed by several older men who drifted in to study Torah. He heard them murmuring, chanting, sighing, and sometimes sobbing. Every day, except Saturday of course, a group of young men in threadbare trousers and shabby capotes came to the Wladno Synagogue and sat at the long wooden table with their books open before them, wholly absorbed in religious learning. In the afternoon there was a bible lesson for boys, their piping voices repeating in unison the words of the rabbi. In the evening many simple Jews who didn't know how to read, sat and listened to lessons. Travelers from faraway towns and villages came in to rest. Beggars huddled near the stove and settled down to sleep. It seemed as if everyone in the village came to pray, study, bare their souls, gossip, and argue. They came to ask the rabbi's advice and to present him with matters for arbitration.

Some came only for the tea provided by the ebullient boisterous horse trader, Josep Rochek, who was the warden of the synagogue. It was well-known that Rochek had smuggled revolutionists across the border during the Insurrection, and it was rumored that even now he did a thriving business in transporting horses and contraband between Prussia and Poland. People came on holy days and festivals for the egg biscuits, honey cakes, herring, and wine that Josep paid for out of his own pocket. And from all over they came to plead for the guidance and seek the wisdom of the young Wladno Rabbi.

Each day, Tova served Herschel his meals, which he ate at the table with the rabbi, and often with some traveler from another village or faraway city. It was odd, Herschel thought, that neither the rabbi nor Tova had ever questioned him.

"They never ask me why am I running, or where I am going," Herschel thought. "In the time of my illness, God only knows what I uttered in my delirium. They fed me and clothed me, and never asked me why I was fleeing and from what."

Apparently the young students who daily sat at the rabbi's long cluttered table, and the shopkeepers who came before the sun had risen to start their day by reciting the morning prayers, did not find it odd that a stranger had suddenly appeared out of thin air. They were accustomed, he supposed, to travelers who came to Wladno, buying grain or tanned skins, or selling implements, or bringing delicacies from the big cities as far away as Lodz, Plock, or even Warsaw.

Josep Rochek was the exception. He was curious. Though Herschel didn't recognize him, Rochek remembered Herschel well.

"This is the timid frightened boy who sheltered from the blizzard at the edge of the pine forest with the group of travelers," he recalled.

In his bantering manner, Rochek belabored Herschel with questions - the same questions he had asked him on the day they parted weeks ago.

"Where did you come from?" Rochek asked. "Where are you going?"

Rochek was a large, broad-shouldered man of middle years. He usually dressed in the Russian manner - a commodious blouse cinched at the waist by a broad leather belt, his pants tucked into high boots. He had a wiry black beard framing a sunburned face that was furrowed by wind and rain. His voice was like a force of nature, and his laughter was like gravel pouring into a bucket. He loved life. He liked nothing more than a flavorsome dish, a proper gulp of schnapps, and a young, spirited horse.

Any Jew who came from out of town would wander in to Rochek's house, not necessarily with anything particular in mind, just a desire to find out what was going on, and perhaps to partake of the beer, the chopped herring, and the egg cookies he always had on hand. To be in town on Saturday and not come to lift a glass at Josef Rochek's house was considered outright sacrilege. When anyone came to the house, first of all Rochek's plump giggling Polish serving girl – always a pleasure to behold – would serve him a glass of schnapps. Then he was asked to sing a new tune, tell a folk tale, or recite a poem. Here, tall stories and jests flew. The whole world was a joke, and no one took anything seriously.

As for Herschel, Rochek knew something, as he put it, was not kosher. The boy spoke no Yiddish, getting by with German. His Polish was abominable. He had no Russian at all. He had the look about him of gentry. He could almost pass for a *goy*!

"Where did he drop from?" Rochek wondered. "He arrived in rags. And ill."

Rochek thought the boy probably would have died without the ointments and salves that the "doctor", Mattes Cohen, produced from his little black bag. "Or, who knows," Rochek thought, "maybe he was saved by the brew of fermented forest berries that the midwife, Rivka Lichteneger, forced down his gullet to make him sweat."

On second thought, Rochek believed that maybe he would have lived anyway, without their nostrums and potions.

"Chaya Czizewer had seen a white dove alighting on the roof of the synagogue," Rochek recalled. "Definitely a sign that an angel bearing good tidings has appeared."

If you believed in such things, which of course Rochek didn't.

•

Wladno, Herschel discovered, was a strange but wondrous place. Poor almost beyond words, but nevertheless apparently contented with its lot, at ease with the rhythm of life that had not changed for centuries. On Sunday, the market square was filled with peasants waiting in front of the church for the priest. They sat on the curb with their feet in the ditch, eating groats, sauerkraut, and bread dipped in mead or wine. On Sunday, Jews stood guard in front of their stores and homes. Troubles and persecutions always began on the *goyim's* holy day.

Thursdays were market days. Herschel watched in amazement as from every direction man and animal flooded into the market. The village was in a frenzy. The streets bustled with activity and with the commotion of commerce conducted in a cacophony of German, Russian, Polish all the languages that a succession of foreign occupiers had inflicted on the town – and, of course, Yiddish.

Peddlers hawked their wares in a incessant chant. They sold fruits and vegetable of every kind - blackberries, purple grapes, yellow melons, red apples and green pears, onions, potatoes, cabbage, radishes, carrots, and turnips. And everywhere Herschel inhaled the sickly-sweet odor of fruit mingling with tobacco, kerosene, and animal dung.

Polish peasants, dressed in little more than rags, sat on overturned boxes. They rubbed shoulders with elderly long-caftaned Jews. Women with shawls over their heads went from stall to stall, poking and prodding meat, fowl, and fish. A horse cart's cargo of wheat overflowed into the street. A man driving a wagon carrying wooden cages of geese, ducks, chickens, and turkeys looked in vain for a place to settle. A frisking colt and a lowing cow were tied to the back.

Herschel saw farmers and their wives and children carrying straw baskets filled with butter, cheese and cream in earthen pots. A decrepit woman struggled with a cart loaded with cherries and strawberries. An old clothes dealer, Benyamin Soldanski, had set up a booth that looked like a tent with walls of canvas, from which many old suits hung. Next to him was the cap-maker, Mendel Yohanan, and a few feet away was the workbench of Lupczak the clockmaker. It was said that Lupczak owed the Tsar three hundred rubles, which was the fine he had to pay for his brother Mottel, who had run off without serving his time in the army. Three hundred rubles was a sentence of life-long labor for Lupczak.

Herschel marveled at the lavish display of loaves of bread, white rolls, butter and cream, and the bottles of mead, wine, and vodka that were arranged on tables in rows, Next to them were barrels brimming with sour pickles and herrings. An ancient *Hassid* passed his hands through grains of rye to assess its quality. Another grabbed a chicken from a cart and blew at its back feathers to determine its plumpness.

A peasant painstakingly examined a scythe. His wife was buying kerosene.

Herschel saw a young girl admiring a flowery kerchief. Two elderly men were leading a calf away, one pulling it by the head and the other twisting its tail. Hershel walked to the corner of Stankowicz Street, near the church, where he saw a dealer selling secondhand goods to housewives who were jostling each other to get to the pushcarts.

Later in the day he heard voices growing loud and raucous, and then he saw a number of peasants and some of the village Poles emerging from the tavern. They rushed out into the street, arms waving wildly. One claimed that an old *Hassid* overcharged him.

"Where is my change, *Zhid?*" the man yelled. "I gave you two rubles! You think I am stupid? I know when I have been robbed!"

They ran up Lomza Street and spilled out into the square. Awaiting them was the timber-hauler, Itcheleha Zloczewer, wielding his axe. At his side, brandishing a stout club, was the broad-shouldered big-bellied blacksmith, Salman Lidzbarski, known as Lidzbarski the Tall. With great pride the Jews told of Salman's prowess; he could fell a *Polack* with one resounding blow.

Soon screams and curses echoed through the market. Blood flowed from a nose. A skull was split. A frightened merchant ran for Rabbi Mordoviscz; a peasant fetched the district administrator, Zabladovich, the massive purple-faced Pole, from the *Starostrow*.

Then, Zabladovich and the rabbi stood nose to nose, and with much fist-shaking, gesticulating, and spittle-flying, they negotiated a peace. The problem was solved.

Herschel learned that the rabbi and the Pole had a clandestine relationship, an unspoken compact. He heard that they often met privately to work things out together.

In the midst of the chaos, the market continued uninterrupted. Deals were made and goods were sold. At dusk, the peasants began to leave for their villages. The craftsmen dismantled their stalls. Wearily, they dragged their feet homeward. Debris and cow dung were everywhere. There was silence in the marketplace.

•

On Friday, when Herschel walked to the square, he found the market practically deserted. A few bored Jews wandered about, and others sat in front of their shops reading, or gathered in small groups to grumble about how poorly they had fared during yesterday's market. On the steps of the synagogue, Herschel recognized Areah Leib Fried, studying a religious book in the pale sunlight. On a bench nearby, two elderly men had set up their chessboard; they sat facing each other on crates, absorbed in their game.

Herschel recognized the sallow-faced, wispy-bearded "doctor", Mattes Cohen, who had swabbed Herschel's throat with a tincture when he was ill. An elder of the synagogue, he was dressed, as always, in a clean black capote. He ambled slowly across the square, muttering to himself, perhaps inventing a new remedy.

•

The hour was late. As darkness descended, Herschel walked the narrow streets and crooked lanes. The shadows grew longer. Sabbath was drawing near. He knew that the women were preparing the Sabbath table: the two candles, the cut-glass decanter of wine, the silver cup, and the braided challah loaf. The chicken soup was ready, and the plump boiled chicken, *kasha* with mushrooms, and the dessert - stewed apples and prunes.

Before long, the walls of the synagogue would echo with prayers of deep yearning and fervor, with heartrending laments of sadness and longing. In the gentle dusk, men would huddle around the table with their prayer books, detached from the world around them. Tears came to Herschel's eyes. He was immersed in thoughts of home.

•

Though Wladno was usually a quiet peaceful town, far removed from the cares of the wider world, Herschel found that one never knew when the serenity would suddenly be shattered. Almost every week, mounted Hussars roared through the village. No one knew why. And who was going to ask? Their arrival was heralded by a blaring cavalry bugle, followed by thundering hooves and bellowing officers. Their sabers drawn, they drove their plunging beasts forward in the ferocious charge for which the dreaded Hussars were justly famous.

Herschel peered out of the window of the rabbi's study, watching shopkeepers in the market square scurry frantically, swiftly removing the stands from in front of their shops. The clamor of the workshops ceased and the smithy's hammer was silenced. Mothers gathered children to their skirts, bearded old men drew their caftans around them and stumbled from the square into the alleys, and young women fled behind shuttered windows.

Captain Sergei Sergeiovich Zakharov led the charge. His side-whiskers flying in the wind, his fierce coal black eyes burning, he was as one with his charger, his entire being exuding brutal strength. He led the plummeting Hussars past Itzchok Karpen's inn, Mottel Levine's dairy, Henodh Schrier's cobbler stand, Isaac Sternberg's bakery, past the church, and the *Starostrow* building. In their wake they left a cloud of detritus swept up by the steel hooves clashing on the cobbles.

Herschel knew that though the villagers loathed and feared the Hussars, they needed the abundant stream of income they provided. The garrison had to be supplied with flour, milk, meat, and vodka. The cavalrymen needed leather for saddles, harnesses, belts, and boots.

As suddenly as the horsemen appeared, they disappeared. They wheeled about and cantered back to their garrison, which brooded behind its filigreed iron gates, just a few versts from the border with Prussia.

Herschel had been warned never to permit his curiosity to take him to the high gates, surmounted by the red and-black coat of arms of the regiment, where two soldiers always stood at rigid attention. On the broad expanse of the regiment's parade ground, on three sides of which stood the bleak gray military barracks, on any given day one could find a bellowing sergeant drilling soldiers. Officers strutted back and forth importantly, swords and spurs gleaming in the sun. Beyond the barracks were the stables sheltering the cavalry mounts, their sleek black coats glistening.

The villagers said that the sentries at the gates were there, not to keep the townspeople out, but to keep the soldiers in. It was unimaginable that any peasant, and certainly no Jew, would of his own free will dare to cross the sinister threshold.

• • • •

19

ZAKHAROV

From his squadron headquarters on the top floor of the *Starostrow* building, Sergei Sergeiovich Zakharov looked out at the dense fog descending over the village. He watched the rain falling over the wretched farms, drenching the stubble in the fields and filling the ruts in the road. Autumn in Poland! He cursed autumn in Poland. His thoughts were occupied with all the hopes and dreams, comforts and joys that had somehow eluded him.

On his right hand, circling his finger, was a replica of a horseshoe nail with the star of the Guards emblazoned on it. This was the silver ring of the Nicholas Cavalry School. As a cadet at the school from the age of ten, he had lived a Spartan existence, sleeping with his weapons and achieving automaton-like efficiency in arms drill. He suffered the privations of living out of a pack in the field, sleeping where he could - in the back of rattling wagons, stretched out on a ground-cloth in wet fields and muddy meadows, or under the trees in hastily erected lean-tos.

He lived with his horse and spent his time combing, currying, and grooming it; he mucked out stalls and polished his saddle and tack until his leather gleamed. And he rode. He rode on parade, he rode in battle formation, in cavalry charges with lance extended, in drills with the sword, and while firing muskets from the saddle. He rode in jumping demonstrations, acrobatics, and dressage. He rode bridle-less horses, bareback, perfecting his form. On more than one occasion he felt the instructor's long driving-whip on his back when he responded tardily to the bellowed command, "Swords out! Lances for the fight!"

He forded swiftly moving rivers and streams. He rolled up his greatcoat in the regulation manner. He mirror-shined his boots. He stood guard under the stars, and in the rain, and in the snow.

Thus was he prepared for the life of the hero, the life of glory in combat that is every soldier's dream. But now he was living another far less alluring aspect of military life. Now, his days were an endless round of petty details inspecting stables, drilling illiterate soldiers. He was preoccupied with lame horses, missing buttons, and lost bayonets. Every after-noon, there was chess and vodka. In the evenings, cards and vodka. The best part of his week - a visit to the whores in Plosk, where, walking in the halls, he would often hear the grunting of some brother officer and wonder, "My God! Is that what I sound like?"

Fifteen years of his life he had spent in the Tsar's ser-vice. And this was his reward: a godforsaken post at the bor-der. The squadrons of the regiment were scattered among border towns and villages; his squadron was billeted outside Wladno. Danger, the opportunity to distinguish himself in battle, even at the risk of death, was infinitely preferable to the tedium and anonymity of service at the border. Customs duties! Pursuit of contrabandists!

"For God's sake," he lamented, "I am a border guard!"

Suddenly he remembered that the troops were to receive five rubles each for the contraband they intercepted the day before.

He tried to console himself with thoughts of the richness of the years he had lived. He was well-off, still youthful and vigorous. But he was now twenty-five. How many years were left to distinguish himself, to advance to the command of a regiment and, why not, a division? He was tortured by his aspirations.

He must remind the sergeant-major that Smulski, that *Polack* slob, was not to share in the reward. Once again he had been absent and been brought back drunk. By rights he should be run through the gantlet of the squadron to receive one hundred rods. But now, in this "new army" it was absolutely forbidden to inflict corporal punishment on the lower ranks.

Zakharov's days were endless rounds of quibbling, like some old *Zhid*, he thought, driving bargains for grain and fodder. He traversed his territory across the river to the border, to the far edge of town, and as far as the lines established by the other squadrons in the surrounding villages. He seized property in the name of Tsar, he purchased cattle and produce, and he was ever-vigilant for smugglers. And, maddeningly, he was forever mediating disputes between the *Zhids* and the *Polacks*.

Though this posting was distasteful and demeaning, training, tradition and principle compelled him to carry out his official duties diligently and with dispatch. He was after all a creature of the military code of dignity, of class and rank. His father and grandfather before him had been cavalrymen. He had been reared as a soldier.

It must be noon. He heard the guard changing below at the entrance to the *Starostrow*. He had to be sure that the sergeant-major was feeding the men in accordance with Colonel Arkcheev's new standing order. He shuffled through the mound of papers on his littered desk.

"Every day, a hot meal from the squadron's communal kettles," he read. "Two meals a day. For the midday meal, on meat days, cabbage or beetroot soup with a half-pound of meat for each man, and sometimes buckwheat gruel with fat. On lean days, for the midday meal, cabbage soup with herring or peas. And for supper, buckwheat gruel. Three kopecks to be allocated for food supplies for each man per day."

Every man also received two pounds of black bread daily, which he kept under lock and key in his wooden chest, together with his extra pair of boots and, often, his dirty shirts. The troops ate in their barracks, sitting on their beds. They slept in their overcoats; there was no bed linen. They wore no underwear or stockings. They followed the peasant custom of wrapping their feet in long narrow strips of cloth.

Had he received extra rations for the infantry riflemen who had been attached to the squadron? He made a note to check with the sergeant-major.

•

Sitting by himself in the drawing room of the Officers' Assembly, as he did every evening, Zakharov's gaze traversed the banqueting hall, the billiard room, and the museum, which displayed uniforms, shakos, swords and guns of bygone eras, and the regiment's enormous silver punchbowl, which was decorated with enameled medallions depicting soldiers in historical uniforms. He was irritated by everything in the Assembly – the faded battle pennants on the wall, portraits of colonels of another time, trophies on the mantle, tattered rugs, and threadbare leather chairs.

He no longer had the heart for gambling. In any case, he had lost his allowance for the month. His mess bill was long overdue. He looked around the room for someone to talk to. Once he had friends with whom he had actually been able to discuss a book, argue about politics, and conduct an intelligent conversation. But now the companionship available to him was interested only in the whores, or lounging at the bar, exchanging tall tales.

A burst of laughter came from the bar. It was the forced gaiety of lonely men. Men far from home. Men in despair.

Zakharov watched the casual way they drained one glass after another. He saw them, not as faces, but as masks - hollow-eyed and expressionless, their red lips frozen in grotesque grins. Sergei Naryshkin, a lieutenant in his squadron, his yellow skin taut over his cheekbones, his hair thin and greasy, sat with his tobacco-stained fingers quivering over his fan of cards. Behind a façade of bonhomie and bombast, Naryshkin was reticent and fearful.

The new coronet, Count Nicholai Krawet, a gangly, light-hearted adolescent, was sitting quietly on the bench by the stove, writing to a girl in Petersburg. Another coronet, Prince Sergei Vorontsov, entered the room. He had prominent puffed-out cheeks and large yellow buckteeth. They called him, "Woodchuck." Vorontsov was one of the most bizarre among them. He liked to affect the look of an elegant Hussar of a bygone time. He added certain little archaic stylizations to his uniform. Sometimes, when the fancy took him, he wore a *mentik* to the mess – a second jacket draped over one shoulder, on top of his usual tunic, which a Hussar would wear only on special occasions. He tried to hide the fact that he was newly commissioned by giving his Hussar's cap an aging treatment, which involved several immersions in hot water.

The esteem in which Vorontsov was held was such that, despite his junior rank, he was given a command. He was placed in charge of the outhouses that the officers used in the field. They were wooden booths on wheels, which on maneuvers followed behind the supply wagons well to the rear of the formation. It was in that capacity, at a demonstration for foreign cavalry officers, that his name became legend in the annals of the regiment.

The regiment had assembled at a gallop and formed up in two lines of 450 horses to each line. A full mounted regiment with hundreds of lowered lances is a beautiful and menacing sight. It is not an easy matter to maneuver with nearly a thousand horses, preserving the aspect of a solid mass while changing gaits, turning, and opening and closing formation.

At the command, "Wheel by the right flank!" two platoons on the left flank turned slowly in place, the next outward platoons moved at a slow walk, the next somewhat faster, while the next was trotting. The outside platoons would be galloping at a good clip. When the trumpeter sounded, "Wheel about!" the echelon that started out in the rear of the formation now rode in the front.

The maneuver was performed with exemplary skill and precision. Then, when the trumpet sounded, "Charge!" one thousand horses thundered toward the reviewing stand. The terrified dignitaries shrank back in fear of their lives. But as planned, the formation came to an abrupt halt in a cloud of dust with inches to spare - led by Coronet Vorontsov's six latrines.

•

At home that autumn the peasants were rioting. Zakharov had heard reports that the Insurrection in Poland had now spread to Lithuanian and White Russian lands. His cousin, Dimitri Nikolaevich, an officer guarding the Tsar's Winter Palace, had written from Petersburg that leaflets urging revolt were even appearing in Russia. There was talk of abolishing censorship, of substituting the Roman alphabet for Russian Cyrillic, of creating a federal constitution, and of instituting agrarian reform. There was even talk about abolishing the army!

Two years earlier the Tsar had freed the serfs. For a thousand years, maybe longer, a thousand serfs had worked the Zakharov family's lands. How would the estates survive? Dimitri had written that he heard of a landowner in a village near the family home who had been murdered in his bed. In a neighboring estate the barn had been burned to the ground. Dimitri said that the gentry, and even some nobles, were demanding a new order. Unbelievable! In Russia, a new order!

"The world is changing before my very eyes," Zakharov thought. "And here I sit in this Polish backwater. Zakharov, commander of dunces!"

•

With long brisk strides, Zakharov marched to the center of Rochek's riding ring. He gleamed and rattled, his highly-polished leather boots creaking, his spurs ringing. His high-necked blue dolman, trimmed in gold silk piping, blossomed with service badges and rosettes. His long, curved cavalry sword hung from the waist of his brick-red riding breeches on a red leather belt.

Josep Rochek looked at him and thought that, putting aside the comic opera aspect of his elaborate uniform, here is a man who is formidable. Rochek, who was not easily impressed, was moved by the force of the man's personality. Everything about Zakharov seemed precise and faultless. He had a countenance that could have been fashioned from marble, a self-assured carriage, and a confident step.

"How is it possible", Rochek wondered, "that Zakharov has walked through the yard, his impeccably polished boots unsullied by the mud? And that he has ridden here on horseback, a journey of four or five versts, arriving with his tunic un-creased?"

Rochek could understand why the captain's troops were in awe of his intensity, his unpretentious competence, and the impression he conveyed of being efficient and unruffled in any imaginable circumstance.

Zakharov examined Rochek from head to toe.

"Look how he stands there completely at his ease, his bearing is military - standing tall in his sand-colored coat, his pale gray fur cap and yellow rawhide boots. Without doubt this *Zhid* must be endowed with an extraordinary talent. It shows itself in his attitude and in his manner. He has the innate dignity of a leader, one who has won renown in battle or, as it is rumored, at the barricades."

He could see why he had great standing with his people.

"Still," the captain reminded himself, "it is well not to forget that this Rochek is venal. He is wily and cunning. Of course he is wily; he is after all a *Zhid*. And he is a thief."

Zakharov paused. He reconsidered.

"Well, not really a thief. But he buys and sells from thieves. Much the same thing."

He shouldn't make allowances for him. Even had it been possible for a bond to form between them, Zakharov knew that any attempt they may have made to know each other would have been frustrated by the fact that, despite all his squadron's efforts, this *Zhid* was able to collect horses from distant markets and find men to ride them bareback across the border, eluding his troops.

"So, Excellency, what do you think of him?" Rochek asked.

Zakharov examined the big chestnut stallion with a practiced eye. His flanks were suffused in a kind of haze. His forelocks and tail were dusted with snow crystals. Vapor came from his nostrils in long streams. In his great, deep, dark eyes an ember smoldered.

"Well over seventeen hands," Zakharov estimated, as he ran his hand along his flanks. "A golden sheen to the coat." he noted.

He examined his foreleg and thought, "Long legs, slender and strong. Broad between the eyes. Small ears. A long neck, an upright shoulder."

"A Budyonny." He said to Rochek, "And he has Arab in him."

"Your Excellency does know his horses," Rochek said with genuine admiration.

"And Don," the captain said, recognizing the bloodlines of the Cossack horse from western Russia. "And Thoroughbred perhaps."

"Yes," said Rochek proudly. "And he can go like the wind. He can go forever. In any weather."

Zakharov caressed the horse's soft black muzzle.

"There is no question, this *Zhid* is different," thought the captain. "You have to admire him, this Rochek. This is a man to have at your side in battle."

In spite of himself, he liked this *Zhid*. And Rochek had a reluctant admiration for Zakharov.

Rochek thought, "An aristocrat. Of course all their officers are. But not a dilettante like some. Not soft. It would be a mistake to underestimate him. They are well-trained, these Russkis. And disciplined. And ruthless."

But Landau, Zakharov's orderly room messenger, had told Rochek that this one had some human qualities. Landau, a Jew and a lawyer from Moscow, had already served ten of his years of military service. Short and pudgy, his plump body definitely unsuited to a uniform, he was no one's idea of a hero. But he *was* a hero. He had been twice decorated for bravery in the Crimea. For that alone he should have been made an officer.

Of course, he couldn't be an officer, or even a non-commissioned officer; no Jew could, not in the Tsarist army. But at the regimental headquarters they prized his acumen and efficiency, and they acknowledged his value. They assigned him duties in the orderly room, where he addressed all the officers familiarly by their patronymics, and they, forgetting that he was a Jew, treated him almost as one of them.

"The way to get to Zakharov," Landau had told Rochek, "the only way - is a horse."

Rochek handed the reins to the captain. "Would you like to try him, Excellency?"

• • • •

20

A TALK WITH THE RABBI

Herschel had grown to love the rabbi, not only for his kindness, but ironically, also for his piety, which was reflected in his every daily deed. The rabbi never ceased to astonish Herschel. Though he lived in a medieval backwater, he was paradoxically, Wladno's link to the modern world.

The *Hassids* might disparage him and mock him for his lack of piety, but they knew that though he was not their kind of Jew, he was after all, still a Jew. And he performed a vital service: he could talk to the *Polacks*, intercede with Zabladovich at the *Starostrow,* and deal with the Russians. The *Hassids,* on the other hand, had no way of communicating with the people who, after all, ruled the village. The rabbi was their intermediary.

Herschel believed that Rabbi Mordoviscz was in many ways a modern man. He was familiar with Darwin, he quoted Spinoza and Schopenhauer, and he had even read the works of Proudhon and Bakunin. Yet he was immersed in ancient ritual and self-denial, praying, fasting, and preparing himself for the world to come. He knew how people lived in the cities, although he had never visited one. He knew they were starving, diseased, and living out their lives in bleak tenements overrun by vermin.

"And certainly," Herschel thought, "he must see that here in the countryside conditions aren't much better."

During the long winter and into the spring, Herschel had wandered the winding streets and alleys of Wladno. Wherever he looked he saw haggard toothless women, men old before their time, their faces lined with fatigue, and children who were mere bundles of bones, with pasty faces and unkempt earlocks. Even young people were bowed as if with age. Everywhere there was the sound of coughing. Everywhere there was the reek of decaying food and chamber pots.

Herschel was utterly baffled by the world as it was taught in the Jewish schools, where young children, their faces pallid and pinched, led a life of apprehension and fear. They were taught to believe that a watchful eye was always upon them, that their deeds were constantly recorded, that demons lay in wait in every shadow, that the iniquitous are burned and reduced to ashes, and that it was a sin for girls and boys to play together.

"You can't call this life," he said to the rabbi. "You can't believe that this is what God planned for us. Did he really intend that this unbearable existence be life? How can we even call it life when people are perishing by the millions? When whole cities starve? When people burrow into alleys for a place to sleep? Madmen and beggars sit around the market unable to find lodging in the poorhouses. Desperate children scrabble for food in garbage bins. This isn't life. It's a nightmare."

The rabbi looked at Herschel sadly. "Can't you see that man, by betraying his God, has brought this on himself? He has forsaken the old customs and sacred traditions. He has abandoned God. He has put his soul in jeopardy."

"The old customs!" Herschel said. "You speak of the old customs! You speak of the ancient traditions! Everywhere in Europe, even in Russia, even here in Poland, people are moving forward. Even the Jews! Especially the Jews! They go to modern schools. They are educated. They dress like everyone else. They don't cut themselves off from the world. You rabbis are so intent on preserving the artifacts of Judaism that you are depriving us of our place in the world. You don't want us to be Poles, or Russians, or Germans. As though we can't be both Jews and Poles, Jews and Germans, as the goyim are Catholics or Lutherans and citizens of their countries as well. Jews all over Europe speak the languages of their nations, and their children go to modern schools. Here in the east they dress like freaks, they speak in a rude and graceless gibberish, and they bury their heads in their books."

He waited for a reply. The rabbi was silent.

Finally, Herschel said, "The rest of Europe is acquiring knowledge, advancing, and shaping a new world. But Jews here, they know nothing of science, nothing of medicine. Their narrow-mindedness is absurd. They are steeped in superstition. They believe in *golem*, in *dybbuks*. They believe that ancient rituals and amulets will ward off evil spirits."

Finally, the rabbi spoke. "Yes, we do believe in miracles. We have an unshakable faith in the miracles related in Scripture. And you. Don't you believe in Torah?"

"Torah?" Herschel said. "Yes, Torah has its place. But so do mathematics, biology, and history. So do languages. In Warsaw, Jews speak Polish. In Prussia and Austria we speak German. We are doctors, businessmen, and engineers. We are assimilated."

"Assimilated?" the rabbi scoffed. "Are there Jewish judges in the courts? Are there military officers? Are there Jews in the government? You are as assimilated as the *goyim* let you be. God willing, we will never be assimilated."

Suddenly, Herschel's hand, as if acting of its own volition, darted across the table. He took hold of the rabbi's beard.

"What is this?" he demanded. "What does this mean? Straggly beards, fringed garments, long capotes. What does it all mean?"

Shock and dismay clouded the rabbi's face. Unlike his father, he was not unapproachable. He was not remote from the people; he was not like a king before his subjects. He was a man who was deeply conscious of his frailties. Didn't he have a heart, a brain and a soul like other men? Wasn't he sometimes tortured by temptation? He was, after all, a man like all others. He was not a so-called "wonder rabbi" who had the power to bless and to curse. He did not expect his followers to ascribe to him absolute wisdom and supernatural powers. He did not expect unquestioning obedience and unswerving fealty. When it came to points of law, of philosophy, or politics, he was prepared to take on all comers. He expected, even encouraged, heated discussion, disagreement, and debate.

But where the dignity and sanctity of the rabbinate was concerned there could be no compromise. The rabbi was sacrosanct. Disrespect for the dignity of the rabbi was beyond imagining. Ten generations of tradition were the bulwark of the Rabbis of Wladno.

Herschel apologized abjectly.

But nevertheless, his mind recoiled at the fears and superstitions that pervaded every aspect of the life of the Jews of Wladno.

He spoke quietly, but with great emphasis.

"Rabbi, I have met people here who believe that between this world and the next, sinful souls take on the form of dogs, cats, frogs, and other creatures that wander in the fields and forest. They think that if a bird taps at the window with its beak, it is bearing good tidings. If a black crow caws on the roof, a disaster will befall the house. They believe that *dybbuks* can invade a person's body, that each night the dead come to pray in the synagogue, that witches and demons come to visit them. They fear the evil eye. What does it all mean? That God's chosen people will be eternally subjugated and forever cast out? That all your prayers and Talmud study haven't been ardent enough? Doesn't it strike you as puzzling that our people can't liberate themselves from an allegiance to an archaic, prehistoric identity that has brought down upon us vilification and persecution? Judaism has long since lost all its importance. Why can't we rise above ourselves and melt among all the rest of the religions of the world?"

The rabbi smiled disdainfully.

"Don't you think that persecution has played a role in forcing us into this disastrous attitude? The pogroms, the ghettos, all these terrible, despicable things."

The rabbi paused. Then he said, "You resist, but I know you have faith. I know you believe in salvation. You don't really believe that science can explain everything."

What was the use of arguing? Herschel knew that he would never bring the rabbi around to his way of thinking. Though it was clear that a strong bond had developed between them, they could never really be reconciled. The rabbi was oblivious to the contradictions of his faith.

They sat in silence. Outside the window they heard the shouts of little boys chasing each other in the streets. Girls pranced about in a circle, holding hands. An old man with a long white beard stood at his window across the way, eating potatoes and sour milk.

• • • •

21

QUESTIONS

Tova had been listening. Standing in the alcove between the kitchen and the rabbi's study, she had overheard many conversations. And sometimes the things she heard caused her cheeks to burn! Wives brought the rabbi woeful tales of faithless husbands. Men came with laments of wives who wouldn't share their beds. Women came to argue over an insult. Parents came to make a marriage contract. A divorce, God forbid, had to be granted. An agreement had been broken. Sometimes curses would ring out, along with insults, vulgarities, threats and vile oaths, shouting and tumult, tears and screams. Suffering souls came to implore the rabbi to drive out their fears, to assuage their guilt, and to resolve their dilemmas of conscience. There were often discussions about the interpretation of Talmud. A question of law had to be decided. Sometimes it was a question of commerce, or a transaction that required arbitration. But more often, it was a woman with a question about whether a goose she had purchased from Kleniek's shop had been properly koshered.

Questions. There were always questions. Many Tova could understand, but there were so many that were beyond her comprehension - complicated matters, many about the mysteries of the Torah. What does it mean that...? How did it come to be that...? The answer, if it did not reside in the rabbi's head, was usually accessible on his bookshelves. He could always find an answer - sometimes later rather than sooner, but always he had a solution, usually a compromise. He was the wellspring of all knowledge, wise far beyond his years, and his word on questions of law was unchallenged. To question the rabbi's decree - that was unthinkable. God forbid that a Jew would spurn his rabbi's decision and turn to the civil courts, where he would have to stand before a judge, swear an oath on the *goyim's* bible, and sit among criminals!

But here was Herschel. He was actually lecturing the rabbi! He was defiant! Yet she felt he intended no disrespect. It was just that he came from a different world. Could it be that people from the cities lived in a different world? She pondered what Herschel had told her. Could it be true that the old ways were outmoded? Could it be that *dybukks* and demons and werewolves really didn't exist? Herschel questioned why the *Hassids* thought it was wrong for girls and boys to play together. She also wondered why. Just last week a delegation from several of the *Hassidic* congregations angrily descended upon Yonathan, demanding that he stop ruining the town by letting boys and girls dance and sing together.

"Next," they said to him, "you will put on a stiff white collar!" By which they meant European clothes.

As far as the *Hassids* were concerned, this was far worse even than shaving one's beard. "A man without a beard deserves unsparing denunciation. The beard is the badge of his faith." However, they said, "A beard can grow anew. But once a man puts on a stiff white collar, it stays on forever!" Herschel, who had witnessed that scene with the *Hassids*, saw Tova's dismay.

"They don't understand that young people are turning to new ways. "They are creating new values To those old *Hassids* that is a threat, an offense and a poison. For them, nothing has changed in the world. For them, there is no world outside of Wladno. They want it to remain the way it is, unchanged."

He had told her that the Polish national movement, the Insurrection, in which many Jews had participated, was bringing change to the people. It had aroused the people's consciousness and pride. Even here in Wladno, in front of Yehiel Shapiro's house, in Kuba Kleniec's butcher shop, and in Aronowicz's tea store, he heard the Insurrection discussed. It was already legendary. People spoke of it with the reverence of an event of distant history, calling it the "Uprising of '63" though 1863 was only last year. He saw it as unmistakable evidence that times were changing.

•

"You said they were after you?" Tova asked.

They sat in the kitchen together. Herschel smiled grimly.

"They were after everybody. Warsaw was in chaos. There was rioting in the streets. The world was collapsing. Yes, they were after me."

But he didn't say why. He said nothing of the assassination.

"I'm sure there was a price on my head a reward for my capture, but they were hunting down all the revolutionaries, and they were rounding up men for conscription. The army was after deserters. The militia was everywhere. I had to keep moving. I couldn't stop. But I didn't really know where I could go, where I would be safe."

Tova looked at him in awe, wondering, "How could it be that this boy is a fugitive?"

"When I left Warsaw the snow was heavy on the ground, and the sky told me there was more snow coming. In the countryside, I sheltered where I could, sometimes in a hayrick. When I could, I found a barn where I could huddle near the animals for warmth."

It seemed to him, as he thought back on it, that he had been on a journey without end. All sense of time had been obliterated.

"I avoided villages, or passed through them at night. But at night I had to be careful of barking dogs."

"What did you do for food?" she asked.

"When I could, I stole it. I had to. I was starving. Sometimes I took a chance. I stopped at a farm and asked for work in exchange for a meal. I did simple things chores, chopping wood, or cleaning out a stable."

Unconsciously, his finger traced a map on the table. "I walked across Poland. I followed the Vistula through small towns, avoiding the big cities."

"And money?" she asked. "Did you have any money?"

"I had a little, and when I thought it was safe, I looked for work. I was desperate. I had to chance it. I worked in a forest, carrying wood. I herded sheep. I worked for a time in a salt mine."

"A salt mine!" Tova was astounded.

As he thought of the mine his expression altered. His face became somber, and suddenly his eyes were swimming. Once again he found himself immersed in the dazzling, stark white sea. The acrid odor of iodine assailed his nostrils, he felt that once again his lips were cracked and encrusted with white brine, and salt crystals inflamed his eyes.

"In Wieliczka, near Cracow, they needed labor badly," he said. "They didn't ask questions."

He looked into the distance, carried back in time to the mine. "Every day we descended into the bowels of the earth. They lowered us in cages, a dozen men at a time, packed face to face. We fell through space - 200, 250 meters or more. Mules were lowered by ropes alongside our cages. We heard them whinnying and braying in fear. Every day we plummeted into a world of salt. Overhead, a ceiling of solid salt. Underfoot, a floor of salt. On either side, dark gray walls of salt. Everywhere, solid salt. In some places the salt walls are one hundred meters thick."

He told his story with great deliberation. He recalled minute facts and minor aspects he had forgotten. Some details surfaced in his mind that until now he hadn't realized that he knew.

"We were divided into gangs. Each gang quarried out more than one thousand hundredweight each day. The mine is a wilderness of shafts, galleries and chambers. There are scores of winding passages, all sparkling with minute crystals. Great piers of hewn logs and pillars of salt support the roof, which is always creaking and groaning, threatening to collapse. It was dark. We had only Bengal lights for illumination."

He sat for a moment, quietly, lost in the memory of his fears. He remembered the cage plunging through space into the void, the deep rumble of the careening carts, the high-pitched scream of the rails, and echoing off the walls, emanating from somewhere deep in the bowels of the earth, an incessant roar.

Tova studied him in silence.

"Every day, fifteen, sixteen hours a day, sometimes longer, we hacked away at the walls with picks and mallets and wedges. We trundled the wheelbarrows full of hundredweight salt blocks. Many of the tunnels were too narrow for the mules, so we had to carry the blocks to the wheelbarrows on our shoulders, or in our hands, stopping every few steps to rest. To push the barrows up the steep grade took all our strength. Even the strongest among us needed help sometimes."

He thought of Siemanowski, straining under massive blocks of salt, putting his shoulder to the heavily laden carts. Taking perverse pleasure in the labor.

Herschel's forehead was now bright with sweat. He was trembling. Images came to him of sudden random spears of light darting out of the tunnels, flashing along the mirror-slick walls of the caves, illuminating gray hooded figures - ghostly shapes, their eyes peering like black discs out of white faces coated in salt. He felt the stifling heat, the sweat running in trails down his cheeks, pouring into his eyes, and the mist of salt drifting through the air. He sucked it into his burning throat and nose. He gasped for air; he gagged and coughed.

Tova saw that his face had paled.

He looked across at her, searching her eyes. He craved her sympathy. It was important to him to make the mine vivid and real to her, to depict it in all its grim detail. He wanted her compassion. But still, he couldn't bring himself to tell her about the pain of his endless hours of labor in crevasses and fissures, when he was bent double, kneeling or crouching until his back and shoulders, all his muscles, screamed in anguish. He wouldn't speak of the brine that seeped into the wounds in his hands, scored by splinters of salt, or his eyes that were red-rimmed, reduced to slits, all but closed, and constantly tearing. He wouldn't tell her that each night when he sank exhausted into his cot, nursing his wounds and resting his cramped limbs, he resolved that this day would be his last in the mine. But somehow, the next morning he was able to muster enough strength to go on for one more day.

"Just one more day," he had told himself.

He sat hunched, his hands on his knees, idle and feeble, fingers spread before him like legs of spiders. The life seemed to have seeped out of him. He looked up. He saw that Tova's eyes were brimming. "It was not all so bad," he said quickly. "Sometimes we saw things of great beauty. One day we came to a magnificent blue lake that we were told was over four fathoms deep. On another day we saw the cavern they called the Blessed Kinga. It was thirty-six meters high and fifty meters long. It was a cathedral carved entirely out of salt, hung with great chandeliers made of salt crystals, with the walls lined with statues of saints, all carved in salt."

He laughed and said, "I put my tongue to the nose of John the Baptist. Salt. Everything solid salt. On such days as these we were lost in awe, surrounded by such incredible magnificence. Our pain melted away. Out of this single hall a million hundredweight of salt had been taken – enough, they told us, to supply the forty million inhabitants of Austria for a year."

He paused and gazed out the window. The moonlight was bright on the cobbles. Tova sat with her head bowed. She took her handkerchief from her apron. Her eyes glistened like pearls.

He broke the silence and said, "But of course I had to move on. I knew that the mine boss could tell by the look of me that I was running. I could see it in his eyes, the way he stared at me. I couldn't take a chance that he might turn me in."

Tova was shocked. "He would do that?"

He smiled at her naïveté and said, "One thing I have learned, Tova. There are people in this world who will do anything. Some for money. But many simply for the joy of it."

After a long pause, she asked, "And now? Here? Couldn't they find you here? Couldn't someone betray you?"

Herschel leaned forward on the bench, his hands clasped between his knees. He replied tentatively, as though this was a thought that had not occurred to him until now.

"Yes," he said simply.

It had been some time since he had allowed himself to consider the possibility that he might be captured. He realized then that over the months since his recovery, he had drifted into complacency. He had begun to think of Wladno as a safe haven. Gradually, lulled by the warmth and comfort of his circumstances, he had spun the delusion that he could rest at last and that he could even make a life for himself here – a simple, uncomplicated life.

"I shouldn't deceive myself," he said in calm, uninflected voice. "Of course they could come after me here."

A tremor coursed through Tova's body. Once again, tears filled her eyes.

Herschel's heart reached out to her. He gazed at her - a tall, supple girl in full flower, her skin pale and translucent, her hair fine and golden, wisps escaping from her kerchief. Her hands were clasped tightly in her lap, her shoulders were drawn forward, and he could see the beginning of the V at the opening of her blouse. He saw the outline of her thigh through the skirt drawn tautly over her knees.

She read his thoughts. Slowly, she walked across to him and sat on the bench beside him. She was so close that he felt the whisper of her breath on his eyes. He sensed the passion rising from her body. A smile, soft and budding, lit up her face. Gently, he placed his fingertips on her pale hand. He looked into her eyes and felt there was in her manner something inviting, yet uneasy. Something withheld. She searched his face and gazed into his eyes. He ignited a blaze in her imagination.

Her hand remained in his, as if it were beyond her control to withdraw it. Then, to her astonishment, their lips brushed softly. And then they were feverishly embracing, his hands seeking her body. Desire engulfed them. He held her and kissed her deeply. She felt his kiss well up inside her, arousing her. She felt his body dominating her. She cried out. Her resistance melted away. She grasped him and pressed him to her.

Suddenly, she forced him away. "What is this?" The question leaped at her. "What is happening to me?" They stood gasping, staring at each other in disbelief. They were startled and confused, overcome by terror and dismay. They were burning with guilt.

•   •   •   •

21

THE RABBI REFLECTS

The first stars appeared. The Sabbath was drawing to a close. The rabbi sat at the head of the table, the elders of his congregation around him. Tova lit the lamps. Light flickered over the starched white tablecloth and the silver cups. Shadows danced across the walls. The house was filled with the aroma of candles and spices. The evening prayers were recited. Rochek stoked the fire in the stove.

Wladno was in the grip of bitter cold. White winter had arrived with its insistent silence and cloudless frost. The snow was unyielding underfoot, windows were rimed with ice, tendrils of smoke curled above the chimneys, and long spears of icicles hung from the eaves.

The rabbi rubbed his hands to warm them. He looked at the others, sitting across from him in their Sabbath finery, sipping tea with lemon. He felt that his home was suffused with a mysterious spirit.

"Angels are present. God is here in the room with us."

Yet for some curious reason he was uneasy. He looked down to the far end of the table where Tova sat. He saw that she was lost in thoughts of her own.

To her shame, Tova's mind lingered on Herschel. She felt she glowed when Herschel was near. She had feelings she had never had before. She felt warm and open, and she dwelled in another world.

In her dreams, she and Herschel were building a life for themselves. In her imagination, she was a lady in long, sweeping dresses and fancy clothes. She wore her hair long. There were people who talked of things other than the S*hul*, prayer, and the Sabbath. Somewhere, there was a city where the roofs didn't crowd in, a place where women and girls had perfumed soap and pretty ribbons in their hair, where people cared nothing about the price of a chicken, where they never even gave the cost of food a thought, where the streets were not mired in mud, and where there were beautiful things you could buy. Somewhere, there was a place where people had no fear of the dark, of ghosts, or of the realm of death.

Herschel had told her about cities where lights burned all the time - lights that don't sputter and stink and about houses where it was always warm. She had heard Rochek and Herschel talking about places where you can go to watch people singing and dancing on a platform! Where you can sit at a table and have food brought to you - anything you want to eat! Where you can go to school to learn about far-away places.

Herschel's words had ignited a blaze in her imagination. She was seized by thoughts of a far different life. Tova was lost in her dreams.

But then she looked up and saw the rabbi gazing intently at her, a strange, perplexed expression on his face. She quickly looked away. How, she asked herself, could she have allowed herself to recklessly yield to a sudden wave of plea-sure – a feeling she had never even contemplated, a feeling beyond her comprehension. And she thought, wasn't she a wife, dutiful and caring, as it behooved a young wife to be? She respected her husband, the rabbi, who was after all an older man. Though only in his thirties, he was twice her age.

And he was a practical man of common sense who held a mysterious position, who spoke for the Almighty in a sonorous baritone and possessed an aura that had charmed her heart.

She couldn't believe what she had done. She burned with shame and guilt. Yet feeling once again Herschel's kisses and embraces, awakening something in her that she hadn't even known to exist. But how can she face her husband? She looked up at him again and instantly averted her eyes.

He looks at me, and he can tell," she thought. "He knows! The shame! The sin!"

The rabbi saw that Tova's mind was someplace far away. When she first came to him two years ago, a girl of seventeen, the daughter of the rabbi of a nearby village, she had worn her honey-colored hair in two golden braids. She had been lively, sometimes even boisterous and capricious. Lately she had grown quiet, shy, and withdrawn. She often lay on her bed in the middle of the day, daydreaming like a schoolgirl. She seemed to want only to dream.

His hand sought a small piece of bread on the table. Shaping it into a ball between his thumb and forefinger, he rolled it back and forth on the tablecloth. He tried to pry it from his mind, but he had heard Tova and Herschel talking together. He has been distracted by the murmur of their voices coming from the kitchen. He could not escape the feeling that Herschel was not good for Tova. He provoked something in her that the rabbi didn't know how to reach.

Tova sat wrapped in thoughts of Herschel. When she recalled his caresses, his kisses radiating into her body, stirring her blood, she felt a shock of pleasure. She was dazed, and the last vestiges of certainty of her life evaporated.

The rabbi couldn't begin to imagine what a storm Herschel's words had let loose in his wife's mind. He was disturbed - disturbed in ways he didn't understand.

"The charm she finds in this boy is pure emptiness. She doesn't see it, but the boy is a danger to her."

His eyes darted from Tova to Herschel. He stared at them in confusion, and his mind quavered around questions he could not bring himself to contemplate.

•

Herschel sat opposite Tova. He knew that he had caused her pain. He knew that she was chaste and blameless. He could only imagine the depth of her guilt and shame.

And now, as Herschel looked down the table at the rabbi, his mind was troubled. He was confused and riven with guilt. How could this have happened? How could he have corrupted Tova? How could he have betrayed the rabbi, who had taken him into his home, sheltered him, protected him?

Herschel suffered relentless fear.

"The rabbi might be growing suspicious. He might be becoming aware of my feelings for Tova. How could I have betrayed him in this way?"

• • • •

23

A VISITOR

He heard their voices as he climbed the stairs. - Tova and another woman were talking. In the few moments that it took him to reach the landing he sensed that there was something strange, yet somehow eerily familiar, in the air. He paused and stood silently in the doorway. He saw Tova sitting at the table. Opposite her, with her back to him, sat a young woman dressed in city clothes. Their hands were entwined across the table. Herschel gasped. His heart pounded. It was Miriam!

Miriam heard him. She turned toward him. Her hands went to her mouth. They were both so startled they were wordless. Finally, Miriam whispered, "My God!"

That was all that she said. She rose from the table, and slowly, as if in a trance, she walked to him. She walked to him and gently put her arms around him.

"Miriam," Herschel said.

He could say no more than that. He held her close; he clung to her and he could not let her go. Tears rolled down their cheeks.

Tova watched them in confusion. They know each other? How did it come to pass that they know each other?

Questions poured forth from all three of them. What was she doing here? How did he come to be here? Where did she come from?

Herschel paced the room in his excitement. He sat down, got up again. He now remembered that Miriam's father was a rabbi in a small town near the border. She had spoken of her mother and her sisters. But Tova her sister? Yes, he could see the resemblance. Tova and Miriam, two tall, slender girls.

Miriam was thinner than he remembered. And she looked older. She looked tired and haggard. She was surprised to find him so changed. It seemed to her that he was somehow more settled and, that he had grown into his body. She could see through his shirt that his muscles had become solid and sinewy. His large blue eyes, always so prominent, now seemed deeply embedded above his cheekbones. And he had cut the hank of hair that was always falling onto his forehead. His mouth, which had been soft and timid, now was a straight line, his lips turned down at the corners, and his brow was deeply lined. She detected in his face, in his bearing, and in his attitude, something that was smoldering.

He was bewildered. "How did you get here?" he asked.

He knew that the Russians were searching for revolutionists everywhere in Poland. He knew that danger lurked everywhere.

Miriam told her story simply. She had escaped from Warsaw when the Insurrection failed. On the train she had been preoccupied. The compartment was full. Smoke drifted in from the corridor. She was nauseated by the smell of stale food and unwashed bodies. A harassed woman with a hysterically weeping child sat opposite her. An enormous bearded man sat beside her, his fat thigh pressing against her. He was paring an apple with great care, working against the motion of the train, struggling to maintain one long continuous peel. The other passengers, a husband and wife with a little boy, appeared to be uneasy, sitting stiffly in their seats, clutching their bundles on their laps. They did not speak. Their eyes shifted restlessly.

She looked up and saw that the tall gangly Russian soldier in the vestibule was eyeing her suspiciously. Or was she just imagining it? She realized that she was clenching her teeth, and she wondered if the tension was visible in the line of her jaw. In any event, the soldier hadn't bothered her. Though it would have hardly been the first time she would have had to deal with Russian gendarmes. She had no doubt that she could handle one this young and inexperienced. Her papers would pass scrutiny, and she had her story straight in her mind. Her invariable rule was to stay as close as possible to the truth, and the truth, which was, after all, that she was returning home to Vadzilovo to see her family. But it could never hurt to run through her story again, to rehearse it, to be wary, on guard. Caution and prudence. That is how she had managed to stay alive.

"So far, so good," she thought.

•

The wagon lurched along the pitted road from the railroad station to Vadzilovo. Miriam felt her heart pounding. The reality of her circumstances came home to her anew as each familiar sight appeared - the *muzhiks* mending fences in the fields, the cows in the pastures, and the tumbledown straw-roofed huts. She was home. For the first time in three years she was home. She could even now feel her mother's tears on her face. Mama would take her face in her hands. The girls would finger the silk of her city clothes, ooh-ing and ahh-ing. Mama would say she was too thin.

What would the girls, her sisters, look like? Perhaps they are married. They may even have children of their own. Maybe they were not even in Vadzilovo any longer. Much may have happened in the three years since she left. Certainly, much had happened to her.

She balanced on the bale of hay, clutching her valise, as the wagon rocked and swayed on the furrowed roads. The pine forest bordered the road on one side; on the other they passed ravines strewn with boulders. She looked about her. Dun-colored fields stretched out to the horizon. The sky was gray, the clouds touching the ground in the distance. A thin curl of smoke rose lazily from a distant chimney. A flock of birds idly circled a field ahead. Old peasants dozed in the pale winter sun outside their straw-roofed hovels.

The horse slowed as it moved up a short incline. The wagon bounced on a rocky cow path, then they crossed an old wooden bridge over a shallow stream. The road turned sharply and around the bend the town appeared. The wagon entered a narrow street that ran down to the market square. It seemed so much smaller than she remembered. The mis-shapen little houses in the square appeared to be rundown. Tattered curtains hung from some of the windows, and the stalls in the market seemed to be disordered and bare. Then her father's *shul* came into view across the marketplace. Her courage deserted her, and she had to resist the urge to turn around and go back.

Her home, next door to the synagogue, was as she remembered it – a whitewashed cottage with a small vegetable garden in front. In the spring, geraniums would be blooming in the boxes under the windows. At the side of the cottage there was a well from which a young girl of twelve or thirteen was drawing water. She wore a shawl over her head and another wrapped around her shoulders. It was her sister Esther.

Esther turned as the wagon approached, and seeing a woman in city clothes – a sight she didn't see everyday! - she dropped her bucket and ran into the house.

When she emerged a moment later, she was urging an old woman before her. Miriam looked at her mother. She was thinner than she remembered; her eyes were deep ovals in her face, making her nose appear more prominent. Lines like parentheses ran from the sides of her nose to her lips.

Her skin was a tracery of wrinkles. Her mother, not yet forty-five years old, had become an old woman. She clutched her shawl to her bosom in the characteristic pose of humility that Miriam remembered and had always found so abhorrent. She approached Miriam timorously.

"Malcha?" she asked.

She reached out to Miriam and gently folded her into her arms. All the sad yearning of the years of her daughter's absence was in her embrace.

Only Esther, her youngest sister, was still at home. She was tall for her age, a slender girl, pretty, modestly dressed, and overwhelmed with shyness. She was only ten when Miriam left. The other girls were married and gone from the house. Two years ago Tova had married a young widower, a rabbi in Wladno, just a few kilometers away.

Her mother wept. If only she could call the family together – the aunts and uncles, and the cousins, and all the neighbors. On such a day as this a holiday meal should be served. But she could not offer her daughter even a glass of tea. She kept glancing anxiously over her shoulder toward the *shul*, afraid that at any moment her husband, the rabbi, would emerge. For him, Miriam no longer lived.

Of course, it was just as Miriam had anticipated it would be. She knew she was foolish to have thought it could be otherwise. She knew that her father would not see her. He wouldn't even acknowledge that she was alive.

•

Miriam and Herschel sat across the table from each other. Their stories poured forth in a rush of words. Miriam's life in Warsaw had not been the adventure she had imagined it would be. All her work, all the hardships she had endured for the Insurrection, had been for naught. The cell was in ruins, and her comrades were scattered to the four winds. Franzos, her beloved Franzos, had been seized, dragged to the Citadel, and hanged. Tears flooded their eyes. All their idealistic dreams of bringing salvation to Poland had been shattered. Everything had ended in treachery and betrayal. Now Miriam was home. "Why have I come?" she asked herself. "There is nothing for me here. Maybe I should go back. But go back where?"

There was no place for her to go.

•   •   •   •

24

THE MANHUNT

The commander of the regiment, Colonel Alexandre Andreievitch Arakcheev, stood at the head of a long table covered in green baize, his two great Borzois at his feet. A large map depicting the disposition of the six squadrons of the regiment was on an easel beside him. On the wall at the far side of the room hung the obligatory portrait of the Tsar, flanked by paintings of the commanders of the division and the corps. On other walls there were a number of framed pictures depicting the heroic deeds of Russian soldiers: Captain Koutouzov dying on a Turkish bayonet, Private Bobrinsky being executed by the French for refusing to divulge information, and Private Petrov blowing up a powder magazine, and himself with it. The walls were lined with cabinets containing trophies won in steeplechases and riding competitions, and silver trays and urns commemorating the regiment's battles. And in the corner, there was the omnipresent icon depicting the Virgin and Child.

Seated on either side of the colonel were the three junior colonels of the regiment, and down the table, in order of their rank, sat the regimental staff and the six squadron commanders.

Arakcheev, a tall florid man in his fifties, took great pride in his military bearing, which he had honed as deputy commandant of the Horse Grenadiers assigned to the Imperial Palace. When he began to speak, Arakcheev's voice took on the resonance he reserved for special occasions. He recited the facts: Two years of demonstrations in Warsaw, and sixteen months of fierce guerilla warfare fomented by the underground Polish national movement, had ended with the execution of the insurgent leaders on the walls of the Citadel. Eighty thousand Poles were now making the journey to Siberia – the largest of all the political contingents in Tsarist history. The insurgents had survived the winter of 1863, but now the leaders of the rebellion who had not already fled the country had been captured.

"Though many individuals involved in the rising have been executed," the colonel reported, "and many have been deported to Siberia, though thousands of landed estates have been confiscated, the Poles are still fighting Russification." He spoke with indignation. "They are still resisting the teaching of Russian in the schools," he said. "Now, under the new orders, the use of the Polish language is strictly forbidden. Poland will be, forthwith, a mere province of Russia."

Zakharov wondered what it had been all along.

The colonel continued: "We have reports that many revolutionists have fled from Warsaw and have sought refuge in the countryside. Polish guerrilla bands have been seen prowling the forests. It is believed that they are gaining support from artisans and workers, and even from the gentry. Only the lower gentry, of course. They are organizing peasant revolts against some of the landlords in rural areas. And so the regiment has received new orders."

He paused for dramatic effect. "We are to intensify the search for anyone connected with revolutionary agitation.

They are to be dealt with severely. We will flush out and capture the revolutionists wherever they hide."

He scanned the table to gauge the impression he was making.

"In addition, a levy of recruits has been ordered. We will sweep all towns and villages within the regiment's jurisdiction forthwith."

Zakharov groaned. Already about thirty percent of the 150 Hussars in his squadron were Poles. They came to him in their peasant clothes with their long, unwashed hair and their gawky awkward manner. Many of them were withdrawn and in tears. Most of them had never even seen a railroad train before. They had no idea where they now were in relation to their homes. Of course few of them spoke Russian. Most of them were illiterate and unable to read a map. The noncommissioned officers had difficulty communicating with them. There was one saving grace: at least these men, predominantly peasants from rural areas, knew how to handle horses.

But where would he put them? His squadron was quartered on the outskirts of the village, three or four soldiers to each house. Already the peasants whose rooms and barns they had requisitioned were screaming. Where would he put them?

The lieutenant-colonel in charge of supplies, Baron Troubetzkoy, a prissy little man whose major preoccupation was the cultivation of an enormous pointed mustache, was now intoning the list of equipment.

"Squadron commanders are to distribute cartridges, first-aid kits, horse blankets, sailcloth pails, hay nets, new horse brushes, horseshoes, extra pairs of boots, and two extra shirts apiece."

A fellow squadron commander sitting next to Zakharov, Vadim Vadimovich Smirnoff, whispered behind his hand.

"Will Troubetzkoy carry all this shit?"

The saddle and the pack together weighed more than thirty kilos; the muskets weighed eight kilos.

Major Chircovy, the armory officer, was now on his feet.

"In view of the regiment's newly assigned military activities, let us take note of its augmented armament. The regiment has now received fifty-four short Littikh rifles. So the regiment's new rifle companies are almost completely armed with muzzle-loading weapons."

"And we will use them!" Colonel Arakcheev pounded the table.

Zakharov's heart leaped at the prospect of action. Despite constant surveillance, and the harsh penalties the Hussars inflicted when they were caught, the Jewish merchants continued to hold sway over the border. They were always able somehow to get their grain or seeds or oil peas over the border to East Prussia. And they moved horses too! The army needed those horses. Powerful Polish working-horses were needed for farming and mining. When he catches them his retribution would be fierce and remorseless. His victims' pleas for clemency would not move him. He would be without mercy.

•

The regiment's six squadrons of Hussars were assembled in a long line along the river. There were more than a thousand men, all mounted on coal-black chargers, their lances tipped with red, blue, and yellow pennants. Colonel Arakcheev sat facing them on his great stallion, his two Borzoi wolfhounds at the horse's feet. He nodded to the adjutant, who with a dramatic flourish, pointed eastward with his sword and gave the command: "The regiment from the right, by squadrons, at squadron distance - Forward march!"

The regiment advanced as one. A systematic sweep from the River Oder eastward had begun. Anyone attempting to evade the dragnet would be driven into the arms of the

Sumsky Regiment, which was waiting to intercept them five kilometers west of Wladno.

•

In Wladno, the townspeople didn't need the church bells to summon them to the market square. In the mysterious way of towns and villages, the news seemed to float on the air. A large crowd had quickly gathered, larger even than on market days. At first, the Poles thought that the conscription order applied only to the Jews. Most reacted with indifference; some were joyful. But then it became clear to them that they would also be swept up by the Russians. Disbelief, and outrage, fear and anger resonated in the square, rising in a low-pitched drone that was punctuated by sobbing and shrieking. Every home in Wladno was in turmoil. The peasants were in a panic. They scurried from the fields and barns to their homes. Wives and mothers collected their children in the streets. They ran to the priest's house. They ran to the church, where they jostled each other to kneel at the alter rail before the towering painted figure of Christ. They lit candles. They prayed for divine guidance. Where could they hide their boys? Where could they run?

In the homes of the Jews, they cried and wailed. Their young men would be torn from them, many of them, if not all, never to be seen again. Boys as young as twelve would be snatched from their families and taken off to training battalions. Boys over the age of eighteen would be drafted for twenty-five years of service in the Tsarist army. They would go to live among the *goyim*. They would die with them. God forbid, they would be forced to eat pork! They would be forbidden to read or write letters in Yiddish. They would not be able to honor the Sabbath. They would cease to be Jews! Of course, this was exactly what the Russians intended - the conversion of as many of them as possible to Russian Orthodoxy.

The mothers and wives of the *Hassidic* boys ran to their prayer houses. Those of Rabbi Mordoviscz' synagogue implored him to appeal to the authorities and explain that what they demanded was impossible. But of course they knew it was possible. There had been conscription roundups before. And there would be again. As long as Jews lived in the countries of others, they would be forced to die for the countries of others.

•

Zakharov's squadron started out almost silently. All that could be heard was an occasional cough, the creaking of leather saddles and boots, and the chiming of swords, lances, canteens, and ammunition. They climbed up a long steep hill and looked down upon the fields in the valley. Here and there tufts of grass stuck up out of the snow. The branches of the trees in the woods beyond the meadow were bare of leaves and dusted white. Within minutes of the start of its advance, the regiment was in the dense fog of the dark forest that bordered the river, the riders threading their mounts in and out of tall pines. All contact between the squadrons had been severed. Zakharov's scouts couldn't find the squadrons on his flanks. A messenger arrived from regimental headquarters with word that they should be on the alert for a band of armed revolutionists that were reported to be in their vicinity.

•

It began to snow. The sky in the east was red, and the acrid smell of smoke drifted throughout the village. From his window in the synagogue, Herschel looked out in horror at streets teeming with people screaming and running in panic. Across the square he saw an elderly couple peeking fearfully through shuttered windows. The streets echoed with shouted rumors: The Hussars were setting fire to the village. But it wasn't the Hussars. Some of the *muzhiks* had been drinking and had lit a bonfire.

Panicked, Tova ran to her husband. She found him in the midst of a swarm of hysterical women in the sanctuary of the synagogue. Taking him by the sleeve, she pulled him bodily from the crowd.

"Yonathan!" she cried. "Miriam! Herschel! Where will they hide?"

Her eyes were wide with fear. "We must get them away."

She was trembling. The rabbi was completely composed, serene, and self-possessed.

"Be calm," he admonished her. "All these women want to get their young people away. Be calm!" He looked at her sternly and said, "Go upstairs now."

Tova stared at him. Then she turned, and without a word she ran from the synagogue. She must find Josep Rochek.

•

In about two hours the squadron had reached a broad stream that was flowing rapidly under a skim of ice. It had a muddy bottom and could not be forded. Zakharov sent scouting parties out to find a route around the bog, and in the meantime, he ordered the sergeant-major to rest the men and the horses.

In an hour he had the squadron moving again. It was starting to snow heavily now, and the snow was piling up on the Hussars' shoulders and on the haunches of their horses. Soon the advance party reported that there were steep ravines ahead. Once again the captain sent scouts out to find an alternate route. It was now dark. In the distance they heard the barking of the colonel's dogs. The wolfhounds were racing through the forest, crashing through the underbrush in pursuit, thought Zakharov, not of conscripts or revolutionists, but of rabbits and foxes.

His lieutenant, Naryshkin, reported that he had come upon a man from Captain Smirnoff's reconnaissance party who said they had been fired upon.

"Nonsense," Zakharov said. "No gunshots have been heard."

He was exasperated. Though he had rejoiced at the thought of action, the futility of this operation was beginning to pall on him.

•

Herschel could see the market square from the alley. It was pandemonium. The stalls were empty and padlocked. There were no pots or pans, no old clothes or faded uniforms, no artificial flowers or black bread, and no sugar or tobacco. Fleeing families were frantically storing their belongings with friends and neighbors. They were selling or trading furniture and bedding, and clothing they couldn't wear or carry, holding blouses and dresses out to mostly indifferent passersby, offering for sale the possessions of a lifetime.

Herschel watched wordlessly. Fear, which had been absent for a time, returned. He knew that he should be running with the others, but he couldn't muster the strength to run. He had surrendered to the inevitable. He knew of a certainty that his time had finally come. At midday, he walked to the edge of town. The long road running west out of Wladno was now crowded with conveyances of every description, shuddering along the frozen, rutted road. Farm wagons, pushcarts, and ancient droshkies were piled high with whatever possessions could be hastily assembled – chairs, tables, pillows and mattresses, beneath which were hidden bits of jewelry and heirlooms handed down from parents and grandparents.

The wind was sweeping snow and dry brown leaves down the alleys and around the corners, settling into gullies and ravines. Old people in dark rough woolen coats shivered and stamped their feet. Some were accompanied by boys in their teens who, judging by their chatter and laughter, seemed to understand nothing of the gravity of their situation.

Those without children of draft age had remained behind in the village, threshing corn, koshering fowl, and shaping leather for boots – business as usual. Those who were departing implored them to guard their homes and businesses.

"Look," said Baranowitz the wheelwright, clutching Herschel by the sleeve, "already the *Polacks* are casting their greedy eyes on our goods."

Bands of peasants had gathered in the marketplace, walking aimlessly, some of them drunk, stopping and whispering, then pointing to the abandoned shops. Herschel watched as they speculatively eyed Markewitz's shuttered tailor shop and stared greedily at Dudowitz's abandoned sheds of mushrooms.

The snow was beginning to fall heavily now. Herschel pulled his collar up. He should return to town, he knew, but he could not tear himself away. It was as if by bearing witness to their flight, he was somehow lending the village people his support - as if to turn away from them would be a form of abandonment. He stood and watched as the long line walked on in silence, into an impenetrable white haze. Finally, he walked back to town, against the tide of the sad procession.

•

The Hussars guided their horses down a steep ice-covered defile to a broad field undulating under a blanket of snow. They crossed the field and rode uphill into a copse of pines. The sky was black; there were no stars. The wind was rising, raining pine needles down on them. The order had gone out from the regiment that the men were to sleep in their saddles. They rested with their faces buried in their horses' manes, gratefully absorbing the warmth radiating from the steaming bodies of the mounts.

At first light, a messenger from the regiment rode up with a report that partisan detachments had hidden arms, food, and large sums of money in nearby farm houses. The revolutionists were stirring up local populations, recruiting peasants, and planning the destruction of bridges, barges, and steamships.

Zakharov immediately dispatched Naryshkin with a patrol.

"Search for steamships!" he commanded with a laugh.

Two hours later the lieutenant returned. He had found no steamships, but he had found and searched a farmhouse. He reported that they had found hay.

"Hay?" said Zakharov.

"Yes, much hay," Naryshkin replied. "No people. Only hay."

Zakharov laughed, "Well, what else would you expect to find at a farm?"

"Exactly," said Naryshkin.

After a long uphill climb, they reached the summit, from which they could see the broad sweep of the valley below. The steeple of the Wladno church was visible in the distance. Zakharov raised his spyglass. The forest blocked his view of the town, but over the trees he could see that the long narrow road leading west was jammed with townspeople. He shook his head and smiled grimly at the futility of it.

By late afternoon it was snowing harder. Zakharov ordered the men to dismount and loosen their girths. Weary and cold, the Hussars fell to the wet ground, and leaning against the trees, they sheltered from the snow as best they could. Zakharov and Naryshkin, wrapped in their greatcoats, sat under a lean-to on folding stools before a fire. They were eating bread spread with preserves that Zakharov's family had sent from St. Petersburg in a wooden box inlaid with ivory. They sipped strong black tea brewed by Zakharov's servant.

"I am growing weary of chasing shadows in the forest," Naryshkin said. "Is this work for cavalrymen?"

Zakharov did not reply, but he shook his head in disgust. He was tracking down phantom revolutionists and corralling ignorant, pathetic *Zhids* and *Polacks* as conscripts!

"What will we do with them if we catch these *Zhids*?" Naryshkin asked. "What are they good for? They are born cowards. They are filthy. They are usurers, dishonorable and greedy. No one can figure them out. In the *Starostwo* the *Polacks* won't accept that they are even Polish. They speak this strange language – Yiddish – a kind of gibberish, and they dress in the style of a century ago. And those long unkempt beards and greasy earlocks! No wonder it is impossible for them to mix with any other nation."

Zakharov thought of Rochek. He wasn't like the others. A man like Rochek would make a soldier. But he couldn't imagine him swearing loyalty to the Tsar.

According to Naryshkin, the Jews were responsible for every imaginable vice.

Their aim is to obliterate the Catholic faith," he said. "Their instructions come straight from the Masonic high priests." Zakharov was silent.

"All of them are dishonorable and haughty," Naryshkin raved on. "They will not quit until they have dominated the banks and seized control of the wealth of the world."

"Once Naryshkin gets the bit between his teeth there is no stopping him," Zakharov thought. "Doesn't he get tired of hearing the sound of his own voice?"

But Naryshkin was nothing if not relentless.

"How will we ever control them? They have a peculiar kind of self-government of their own. It is as if the state has no authority over them."

Zakharov had to acknowledge that there was some truth in Naryshkin's tirade.

These *Zhids*," he thought, "seem to govern themselves without a governing body, without a central organization, or even a dominant religious authority. They can read and write. They make their own laws. They settle disputes among themselves. They mete out punishment in their own peculiar way. They can't be landowners or masters of serfs. They can be drafted into the army, but of course they cannot be officers. They are nothing other than an extremely infuriating incongruity."

He just doesn't understand them. He believed that by their insularity, by their refusal to admit the outside world, they bring down oppression upon themselves.

Zakharov wondered, "Where do they fit, this mongrel race? On the other hand, these *Zhids* are subjected to pogroms, to insults and accusations. They pay punitive taxes. Their property is seized. We do nothing but persecute them. Is this hatred of them rational? It is stimulated by the very things that should arouse sympathy – their destitution, overcrowding, their frailty. How can they escape their fate?"

•

The silence of the forest was shattered. A horse galloped wildly out of the woods. The rider was Prince Vorontsov.

"We're surrounded! We're surrounded!" he cried.

He was hysterical. Finally, assured that the regiment was not under attack, he calmed down and regained the use of speech. He reported that he had ridden into a large formation of gray horses.

He had stumbled into a reconnaissance patrol of the Sumsky Regiment.

•

On the road, in the long procession, they stamped their feet and blew into their hands to revive numb fingers. They pulled their hats down over their ears. They wore their clothes in many layers, carrying whatever they couldn't wear in bundles on their backs.

Simcha Krelenstein, the cobbler, wore a wooly sheepskin. He pushed a cart piled high with his most precious possessions – bundles of tanned skins of every color, shape, and size, without which he couldn't practice his trade.

Alter Szklaniewitz was yelling, "Not so fast! Not so fast!"

He stumbled along behind his oxcart, which his son Mottel guided. He struggled vainly to keep his teetering cages of fowls from falling from the wagon.

Dina Margolies, her eyes red and her face stained with tears, clung to the arm of her husband Eli. They had been married less than a year. He, at eighteen, would certainly be seized. Every so often, she turned, looking back toward the village, which had long since disappeared from view. Still, she hoped to catch one more glimpse of Mama and Papa, last seen waving forlornly from the steps of their house.

Walking beside them, burdened under a heavy bundle of clothes he planned to sell, was Stefan Rynek, a young Polish fisherman. He was urging them to flee with him to the Mazury district, where he knew that the lakes had an abundance of freshwater fish.

Rumors flew all up and down the long line: there had been many arrests, the Cossacks were sweeping through Wladno, the *muziks* were pillaging the village. Questions flew from person to person. Where could they go? Where could they hide? Where would they be safe? The pork butcher Pachelski and his wife, were fleeing with their teenage son to Lomza, hoping that the conscription order might not be in force in another district.

"Dumb *Polack*," the grain merchant Lwowitz thought. If the Russkies are looking in Wladno, they will look in Lomza."

Lwowitz was heading to Grodno, a large city, where he was confident that he would be hidden by a mill owner he knew. Most of them didn't know where they were running. They knew only that their sons must escape the Tsar's conscription.

So far, they had seen no sign of the Russians, but with their finely honed instinct about such matters, they knew they couldn't be far behind. They knew. This was a people who, for as long as anyone could remember, had witnessed the pillaging of their villages. This was a people to whom mortification was a part of life. So they knew that soon the Hussars – would descend upon them, spurring their charging horses into their midst, their long lances poised, screaming, cursing, and whirling their sabers above their heads, lashing out at them with crops and whips.

The Hussars were justly feared, and even more so the Cossacks, who they knew would immediately go for their wives and daughters.

•

Two days later, when Zakharov and his squadron returned to Wladno, they found the village eerily silent. The only sound to be heard was a dog barking in the distance. Colonel Arakcheev's regiment had been on a forced march in the forest for thirty-five hours. They had not seen a single revolutionist, nor had they run down even one person attempting to evade conscription. Most of the men and boys of draft age had fled, but some were still in hiding in the village. Zakharov moved quickly to close off the streets. He ordered a search from house to house.

Some of the Poles who were in hiding were drunk. The Jews had simply lost their heads and run. Where could they hide? The snow was heavier now, and the wind had picked up. Zakharov looked at the threatening sky. A blizzard was on the way.

The next day, angry crowds poured into the street in front of the *Starostrow* building. The townspeople milled around in the snow, undeterred by the rising wind. They were enraged and fearful. They shouted oaths. Fists were raised toward the windows of the squadron headquarters. A long line of petitioners, begging for exemptions, snaked into the building, up the stairway, and into the corridor leading to the headquarters. The office was in turmoil.

"Good God!" Zakharov exclaimed. "It is impossible to push through the door!"

People were climbing over each other and thrusting documents into the faces of the clerks at the desks. Brawls boiled up. The din – cries of anguish and outrage in Polish and in Yiddish – was overpowering. A young mother shrieked into the face of an overwhelmed clerk. She pushed papers at him, which of course he couldn't read.

"A mistake," she screamed. "Can't you see? Take a look! See here - Yankel Baranowitz is too young to serve."

An absurdly wrinkled Polish woman cried plaintively, "How could you have seized Janusz Boczko? He is far past the age of recruitment!"

Shmulka Zabrewski, the butcher, pleaded for his young helper. "Everyone knows that Chaim Krelenstein is lame!"

The mob outside the *Starostrow* shifted and stirred. People pummeled each other to reach the door. Sergeant-Major Przemysl ordered the Hussar guards, who were usually assigned to the street doors below, upstairs to control the crush of people storming the office. The soldiers were quickly overwhelmed. The crowd swarmed around the entrance to the office, clamoring for justice and howling for mercy. Inside, the clerks fended off the papers – birth records, Baptismal certificates, citizenship documents that were thrust at them. Two of the clerks couldn't read or write anyway. The two others sat with their arms crossed over their chests, indifferent to the noise and confusion.

Coronet Vorontzov, assigned especially to this duty, leaned back in his chair, his blouse undone, thumbs looped in his braces, surveying the scene benignly. The sergeant-major presided over the melee with his usual aplomb.

Zakharov, meanwhile, stood inside the open supply cupboard in too close proximity to the regimental adjutant, Colonel Razdolnoe. He had ridden to Wladno to personally deliver an urgent message. An assembly point had been designated at the railroad junction, to which the captured revolutionists were to be taken.

"Yes, Colonel, but the regiment has failed to capture any revolutionists," said Zakharov.

The colonel looked at him sternly.

"You *will* capture them," he said. "Those are your orders. Revolutionary courts have been set up, and you are to order the revolutionists to disarm and give up their ringleaders. Conscripts who have so far evaded the dragnet are to be warned on pain of death to surrender."

Zakharov thanked the colonel solemnly, assured him that the orders would be promptly carried out, brought his heels together smartly, saluted, and saw him on his way. The colonel's orderly struggled to clear a path for him through the crowd.

As the colonel departed, Zablodovich, the *Starostwo* administrator, heaved his way into the office through the maelstrom outside. Zakharov saw him and was dismayed. The man always moved in a miasma of schnapps, garlic, onions and sweat. The captain was certain that his face betrayed the revulsion he felt whenever he was confronted with Zablodovich's corpulence, his little pig eyes and sallow, pockmarked face. Zablodovich owed his position on the district council to his colossal size. He had a huge head, an enormous mouth, and lips like two slices of liver. He was ugly. And he was ignorant. But he was intimidating.

"Excellency!" Zablodovich called out to him from the doorway.

Spittle flew from his mouth. He was agitated. And as usual, he was obsequious. The captain was always amused that this man, who affected such an imperious manner in his dealings with the *muzhiks,* and who was so insufferable with the *Zhids,* would at the mere sight of a Russian be reduced to a quivering mass. What, Zakharov wondered, had roused this dimwit from the muzzy condition which was his usual state?

Zablodovich stood before him kneading his tattered fur hat in his sausage-like fingers. His voice was barely above a whisper, and the captain had difficulty hearing him over the crowd. Zablodovich reported that he had heard that the boy, the *Zhid* who arrived from out of nowhere months ago, the one who was living with the rabbi - had evaded the dragnet.

"Ah, Wladno is suddenly in peril," Zakharov said. "Is the government in imminent danger of being overthrown?"

Zablodovich was affronted by Zakharov's sarcasm.

"He is a fugitive!" he bawled. "He is a revolutionist!"

"A revolutionist?" Zakharov said. "Really? Who said that?"

"Does it matter who said?" Zablodovich replied.

"Conspiracy. Intrigue. Even this moronic lout is embroiled in plots," thought the captain. "They are like children in their secret scheming. They are so ignorant that there is no dealing with them." Zakharov's irritation was getting the better of him. He demanded, "Who put you up to this?"

Zablodovich's bulging eyes betrayed his fear. He stood nervously.

Zakharov knew that this lout could not have acted of his own volition. His first instinct was to reach out and grab him by the throat. But suddenly weariness overcame him. He was too tired to trouble himself. Besides, he was loathe to touch this walking garbage heap.

"Get out!" he bellowed.

Relief evident on his sweat-slicked face, Zablodovich retreated, jostling several people as he stumbled backward toward the door.

Zakharov stood silently for a moment. He wondered who had put Zablodovich up to turning the boy in. Who wanted the boy out of the way? Then he turned and looked around the room for the messenger, Landau. Nothing happened in the village that Landau didn't know about.

• • • •

25

ROCHEK'S BARN

Salman Lidzbarski, his enormous body forging into the wind, held the lines in one hand and the long whip in the other. The sleigh raced through the village streets into the countryside. The snow was illumined by a wintry moon. It glittered like diamonds. It was harshly cold, and though Miriam and Herschel were bundled to their eyes, the blanket of animal skins provided little warmth.

Over the roar of the wind Miriam shouted, "Where are you taking us?"

"Rochek says come," Lidszbarski said.

Lidszbarski believed that was all the explanation they required. They had thrown their few possessions into the sleigh and sped off into the night.

•

Rochek's cavernous barn was lit by kerosene lamps hung from the beams. Looking down from the loft to the stalls below, Herschel saw Lidzbarski removing the harnesses from the team. Then, kneeling in the sawdust before one of the heavy-haunched bays, he lifted its leg to score the snow and ice from its thick hooves. The big dray horses in the stalls stomped and chuffed. The saddle horses, unaccustomed to the presence of humans in the barn at night, whinnied, tossed their heads, and pawed the straw nervously. The barn echoed with curious night sounds - the scurrying of rats, the creaking of ancient timbers, the random cracking of trees shedding frozen limbs, and water dripping with a steady, rhythmic splash into a barrel somewhere below.

Miriam blew on a window skimmed with hoarfrost. She looked out at the extraordinary night. The moon, which stood high above the barn, was pale yellow and enormous. Its rays filtered though the clouds, casting a blue light upon the snow in the fields. Broad shadows crept over the ground like gray velvet. A harsh wind surged in a broad sweep through fields and towns, through walls and fences. More snow was on the way.

A great weariness had descended upon Miriam. Her life seemed to hover before her. She had always known that she could never return to the life of the *shtetl*, but she was nevertheless deeply saddened by her family's rejection. Now she had no idea where she would go or what she would do.

Herschel had all but given up. He had become reconciled to his fate. He couldn't keep running forever. But what would become of him? Never far from his thoughts was Seimanowski's grim depiction of the death march to Siberia.

They heard the barn door rumble open. They looked down to the floor below. A funnel of loose straw and debris swept up through the hatch. Then they heard Rochek's voice.

"I'm coming up," he called to them.

His head emerged from the hatch. He wore a thick fur cloak. A heavy woolen scarf was pulled over his face and mouth. He walked quickly to the stove, stomping and shuffling, shaking off the snow.

He caught his breath, and then he said, "You must leave. We go tomorrow, as soon as there is a break in the storm."

Herschel looked toward the window dubiously.

"Don't worry, the storm is our friend. There is little the border guards can do to hinder those who wait for a stormy dark night."

He had often waited for pouring rain or driving snow, for the moon to be hidden by the clouds, to steal through the forest and slip around the white-painted boulders that marked the border.

"Some, for whom the border is a livelihood, make a deal with the guards and saunter across like gentry."

He pounded his chest and laughed, "Josep Rochek always rides across in style."

Rochek usually led a string of horses to be sold on the other side. He was, after all, a horse trader by profession, a tradition passed on to him by his father and his father before him. Rochek also had another line of work. He was part of a clandestine network that smuggled army deserters, political dissenters, and illegal residents from Russian Poland across the border into Prussia.

He laughed again. "I don't know why the Russkies even bother to have guards at the border."

Many in the military guard were in Rochek's pocket. It was believed that his influence was so great that the fate of many top officials and provincial ministers – whether they remained in office or were exiled to Siberia – depended upon him.

From the expression on Herschel's face, Rochek could see that he remained unconvinced. Rochek smiled at him.

"Don't worry, boychick. There is no danger. I can usually settle these affairs peaceably with the guard."

"And if you can't?"

"If I can't," he smiled slyly, "then it is time for the guard to move on... to the next world!"

But in truth, Rochek was worried. Earlier in the evening, just as dusk was descending, he had an unexpected visitor. In the distance, he saw a cloud of snow boiling up. Gradually it grew, finally materializing into a sleigh driven in reckless haste by a driver in uniform. It was Josep Landau, Zakharov's orderly. Landau brought the sleigh to a halt in an explosion of snow and ice, barely a foot from where Rochek stood.

"What brings you here, Josep?" Rochek asked.

There was no friendly smile on Landau's face. He looked about nervously. Taking the reins and the whip in one hand, he leaned from the bench of the sleigh and grasped Rochek by the sleeve with the other, pulling him roughly to the side of the sleigh.

He looked about once again, then he whispered, "He says go! Go tonight!"

"Go?" Rochek asked. "Who says?"

"Zakharov, you fool!" Landau said, searching Rochek's face to be certain that he understood.

Then, apparently satisfied, Landau wheeled his sleigh about and raced off.

"A warning from Zakharov!" Rochek smiled and shook his head.

•

Their departure could not be too long delayed. This was not just another routine sweep of the village. This time the Russians were out in force. The dragnet extended along the entire Polish-Prussian border.

Herschel saw that the storm had now blown up into a blizzard. The trees were bowed and swaying in the wind–driven snow. Shreds of clouds raced over the forest. Rolling thunder drowned out the roar of the wind, and flashes of lightning, unusual in winter, lit up the farm buildings and silhouetted the distant mountains in silver against the black sky. Obviously, they would go nowhere tonight, but Rochek said that at the first break in the weather they would be off.

•

It was even colder now. Sleet lashed the barn. Wind whistled through the siding, and in some places snow was actually driven through the cracks between the boards.

Miriam went to the samovar and poured another glass of tea. The enamel plates with the remnants of their kasha and cabbage sat unwashed in a tub near the ladder. The odors of the barn – sweet moist earth, rotting apples and roots, wet hay and horse manure – mingled with the fumes from the small stove.

"Soon we will be away from here," Miriam said, speaking more to herself than to Herschel.

Herschel was silent.

"You don't think so?"

"I don't know," he said.

He was reluctant to let her see his apprehension. But he craved reassurance.

"To me it sometimes seems hopeless."

"Rochek knows his business," Miriam said. "You will soon be home in Berlin, and I will be... well, I don't know where I will be."

She sounded defeated. He was not accustomed to pessimism from her.

She said, "In a month or two, Wladno will hardly be a memory for you. And you won't even be able to recall my name."

"You are wrong," he said.

He resisted the impulse to tell her he would never forget her. But now his thoughts were dominated by Tova, Worried about her safety.

"Come away from the window," she said. "It's cold over there."

She stood with her hands extended toward the stove.

"You haven't told me what you think of my home." she said.

"Your home?" he asked. "Wladno isn't your home."

"Wladno, Vadzilovo, there is no difference." she said.

He saw that she wanted to talk. It was implicit that they would not speak of the Insurrection, nor would they speak about what happened to them after they fled from Warsaw. For Herschel, the months of upheaval and uncertainty, of death and destruction, of fear and flight - all that had become as dust. It was empty and meaningless.

"What do you think of Wladno?" she asked.

"Backward. Dirty. The people are steeped in ignorance."

"But they work so hard," she said. "They suffer."

He was bemused. Why was she so defensive? She had always condemned life in the *shtetl* so vehemently.

"Yes, the Jews work hard. But they are hopeless. Mired in the past in myth and superstition. The village Poles, they are drunks. The peasants are ignorant, and they are dangerous. They burn and loot at every opportunity. And the Russians. What can you say of the Russians? They look for any excuse to attack and persecute. One day they are after deserters, the next smugglers, and the next conscripts. And of course revolutionists."

He laughed bitterly. "But revolutionists, we are fair game everywhere, aren't we?"

"Yes, fair game," she said. "And now we are out in the open, exposed, all our expectations dashed. We had our chance, and the revolution was sundered. But the working class rebelled, which in itself is something. And some day the privileges of the exploiters will be brought to an end."

He looked at her doubtingly.

"Poland won't rest," she said. "The people will rise again."

She shoveled more coal into the stove, and then she stood hugging herself, pulling her shawl tightly around her shoulders. There had been no break in the weather. The storm showed no sign of abating. They settled down for the night. Herschel moved some broken chairs and boxes of old papers to make room for a bed of sorts. They put horse blankets down on top of a layer of hay near the stove and lay down together. They slept a troubled, restless sleep.

•

Suddenly, Herschel awoke, startled. The barn door clattered open and the wind roared in. He heard voices he didn't recognize. Anxiety streamed through him. He woke Miriam, shaking her shoulder gently and putting his finger to her lips. They rose quietly and went to the hatch, where they stood motionless, looking down to the floor of the barn.

Rochek was standing with several men – strangers. They were brushing snow off bulky quilted coats and sheepskin jackets. Rochek called up to them, "Don't worry. They are friends."

The men, revolutionists, had made their way to Rochek through the forest, narrowly evading the advancing Russians. There were five of them. Rochek and Lidzbardski hustled them down into the cellar of the barn, through a hatch hidden beneath the hay in one of the stalls. When Herschel and Miriam joined them, they were removing their coats, stamping their feet, and blowing on their frozen hands, their breath fogging the air. Two of them collapsed where they stood, exhausted, with their backs against the stone wall of the cellar. The others sat down with Rochek at a makeshift table that Libardski had erected from two barrels and some old boards. The lamps hanging from the low beams cast a flickering light, illuminating fragments of their faces.

On Rochek's left, a tall, gaunt man slouched over the table.

"He is a corpse come to life," thought Herschel.

Behind him, against the wall, sat a heavy, fiercely bearded man, his black eyes glowering in the lamplight. A boy, who Herschel thought was probably his own age, slouched at his side. Next to him, almost obscured in shadow, two older men were hunched in fatigue. The face of one was contorted in profound wretchedness. The other had high cheekbones and a shaved head.

"He is an Asiatic, perhaps a Mongol," thought Herschel. "Perhaps a Siberian."

They had tramped through the forest, just ahead of the advancing Hussars. At night they sheltered in the woods or in the barns of abandoned farmhouses. They went on for several days, through the wet fields and woods, staying clear of traveled roads and avoiding villages.

"The Russian troops are right behind you," Rochek warned them. "They are patrolling the forest only a few kilometers from here, searching for partisans – For you!"

He thrust his finger at them to make his point. "They are everywhere, sweeping the village for conscripts."

The older man, named Korno, lay sprawled across the table with his massive head on his arms. He looked up. "Cossacks?" he asked, apprehensively.

"No, not Cossacks," Rochek said. "Hussars. But the Cossacks will come."

"These village people, why are they running?" asked the emaciated man, the one named Wyszjiwo, rising from the overturned keg on which he sat. "Why don't they stand and resist?"

Rochek laughed grimly. "Resist? They don't know how to resist. They are like children. They are defenseless."

"We can organize them and arm them," Wyszjiwo said.

An ironic expression remained fixed on Rochek's face. His voice betrayed his unease.

"And then you will move on. You will expect me to get you across the border. But what will happen to the people who live here, who must remain here? Do you think there will be no reprisals?"

The bearded man, Nadwszki, swore to himself.

"Has it come to this?" he thought. "Do we really have to cast our lot with these *Zhids*?"

He sprang to his feet and shouted, "Don't your people know what sacrifices we have made for their freedom? Don't they know that hundreds, maybe thousands, have died at the Citadel? That we have been slaughtered in the streets and marched off to slavery in Siberia? Why did we do it if not for them?"

He looked at Miriam and Herschel, and he could see that it was futile. They were not made for the harsh, bitter life of the revolutionist. They would never stand and fight.

Nadwszki thrust a finger at them and said, "You imagine you are heroes. You admire yourselves. But you are too soft."

Herschel laughed to himself. "Ah, I see. They plan to attack the Hussars with words. Words. More words."

Their words carried him back to the impassioned tirades of the revolutionists in Warsaw and to the lofty oratory of the comrades in London.

"These insurrectionists make terrorism out to be some kind of game." Herschel thought.

"They talk in abstractions. 'The Cause' and 'The People.' They use such arrogant terms as 'the meaning of life' but give no thought to the meaning of *lives*. They declare their love for the masses and the underprivileged, but they despise them for their ignorance. So much for brotherhood! So much for solidarity!"

The idea of the Insurrection was now more odious to him than it had ever been.

Rochek roared back at Nadwszki. "Don't you understand that the village is surrounded? Maybe you are willing to die for the Cause, but these people they don't even know what the Cause is. For them the highest cause, the most noble cause, is just to stay alive!"

Nadwszki said to his comrades, "What can you expect from these *Zhids*? They are aliens in the house of Poland. They may speak Polish, but they conduct their dirty, secret business in their own strange language. Clever and cowardly, the Christ-killer follows his own incomprehensible evil precepts!"

The Asiatic, the one they called Casmir, rose from the table. He walked with a stoop, his shoulders hunched, his hands thrust deeply into his pockets. Looking at Miriam and

Herschel, he sensed their cynicism. He shouted, "You Warsaw people, what have you done for the Insurrection?" Thrusting his fist at Herschel, he screamed with demonic intensity, "You are parasites and cowards!"

Rochek felt the sting of their contempt. He was angry. He could lead them onto the ice in the river and let them drown. He could lose them in the forest and leave them for the wolves. He could. But he wouldn't. There was nothing for it, he would have to accept them, take them in, shake their hands, feed them, drink vodka with them, and help them to escape. That was his solemn obligation.

•

The storm was unrelenting. It continued to howl into the afternoon, building in intensity. The partisans were growing restless and increasingly argumentative. They quarreled among themselves. They shouted over each other, their words becoming more brutal and vicious.

Herschel thought that the idiocy of the one was exceeded by the folly of the other.

He heard the tall, emaciated Wyszjiwo say, "We can manage it with just five men, I guess."

"If one of them knows the garrison, I suppose we can do it," replied Nadwszki.

The Asiatic said, "But we need more weapons."

Their first act, he suggested, should be to raid the regimental garrison to get firearms, and powder to blow up the ammunition dump.

"We all know our jobs," Nadwszki said, turning to Rochek. "But we need someone who knows explosives."

At this, Herschel saw Miriam's body stir. Then, in a flash, her eyes darted across to him. She saw that he had not failed to notice her interest. She looked away and began to roll a cigarette.

Rochek rose to his feet. "Listen to me. I will help you any way I can. You need food, supplies, horses," he pounded his breast with his fist and said, "You can count on me." His fierce gaze swept their faces, "But leave our people out of it! Do you understand? I want the village people left out of it!"

"*You* listen!" Nadwszki shouted. "It is your duty to help. Your sacred obligation! With the help of the villagers we can destroy the garrison."

"We can attack tomorrow," said Wyszjiwo. "If we move quickly, we can strike before dawn."

"No!" Herschel screamed. The word seemed to explode from his guts. They looked up as one, startled. This was the first word Herschel had uttered. Now he leaped to his feet. "Fools! Idiots!" he yelled. He was frantic. He wanted to strike out at them. "You will kill us all!"

Miriam stared at him in amazement. His eyes were flashing. He was like one possessed. Miriam knew that the very thought of bloodshed was an abomination to him. He would never raise his hand in violence again.

• • • •

26

ENVY THE DEAD

The air rushing against his face was frozen. He was blinded by the wind-driven snow. He now knew that he had made a mistake riding out into the blizzard.

He felt pangs of guilt for abandoning Miriam, but the thought of her with that mob of partisans assaulted his mind. He was outraged that she would even consider helping them.

"To go against the Russian cavalry is lunacy! Well, Miriam can help them if she wishes, but not me. I have had enough of bloodshed."

He headed his horse toward the village. What he would do when he got there he didn't know. He was determined to put as much distance between himself and the partisans as possible. He was not insensible to the deprivations the partisans had suffered and the dangers they had faced, nor was he unaware of their courage.

"After all," he thought, "I was not just a bystander, an onlooker, to other men's courage. Hadn't I conquered my own terror, faced my own demons, and placed my own life at risk?"

But he failed to see the heroism in a futile gesture.

Riding was becoming more difficult now. He had to guide the horse past snowdrifts too high to traverse. He tried to follow the line of the fields, but in some places the fences had been carried off by the wind; in others the snow had built up in drifts, obliterating the fields. A mask of snow had formed on his face. The intense cold had penetrated his cloak. The horse was shying, tossing his head and whinnying.

The tempest continued, and now he was gripped by fear. For the first time he was afraid that he would perish in the storm.

"Perhaps," he thought, "that is the appropriate fate for a man who can't control his rage."

Then, in the distance he made out the dim outline of Zloczewer's barn. As he rode closer he saw the inviting yellow glow of flickering lights, and in the window of the barn he could see the passing shadows of people inside.

•

He was blinded momentarily by the sudden blaze of light when he entered the barn. He shielded his eyes with his hand. When he looked up, he was startled to see a dozen men and boys. He recognized many of them. Biezunnski, the rotund old baker, and two others had ancient muskets slung over their shoulders. Several men had knives and clubs; some had scythes and other farm tools.

Itzchok Yankl, the innkeeper, was kneeling on the floor, siphoning kerosene into cans held by two Yeshiva boys, their side-curls dangling and their fur hats tilted back precariously on their heads.

He was astounded. "What are you doing? What do you think you are doing?"

Kuba Kleinac, the muscular butcher, turned to him and said, "We have nothing to lose."

Zilbergerg, the cobbler, sobbed, "The *Polacks* have taken our houses. The young men are gone, driven away by the

Russians. The livestock is gone, the shops and stalls are destroyed, and the *shul* is desecrated."

Herschel was stunned. His breath caught in his chest. Itcheleha Zloczewer walked over to him. He had a puzzled expression on his face. "Haven't you been to the village?"

"No," Herschel said.

"You haven't been to the *shul*? You don't know what happened at the *shul*?"

"No," Herschel replied, his heart sinking.

"They took the rabbi. The *Polacks* took him."

"Took him? Where?"

Zloczewer shrugged, "God only knows. But of this you can be sure - he is dead."

Herschel's body sagged. He thought he would drop to the floor. Zloczewer gripped his shoulder and looked squarely into his eyes. "Listen Herschel, he is better off dead. Believe me."

"Who took him?" Herschel asked. "Who took the rabbi?"

"Zabladovich and a mob of his *muzhiks*. They dragged him through the square."

Mattes Cohen said, "I was there. I saw it. Zabladovich told us, 'I want all of you to go away.' He said, 'This is our land, and you Izraelici have already caused enough trouble.' And they took him."

Herschel's head swam. He turned to Zloczewer.

"Itcheleha, please," he pleaded, "where is Tova?"

"I don't know," Zloczewer said sadly. He could not meet Herschel's eyes.

"Listen, Itcheleha, please," Herschel begged, grabbing him by the shirt. "I don't know," he said again. "The *Polacks* were rioting and plundering. We ran with our families."

Herschel broke away from him. Frantically, he ran to the door.

"Where are you going?" Biezunnski said, grabbing him by his coat.

Yankl ran to him, "Are you mad?"

The others gathered around.

"You can't go anywhere in this storm," Zloczewer said. "Besides she is probably safe with other people in the village."

Herschel looked up at the women who were peering down from the loft. He saw faces he recognized – Biesunnski's wife and Yankl's daughter. They looked down at him from under their shawls.

He called up to them, "Have you seen Tova?"

They didn't answer. They shrank back from the railing.

Herschel was close to collapse. "When did this start?" he cried.

"Last night. Sunday," said Yankl. Yankl's bald pate was glistening. Tufts of gray hair stuck out above his ears, creating the impression of some plump, exotic bird.

"When does it always start? Sunday. They probably thought with the Russians on the rampage, this would be a good time. Not that they have ever needed an excuse."

Biezunnski said, "It started in the afternoon when they stole Reb Baruch Stecher's hat and used it for a *Judosz*." "For a *what*?" Herschel asked.

"A *Judosz* – a Jew puppet," Biezunnski said. "A puppet the size of a man. They dressed it in black, put a beard on it and ear-locks, and danced around with it in the square. Soon the *muzhiks* came from their *zajazdy*. Dozens of them, all drunk. They began beating the puppet with sticks. They dragged it over to the steps of the church, and when the priest came out – he should burn in hell! – they screamed and yelled and went crazy. They hung the puppet by the legs from the belfry and screamed and cursed and danced like *meshuganas*."

A balding, portly young man named Goodman came over.

"We stood on our side of the market and watched helplessly," he said with a shrug.

With his arms outstretched, his palms heavenward, he stood in the posture of inevitability that was so common among the villagers. "What could we do?"

"Then they started to break into the shops," said Itzchok Yankl.

Goodman said, "First they took the puppet down from the church and took it to Rabbi Mordoviscz's S*hul* and threw garbage."

"Then they poured kerosene on it and lit it," added Zloczewer. "They paraded it around the market on fire."

"By then," Yankl said, "they had broken into Nachman's wine cellars and rolled his barrels into the square."

Kuba Rosenblum, the bowed old butcher, spoke with tears in his eyes. "The *muzhiks* came from the fields, running into the market, screaming, 'Kill the *Zhids!*' The boys who work in my shop grabbed picks and shovels, ready to beat them off, And these two Yeshiva boys from Plock, they joined them."

Goodman said, "Two of the *muzhiks*, who had been jailed for stealing wood from Chaim Rosenbaum last year, ran to his house. They killed him."

With great sadness he murmured, "He has a wife and three girls."

Biezunski's face was taut with anger.

"Fedya saw his two cows driven out of his yard by two *muzhiks*," Biezunski said. "Manya's tall clock, the one in the painted case, was carried away on the shoulder of his neighbor, Racionz."

"Neighbors!" Zloczewer spat the word. "Our neighbors, the *Polacks*, they stood in the streets watching our suffering as if they were at a carnival. They clapped and laughed, encouraging the *muzhiks*. Some of them lay in ambush for us, waiting to move into our shops. The priest, the snake that he is, spread venom among them, encouraging the pillaging."

Herschel was struggling to take in all that he was hearing. But his thoughts were on Tova. Where is she? Is she safe?

Melkmann the lumber merchant, was weeping. "My Papa knew," Melkmann said. "He knew. On *Shabbat*, when we were coming home from *shul*, Papa looked up. He said, 'See the sky?' The night was dark, and there were no stars. Papa said, 'I see bad times. Bad times are upon us. Those who live through these days will envy the dead.'"

•

The wind was high and blowing in gusts. The sky, though it was barely visible through the steadily falling snow, was tinged with red. Smoke was in the air. When he came to the blacksmith's stables at the end of Stavisky Street, Herschel left the horse and continued on foot. There was no life in the streets. There were no merchants. No children. No sound but the lamentation of the wind.

He felt a strange loneliness. The absence of people and the vacant streets filled him with dread. He trudged through drifting snow toward the synagogue, keeping his back to the walls of the houses, slipping into the narrow alleys, avoiding the streets.

Though the Hussars had thrown up barricades at the crossroads, he didn't see any soldiers. But then, through the curtain of swirling snow, he saw the glint of the weapons carried by the troops who were standing concealed in the shadows. Suddenly, he was startled by the pounding of horses' hooves in the snow. He shrank back against the wall. Then all was quiet again. He moved through the alley. Then, from somewhere far away, he heard a cry - a wail of pain so deep, so profound, that no mere corporeal wound could have been its cause.

"My God," he cried, "What has happened here?"

He ran, bent low, close to the walls of the windswept streets. His eyes teared. He scuttled along in the snow, gasping deep draughts of frigid air. He ran down the alley to Warta Street, and then to the market square. Through the wind-driven snow he could barely see the shops and the dwellings on the western side, the "Jewish side" of the square. Strangely, they appeared to be visible only in outline.

Shadows of the old shops lengthened on the snow like dark macabre creatures. Then to his horror, he realized that what he was seeing were the skeletons, the bare bones, the remains of buildings that had all been burned to the ground.

Black smoke rose from the ruins. It whipped through the falling snow into restless red clouds stained by a fire burning somewhere in the distance. Then, he saw that what he had taken for abandoned bundles were several bodies lying sprawled grotesquely on the ground. Struggling to bring his trembling under control, he remained concealed in the shadows at the corner of the street.

"Oh God!" What will I find at the synagogue?"

Across the square, a detachment of mounted Hussars drew up to the *Starostrow* building. Light from the windows cast yellow rectangles onto the snow, the only illumination in the square. One of the riders dismounted and made his way up the steps through the drifting snow.

Herschel turned to his right, remaining in the shadows, following the square to Synagogue Street. He stopped at the corner. Two guards were huddled around a fire at a barrier that had been erected from bales of hay and what appeared to be boards torn from a market stall. Three cavalrymen were leading their mounts across the square. They stopped at the barricade to talk to the guards. He heard their laughter. He slipped past unnoticed.

From the corner, the entrance to the synagogue was barely visible through the snow. But he saw with foreboding that the two great iron-studded oak doors yawned wide. He ran, struggling his way through drifts, across the street and up the steps. Warily, he entered the sanctuary. Apart from a sickly light that filtered through the remains of the stained-glass windows, the great vaulted room was in darkness. The Eternal Lamp above the ark had been extinguished. The doors of the ark were torn from their hinges. The Torahs were gone. At the center of the sanctuary, smoke rose from a smoldering pyre of books.

Tova! He desperately wanted to call out for Tova, but he was afraid that he would bring the soldiers who were patrolling nearby. He ran up the stairs leading to the balcony and to the rabbi's rooms. He gasped for breath. At the top of the stairs he leaned against the wall, struggling to bring himself under control. He peered down the passage into the open doorway. He called out softly to Tova. But in his heart he knew she wouldn't answer.

When he entered the rabbi's rooms he heard the grinding of broken glass under his feet. The floor was covered with plaster, splintered wood, and shards of glass, which glinted in the pale light. He heard a plaintive moan that was almost imperceptible. His heart pounded. Then he realized that what he heard was a sob that had escaped from somewhere deep within himself. He closed his eyes and gathered his strength. He forced himself to walk to the bedroom.

He called out softly. "Tova," he whispered.

From the doorway he could see the foot of the bed. He saw her leg, clad in a coarse gray woolen stocking. She was wearing no shoes. One hand lay palm upward on her thigh, listlessly, in what appeared to be a posture of pleading. The rest of her body was in shadow.

He called out, "Tova" His voice broke.

He entered the room. The floor was moist under his feet. Tova was sprawled on the bed. Her blouse was open, pulled aside, exposing the pale skin of her high young breasts. Her hair had escaped from her kerchief, falling in ringlets onto her forehead. Her expression was serene but melancholy. She smiled up at him with gently swelling lips. In her eyes there was, he thought, a look of bewilderment, as if she were deeply immersed in a dream she didn't understand. He remained motionless, scarcely breathing. His feet were fastened to the floor in her blood.

•

On the street he stood with his back against the syna-gogue wall. His body was racked with sobs. He breathed deeply, greedily, sucking in the cold night air. Slowly, his heart regained its rhythm, and his trembling grew less vio-lent. Awareness returned.

How he found the reserves of strength, and the cour-age, to enter the synagogue again, he didn't know. Dreading every step, he once again climbed the stairs to the balcony. The hallway loomed long and dark before him. A slowly mov-ing curtain cast a shadow on the wall. Somewhere below, a current of air slowly eased a door shut. His heart pounded convulsively.

Just a few feet from where he stood, Tova's body waited. He thought of her eyes in deep shadow, staring blindly. He thought of the blood on the sheets. He stood motionless, scarcely breathing. His mind drifted back to the ominous somber dreams of his childhood. He was alone. He was alone in the dark with death.

Why did he linger? He could not tear himself from Tova's presence. He went to the window and looked out at the silent, unforgiving night. The wind had subsided, but the snow was still falling. The moon shone down, casting a pale yellow light on the intricately winding streets, the tumble-down houses, the decrepit market stalls.

He wondered how it came to be that suddenly the vil-lage seemed so astonishing to him, that the people of the village suddenly seemed so heroic. All at once everything was uncomplicated and effortless. The clouds of this sorrow-ful night were swept away. He had come to a decision. He had observed other men's bravery. He watched them con-quer their dread of death, he was aware of the sacrifices they made and the risks they ran. He could not be a bystander. He drifted from a condition of profound melancholy into fierce, unbounded loathing.

He raced down the corridor, averting his eyes, shrinking from even a fleeting glance into the room where Tova lay. He threw open the door to his room and ran to the cupboard in which he kept his few possessions. From behind a pile of books on the floor, he pulled out a bundle tied in twine. He placed it on the floor. With trembling fingers he untied it and unrolled the stained flannel. He took the heavy cavalry revolver into his hand.

•

When Herschel awoke he was confused. He didn't remember how he made his way back to Rochek's barn. He sat heavily on a bale of hay, his head in his hands, awakening to the realization that all that had occurred yesterday was real and not a nightmare. He gazed down at Miriam. Her features betrayed no hint of her anguish. She slept on, expressionless. But when she stirred, her smooth brow tensed and her eyelids fluttered, and he could now see her pain.

How difficult it had been for him to return to the barn. How was he going to find the words to tell her? But it had taken only one look at him for her to know that something had gone horribly wrong. For the longest time they held each other. The tears on their faces mingled. Slowly, still wrapped in their embrace, they sank to the ground and sat facing each other, cross-legged on the straw-scattered floor, knee to knee, their foreheads touching and their arms around each other's shoulders. They sat that way for the longest time, sobbing and unmoving. Miriam's skirt was stretched across her knees, a bowl into which their tears fell.

Finally, exhausted, they drifted into sleep, lying side by side.

He awoke a few hours later and forced himself to his feet.

Then he sat once again on the bale of hay and slowly he turned a full circle, surveying the loft. It was piled to the rafters with empty crates and steamer trunks, discarded tools, and remnants of old furniture. He peered up into the high shelves and into the dark corners. And then he went straight to the place where he knew she would have hidden it. He found it immediately. The bomb was in a keg about one hundred centimeters long and perhaps twenty-five centimeters in diameter. He lifted it with great care and cradled it gently in his arms.

•   •   •   •

27

VENGEANCE

The great *Starostrow* building in the center of Wladno's market square, loomed out of the snow like a fortress rising from
the depths of a vast white lake.Its grandiose turret appeared
to float in the air, suspended above the white walls of the
building. A nimbus of yellow light glowed from the windows
on the ground floor, casting gray shadows onto the snow.
Herschel looked at the lights in the windows. They flickered
in the falling snow and swirling fog. He heard the bite of the
snow under his feet and watched his long shadow advancing.
Blowing snow and drifting fog obliterated the streets reaching out from all sides of the square.

The silence in the square was interrupted only by occasional bursts of drunken laughter from a small knot of men
gathered on the steps at the entrance to the *Starostrow* building - Zabladovich and some of his fellow members of the civil
administration.

A few villagers trudged along in the snow, carrying lan-
terns, some with packs on their backs, and others pushing
carts on sleigh runners. Apart from them, there were only
the restless troops at the barricades at the perimeter of

the square and the two guards at the door of the building. Herschel plodded across the square. He was unhurried. He carried the keg under his arm. It was surprisingly light. In the other hand he carried a lantern.

He gazed up at the stars flickering red and white in the pale blue dome of the sky. He was seized by an exultant sense of clarity, which surged through his heart in a single wave. On this night, fear had no meaning for him. He knew that he would not return, but he felt no fear, no anxiety. It puzzled him as he thought about it. He wondered why it had ceased to matter if they captured him, or even if they put him to death. He was bemused by this sudden awareness, this certainty of death, which apart from its novelty, held no interest for him. He had come to a decision, and now, on this night of devastating sorrow, it was as clear as a new dawn.

•

Itchelaha Zloczewer shifted his hunting gun from one hand to the other. He was in a state of high excitement. But he had to restrain himself. He knew that he must remain calm. He must be cautious. Five men kneeled beside him. Some of them had guns they used for hunting, others were armed only with axes and barrel staves. The two Yeshiva boys had assembled piles of rags. Cans of kerosene were at their feet. Goodman, who was armed with nothing more than an axe handle, looked at the boys curiously. Are they really going to war wearing those long capotes and fur hats? They were crowded together, pressed against each other, so close that the vapor of their breath mingled in the cold air.

Zloczewer could see practically nothing. Blowing snow merged with the smoke and fog before the shops and stalls in the square. They were startled by a horse galloping by in a nearby street. In the distance, they heard rifle fire and men shouting. Cautiously, they peered down the alley. They saw nothing. All was again silent. And then several Hussars thundered across the square, their mounts kicking up clouds of snow. They disappeared into the darkness of a street on the other side.

Zloczewer signaled his men. They got off their knees, weapons in their hands. They ran through the twisting streets of the village, hugging the walls. They ran to the end of Jerome Street and vanished down an alley behind the ritual bath house.

On the other side of the square the "Polish side" Kuba Kleineck's group advanced on the houses and shops, most of them old, flimsy structures with thatched straw roofs. Some of the Poles in the houses heard them and, saw their advancing shadows.

"They are already running from the buildings, slipping along the walls and scampering like cockroaches," Kleineck thought. He stood at the door to Vernatz's apothecary. He heard the sound of feet frantically clattering down the stairs. A door crashed open, and Vernatz came bursting out into the snow. He was in his underwear, his boots and clothing in his arms. He ran by in such haste that he passed Kleineck's men crouching in the shadows without seeing them.

Kleineck put a man with a musket on the roof looking out over the square. He signaled to the others to advance to another building down the street. The street was Priests' Lane, where the priest lived, next door to the church.

Across the square, at the corner of Lobo Street, Zloczewer held up his hand. He paused for a moment and looked about. They were about fifteen hundred meters away from an old log building, the largest of the *zajazdy*, the *Polack* taverns. He signaled Yankl, who was with the boys carrying the kerosene cans. Yankl waved at them vigorously. They picked up the cans and ran. They ran with their side-curls and the skirts of their long gabardine capotes flying. At the inn they frantically poured out the kerosene, splashing it on the walls and doors. They smashed the windows and poured kerosene on what furniture they could reach.

Itzchok Yankl commanded, "Now!" They threw burning rags into the building. A loud roar and a sudden rush of air thrust them back violently. The inn burst into flames.

•

Standing outside Josep Rochek's barn, Salman Libardski heard a muffled, echoing explosion. The sky over the village suddenly lit up. He ran to the barn and threw open the door. He called to Rochek and Miriam.

"The village! An explosion in the village!"

Miriam and Rochek scrambled up the ladder to the loft and ran to the window. The sky over Wladno was aglow. The undersides of the furrowed clouds were tinged with red. Abruptly, Miriam turned to Rochek.

"Josep, where is Herschel?"

Without waiting for the answer, she ran to the corner where she had hidden the bomb.

"It's gone!" she cried. She was in a panic. "Josep, the bomb I made. It's gone!"

Rochek and Lizbardski ran for their horses.

•

Itchelaha Zloczewer watched from the corner, his group of men arrayed behind him. The blaze lit up the entire square, illuminating the burned-out shops and the remains of homes whose beams reached like splintered bones into a sky streaked with smoke. Windowpanes burst from their frames, and glass tumbled to the street, where it sparkled like diamonds. By the light of the flames he saw people running toward the back streets and alleys, jostling each other and trodding on each other in their panic to escape. To escape from what, they didn't know.

Zloczewer shook his head. How meaningless it all was. From a distance, they he heard the sound of galloping horses, their hooves pounding the snow as they raced back and forth through the village. The Hussars were firing their guns into the air. They had no idea what they were looking for.

Bullets bit into the doorway above Zloczewer and his his men. Splinters of wood and slivers of plaster fell from the wall of the building, where they lay flat on their bellies in the snow.

That is where they died.

•

Herschel ignored the gunfire. He advanced across the square, a dark figure in the long dark shadows. He stepped forward into a cone of light streaming from the *Starastrow* building. He ran the next few steps. He ran with the ecstatic joy of a child at play. He stopped abruptly a few meters in front of the building, his feet sliding in the snow. Calmly and deliberately, he lifted the glass from the lantern and lit the fuse of the keg. Then, raising the bomb high above his head with both hands, he thrust it forward, heaving it as far as his strength would allow.

In an instant a terrifying incandescence enveloped him. The men on the steps of the building stood unmoving and frozen, embraced in a halo of bright light. He saw their faces with a supernatural clarity. He saw their chapped lips and their rheumy eyes. He saw the stubble of the beards on their chins. He saw their rotten yellow teeth in the yawning ovals of their screaming mouths.

A fearsome blow lifted him from his feet. His arms danced wildly in the air, puppet-like, in a vain effort to regain his balance. There was no sound. He could hear no voices. A curtain of silence had descended upon him.

He wondered, "Am I going mad? Have I crossed some ominous threshold?"

Then, as abruptly as sound had vanished, it returned. An explosion of sound smote him, echoing off the distant hills. Now the screaming of the injured and the pathetic cries for help came to him quite clearly.

Herschel lay on his back. The snow was stained with blood. There were several bodies lying nearby. In the light of the leaping flames, they appeared to be moving and writhing. He struggled to his knees. Glass was raining down on him. He ran his hand over his face. His nose was bleeding. His eyes burned. His coat was in tatters. He was trembling and his teeth were chattering. Kneeling in the snow, he looked across the square, amorphous in the fog and smoke. Several buildings were aflame. A troop of Hussars wheeled their horses in one direction, then in another. Behind him, a few feet away, the *Starostrow* building was a hill of rubble, smoke pouring slowly through the windows and billowing up into the sky. In the one wall that remained standing, shattered glass shone, reflecting the light of the fire.

He could no longer see clearly. He was becoming aware of pain. He felt a throbbing in his chest when he moved. Tears rolled from his eyes. The smoke was choking him. He retched in spasms. Sweat poured from his body. He was thirsty. He was very cold.

"So this is what death feels like." He was prepared for death.

He was beset by a procession of withered memories. He saw images of home, of his mother and father, of all the things that most men cherished – love, family, peace. How had they managed to elude him?

The wind was bitter now, and the snow came at him from the north. He raised his head to the churning sky. Clouds were racing past the pale moon. Everything was turning slowly, inexorably rotating around a great sphere. The nocturnal winter world revolved about him in an impenetrable vapor. Billowing clouds swept him up. He looked down at the earth from a great height. He saw the quilted earth drifting below. The dun fields, the tumbledown village, the river of faded green - all were all spread out before him like an atlas.

He hovered over the village. The clamor of the market square floated up to him. He heard children's laughter, the rumble of carts and wagons on the cobbles, and the chorus of the merchants shouting over the din of the crowd. From the windows of the tiny *shuls* of the *Hassids* came the sweet sound of children chanting their lessons. And everywhere the whisking, whisking, whisking of straw brooms in the gnarled hands of women in *babushkas,* ceaselessly sweeping the dust of the market from their front steps.

He breathed in the mingled aromas of spices and frying food. He smelled the pungent odor of barnyard animals and overheated bodies. He saw the neatly hoed rows in the small front garden patches and the geraniums nodding bravely in the window boxes of the thatched-roofed whitewashed cottages. And he beheld the old people leaning on their elbows in second-story windows, delighting in the endless drama of life unfolding in the square below.

And then he heard the drumbeat of horses' hooves in the distance. Someone was fast approaching. Dimly, he saw two men on horseback. He heard a voice calling out to him. "Herschel! Herschel!"

Then, floating in a cosmos so vast that it seemed to be infinite, hovering before him in a vague realm of her own, appeared the celestial girl of his childhood dreams. She slipped out of the shadows of the garden. She smiled at him. Her arms opened to him. Arms of enchantment beyond words, promising comfort and warmth. He reached out to her and gathered her to him, dissolving in longing and wonder.

• • • •

EPILOGUE

Summer 1914

KIEL, GERMANY - NEW YORK CITY

June 24 August 4, 1914

Kiel Harbor, bathed in brilliant summer sunlight, swarmed with motor launches, private yachts, and boats under sail of every size and description. White-funneled ocean liners, brightly bannered steam vessels, tugboats and barges, were draped in red, white and blue bunting. They sailed past long lines of gray German warships decked out in many-colored signal flags. A zeppelin circling overhead looked down on thousands of wildly enthusiastic spectators.

The British Fleet was steaming proudly into Kiel Harbor for a weeklong celebration - a friendly ceremonial visit and an opportunity for the Germans to put their naval might on display for their rivals.

The harbor resounded with a twenty-one gun salute as the Kaiser arrived on board the gold and white royal yacht Hohenzollern. British sailors in gleaming white uniforms and marines in bright crimson jackets stood rigidly at attention, lining the decks of the enormous dreadnought King George V.

In the evening, British officers were received aboard Hohenzollern by a jovial smiling Kaiser, who wore the uniform of a British Admiral of the Fleet.

On June 25th, the Kaiser returned the visit, dining aboard the British dreadnought, while an orchestra played works by German composers. On shore, German officers hosted their British counter-parts at tennis matches, tea dances, and lavish dinner parties and balls.

On Sunday, June 28th, the Kaiser went racing aboard the yacht Meteor. That afternoon, at 2:30, a launch carrying the Chief of the Imperial Naval Cabinet sped out to the Meteor. He called across the water to the Kaiser. He was the bearer of grave news. The Archduke Franz Ferdinand, the heir to the throne of Austria-Hungary, had been assassinated in Sarajevo.

Early the next morning, the Kaiser left to prepare for his journey to the Archduke's funeral.

One day later, on the morning of June 30th, when the British squadron weighed anchor, from the masts of the German warships flew the signal, "Pleasant journey."

From the British flagship came a message in return: "Friends in past and friends forever."

On August 4th, Britain and Germany were at war.

•   •   •   •

New York City, August 4, 1914

Friday evening. The family is gathering. Their voices echo from the entrance hall up the winding marble staircase to the drawing room above. From the enthusiasm of their greetings, one would never know that they had been in each other's company only one week earlier. There were often twenty-five or thirty, and sometimes more, at the table on Friday evenings – Harry Hart's sons and daughters with their spouses and their children, and a collection of aunts and uncles and cousins.

Friday evening dinners had a glow about them, a radiance and a warmth, that emanated from the knowledge that each member of the family was a link in a long chain of tradition that spanned time and distance, carried forward from Harry Hart's father's days in Berlin, from *his* father's time in Lübeck, and for many generations long before that.

A formidable family, renowned throughout the world as brilliant bankers, they are intellectuals, legendary statesmen, and distinguished scientists. They are humanitarians, philanthropists, socialites, and patrons of the arts. Remarkable not only for their power and influence, and accumulated wealth, but also for their solidarity. The family had long been a bastion against a world that, if not overtly hostile, had certainly not always been hospitable. What they had gained over many generations they had often achieved in the face of prejudice, chauvinism and bigotry.

Guests were often surprised when they first met Harry Hart, the head of the family and the leader of the Hartenstein banks. From his photographs, and influenced by his celebrity, they often expected someone more formidable, taller perhaps, or more distinguished. He was in his late sixties, of middle height, slightly built, with a full head of wavy gray hair. His manner among strangers was reserved, some would say cold. But the truth is that he was a shy, retiring man who went to great pains to avoid notoriety.

Dinner began, as always, promptly at eight o'clock. The drawing room doors swung open, and the family filed down the stairs, through the entrance hall, and into the long, brightly lit dining room. Overhead, chandeliers cast prisms of color onto the walls and mirrors. Silver and crystal glowed in the light of candelabras placed among the flowers along the length of the table.

There is nothing unusual in their manner as they take their places for the ceremonial lighting of the Sabbath candles, their voices ebbing and flowing and merging like the tuning of an orchestra. But this was not to be the customary celebration of the culmination of a week.

In the past week, Austria had declared war on Serbia. Germany then declared war on Russia and, two days later, on France. And just today, church bells had tolled across England. Great Britain had declared war on Germany.

Europe had gone to war.

•

Harry Hart's thoughts are with his brother Simon and Simon's family in London. He thought of his brothers, and cousins, and his many in-laws in Germany and Austria.

In Germany, his brothers Elias and Kurt had rushed to Berlin to confer with the Kaiser about financial preparations for war. Elias had told Harry that enthusiastic crowds of young people had thronged the *Unter den Linden* and surrounded the Kaiser's palace, chanting "We want war!"

"Exhilaration is rampant throughout Germany!" said Elias, who did not sound particularly unruffled himself. "The crowd bellowed the national anthem. People cheered hysterically, hugging one another and waving banners and flags. The Chancellor is so confident of victory that he is already discussing the reparations that Germany will demand from its defeated enemies."

Elias had volunteered to apply his considerable knowledge of international banking to the war effort.

Harry's brother Kurt, a patriot to the bone, in spite of his advanced age, had immediately responded to the call for service to the *Vaterland* by rushing to his reserve mobilization depot.

In London, Harry's brother Simon, long a confidant of David Lloyd George, the Chancellor of the Exchequer, had been warning for many months that an escalating xenophobia was taking hold of Europe. To the last, he had clung to the hope that England and Germany would settle their differences. Simon, a benevolent, rational man, viewed the war as mass suicide. He had been asked to serve in the war cabinet – a duty he could not refuse.

Harry Hart looks at his sons seated across the table. Lincoln, the eldest, is showing his years. Approaching forty, he is balding and putting on weight. His younger son, Judah, is still boyish in his thirties, and is like a boy in his liveliness and enthusiasms. Their wives, their eyes shining, are in animated conversation with his daughters. He loves his four daughters. There is a luminescence about them, something madcap and frivolous about them, an energy and vibrancy that enchants him. Hannah, the eldest, is so much like her mother, especially her laughing eyes. Gone now twelve years, his wife Dora. Passed away within a few months of his sister Rachel.

He hears the voice of Rachel's son, his grandson Eduard, who is visiting from Germany. He is addressing Hannah's husband, Marcus Goldsmith, defending Germany.

"Uncle," the boy says in his clipped Berlin accent, "In your childlike enthusiasm you Americans believe that there is only good and evil, and that the choice between them is always perfectly clear."

"Eduard is speaking nonsense," Harry thinks.

But still, despite his zeal, Eduard maintains a meticulous civility. Goldsmith, on the other hand, is growing hot. He is a tall spare man in his late thirties, with a powerful stentorian voice that is strangely at odds with his appearance. He parked his knife and fork on his plate with some emphasis.

"Be that as it may, it would not be wise for your Kaiser to underestimate England and France." He paused dramatically. "And soon *we* will be in it!"

Goldsmith could be a supercilious bore, thinks Harry Hart. Why did he always feel that Goldsmith is looking down his nose at him? Perhaps it was because he knows that Goldsmith has a superior mind. He is a physicist. He deals in matters of such bewildering impenetrability. Who in the world can understand the complexity of atoms and molecules?

Looking at Eduard, Harry observes that his nephew has his parents' beauty.

"Beauty," he tells himself, "is the word for the boy's astonishing handsomeness."

Eduard is saying something about Berlin, and he and Goldsmith turn their gaze toward Harry. He had just returned from Berlin, where he visited his brother-in-law, Eduard's father.

He had traveled into the misty Berlin suburbs, hastening through the darkly glistening streets, past the pompous ornate buildings he had always abhorred, and through the stone archway to the gates of the sanitarium. When he saw his brother-in-law, he had been shocked by his appearance.

He had altered almost beyond recognition. His eyes were feverbright, red at the rims, and sunk deep into hollows in his face.

"Jo," Harry Hart called out to him, "It is Herschel."

For a long moment there was no response. Then, languidly, Malkovitz turned to face him. Whenever Harry Hart thought of Joachim Malkovitz he saw him in his many personas: an ambitious careerist, a swaggering bully, and, paradoxically, a self-sacrificing family man. But Harry knew him for what he really was - a coward. His cowardice manifested itself in self-indulgence, self-pity, and chauvinism. And sometimes, strangely, as courage. He was a man who was afraid to acknowledge fear or express caution. But still, behind his mask of self-confidence, he was a coward.

Over the years, Harry had come to understand that it was probably Joachim's fear, and his relentless ambition, that drove his success in business. He had been a formidable partner in many of the Hartenstein Bank's enterprises. That night, he was like a man struggling to rise fully clothed from a pool of water. He was overwhelmed and utterly defeated. That night, it appeared to Harry Hart that he had given up all hope.

Looking now at Malkovitz's son, Harry is struck by how confident and self-assured Eduard is, how much like his father.

He hears Julian, his brother Simon's grandson, chatting amiably with his cousin Anne. What are they going on about? They are talking about Nijinksy and Diaghalev. Julian is explaining; she is protesting that he is wrong. Harry Hart is relieved to hear someone speaking of something other than the war.

Then came Lincoln's voice, calling to him above the dinner table conversation:

"Papa, when do we hear about Uncle Simon's party?"

This is the first Friday dinner since his return from Europe. He had gone to London to join in the celebration of his brother's seventieth birthday. He was four years younger than his brother, but none of them knew that. Whenever the children asked how old he was, he challenged them with mock hauteur.

"Why, I ask, should you know my age? I have no idea how old you are. And I don't believe it would be good form to inquire."

"Papa," they cried, "You know everyone's age to the minute!"

He did in fact take childish delight in remembering the birthdays of others. He plotted elaborate surprises and planned lavish entertainments. He insisted, however, for some mysterious reason, that the anniversary of his own birth go uncelebrated. Of all of the family assembled that night, only his cousin, Adam Hart, who sat by choice at the children's end of the table, knew his age.

Looking at Adam, laughing and chatting contentedly with the children, his mind is flooded with remembered images.

It was 1865. He had recently arrived in America from Berlin. He was peering through the train's misted windows into a black night. The train passed under arches lit by torches that were draped in black. He glimpsed roads leading to a city crowded with long lanes of carriages and people on horseback and on foot.

When the train finally drew into the station, he saw the sign. "Springfield," he read. From the vestibule of the railroad carriage he looked out upon a city swathed in black. Most of the buildings were draped in mourning weeds and festooned in black cloth. Black curtains and valances adorned the windows. The assembled crowd, gathered at the station and in the streets, stood shoulder to shoulder. How strange it was, how eerie, to see such a vast throng standing so quietly, almost in silence.

At last he saw his cousin in the crowd. Adam Hart was a tall thin man in his twenties. He was wearing a soft-collared shirt and a broad-brimmed hat. He lived in Springfield with his wife, the daughter of a prominent mercantile family. Herschel had come to live with them for a time.

Adam had waited for him on the platform for almost five hours. The entire railroad had been in confusion. Schedules had been abandoned to clear the tracks for another train making the nightlong trip from Chicago. They stood together watching, as at last the train slowly entered the station. Its cowcatcher was draped in black. A large picture of President Lincoln was mounted on the front of the locomotive.

The honor guard of blue-clad soldiers descended and lined the way from the funeral car. The coffin was lifted from the train and placed in an enormous gold, silver, and crystal hearse.

Adam, a poet of some renown, showed him his notes for the poem he was composing for *The New York Herald*. He called it "*Home*", noting the banners displayed along the Chicago and Alton Depot: "BEAR HIM HOME TENDERLY" and HOME IS THE MARTYR."

Bells tolled mournfully. The crowd murmured. Adam Hart watched, puzzled, as tears filled Harry's eyes.

•

"Tell it, Papa! Tell it!" The children's voices came to him from down the table.

The family is impatient to hear about the festivities for his brother Simon. Harry Hart loved to tell a story. But he also enjoyed their entreaties, so he allows them to beseech him. He spoke with great style, and when he addressed a group, even in the intimacy of his own family, his speech took on an oratorical quality, and his German accent, which had virtually disappeared over the years, became more pronounced.

Finally, holding both hands in the air in surrender, he begins. "The cake was of modest size – only – four tiers high. It was adorned with flowers and surmounted by cherubs dancing attendance on several buxom maidens who were in a shocking state of dishabille."

He glanced theatrically down to the far end of the table, where the youngsters sat in strict order of their age.

"Tittering? Do I hear tittering down there?" he asks sternly.

He paused to allow the laughter to subside.

"The cake was covered in writing. More writing than the Treaty of Ghent."

"What did it say?" asked cousin Fanny Germain, who with her sister, Amelia DaCosta, was an honorary *tante* to the entire family.

"It was silent. The cake said nothing."

"No! No!" they cried. "What was written on it?"

"I'm sure I don't know," he said, feigning indignation. "I was taught as a boy that it is impolite to read other people's birthday cakes."

Why, he wonders, in the midst of their laughter, does his attention stray? Unaccountably, he finds that he is reviewing the list of the wars and revolutions the family had endured: the Seven Years War, the French Revolution, the Napoleonic wars, the Crimean War, the Boer War. He pauses. Had he skipped any? The Franco-Prussian War, the Spanish-American War, the Boxer Rebellion, the War Between the States, and Lord only knows how many in the centuries earlier. The family had survived them all, as they had endured economic upheaval, the failure of banks and railroads, and panic on the stock exchange.

But this war, which he knows will be on a scale the world had never known, could bring to an end much that the family had achieved over the centuries. He struggled to comprehend a conflict that seemed so inchoate and irrational, a war that could shatter the Hartenstein world.

His thoughts are disrupted by the dinner table chatter. He wonders, with some annoyance, what is it they are talking about now? Churchill at the Admiralty. Lloyd George opposing him. Kaiser Wilhelm's ambitions. German atrocities in Belgium.

His daughter Elissa's husband, James Rothschild, is going on about the disruption of international credit. Harry Hart fumes.

"What in the world can he possibly know about it? He is a physician. What the Dickens does he know about it?"

His daughter Marisa's husband, Marius Blechman, rushes to get a word in. His broad face is red, and his bushy eyebrows are dancing like semaphores. He is a banker. He at least is qualified to speak. He is denouncing the ineffectiveness of the International Court.

"Off again," Harry Hart thinks. "They are off again, enthralled by the weight of their own opinions, their convictions and their pretensions - enraptured by the sound of their own voices."

"America will soon enter the war," says one with great assurance.

"No, we have no essential interest at stake," says another with equal vehemence.

Harry's eyes dart from one end of the long table to the other. He observes them. He listens to them.

"Why," he wonders, "am I so irritated?"

Three days earlier, his cousin, Max Hartenstein, had called from Berlin to tell him that several members of the Berlin Hartenstein and Malkovitz clans had joined the crowds celebrating at the *Rathaus*. According to Max, they screamed, "War! War!"

Max said the family stood at attention and sang *Deutschland, Deutschland über alles.* "The children are terribly excited by it all."

Though he had been enthusiastic in his support of peaceful relations with England, Max and the other Hartenstein cousins, and their Vienna in-laws, the Oppenheims, were in sympathy with Germany's global ambitions. They, like other Jewish bankers in Germany, had an important voice in German state councils, and they believed that the *Vaterland* deserved a new consideration in world affairs. But in America, the conflict created appalling distress for Harry Hart. Already he, and other Jews of German ancestry, were enduring intolerable smears of disloyalty.

"How long do you think it will last?" Amelia DaCosta asked Harry's son-in-law Matthew Wilder.

Eduard Malkovitz burst in before Matthew can answer. "It will be over by Christmas!" he said with utter confidence.

"I don't believe that," piped up Julian, surprising everyone, for this was a young man who rarely asserted himself. He was always an observer; someone who listened, looking from one speaker to the other with his rather opaque eyes.

They speculated about when America would enter the war. Eduard, a reserve officer awaiting his call from the German army, is shining, smoldering, destined for heroism. Julian said he planned to return to England to join the Royal Flying Corps.

"Come Josephine in my flying machine," The tune invades Harry Hart thoughts. He hums the tune to himself. "Up we go! Up we go!"

Miriam's husband, Matthew Wilder is dismayed.

"Isn't it inevitable, Papa, that our British and German banks will be used against each other?"

It was a certainty that the funds of the Hartenstein Bank in New York would eventually be used to finance the war against Germany, the Hartensteins' ancestral homeland. Wilder is an editor of the *North American*, a newspaper in Philadelphia. Harry thought of him as a practical man of uncommon judgment.

"Matthew," he says, "*The Times* has already raised questions about our American bank's connection to our German and Austrian banking houses. And your paper has written that we are refusing to aid the allies, that the family is a 'sinister influence." Matthew laughed. "Who would know better just how sinister than your sons-in-law, Papa?"

There is a void after the laughter had faded. Their mood has altered. Harry Hart folds his napkin neatly. He looks at their faces shifting in the candlelight. They seemed to undergo a subtle transformation. They sit together around the table, but he thinks that now, somehow, it is as if they have suddenly become aware of what is happening in the world; that they have finally seen the incongruity of a Friday evening celebration while civilization is falling to pieces around them.

•

The sounds of the traffic are muted, drifting up to the terrace from the streets below. The air is warm. The drone of the city's life wafts up to him on a perfumed evening breeze. Harry Hart looks down over the parapet. The river sparkles, reflecting the moon in long golden swells. The Palisades across the river on the New Jersey side are lofty purple shadows. At the base of the cliffs, at the water's edge, a few lights glimmer.

"Homes," he thinks. "They look snug and inviting."

His thoughts drift to the events that are enveloping the world. He is fearful – a feeling kindled by the euphoria that humanity was experiencing. Every nation was so blandly confident of victory as they plunged headlong into catastrophe. He anticipates the panic that will soon engulf Europe, and eventually the rest of the world. He envisions the charred landscape of Belgium and France. He sees cavernous halls transformed into overcrowded hospitals. He hears the long roll call of the dead, the wounded, and the missing. He worries that within his family, renowned for its unity, that the reality of war will set brother against brother and cousin against cousin.

He ponders man's malevolence. He broods over man's consummate cruelty. "How," he wonders, "do we manage every day to go about our lives – lives that are indolent and uncaring, false and insincere?"

He stands quietly, gazing somberly at the evanescent moon, at the golden tinted river, and the colors of the summer sky layering the clouds.

As he stares out into the evening, inexplicably, he becomes uncomfortable. He is ill at ease. He has an eerie sense that he is not alone on the terrace. Of course he knows that no one is here with him. Still, though it is obviously ludicrous, he feels a compulsion to turn and look around. Of course he is alone. But why can't he shake off the feeling that some other being is standing close to him?

"This is only an illusion," he tells himself, "A waking dream. A bizarre flight of the imagination."

But no, he realizes, this is no fantasy. Someone is here, sharing his space, breathing his air. He recoils, certain that something appalling is about to befall him.

Then, he sees the slender boy with large sad eyes.

As he stares at him, transfixed, he knows that in some mysterious way he is conjoined to him. Suddenly, it becomes clear to him, though it is no less mystifying, this companion, standing beside him, is without question, Herschel.

This is Herschel. Herschel, with his extraordinary intelligence, his mental gifts, instinctive kindness and compassion, with his noble aspirations, and lofty ambitions. This is Herschel, with his impatient mind, ideas flying like sparks, reaching out passionately, always in ardent pursuit of a more sincere side of life.

To his utter amazement, this Herschel speaks to him.

"You know, you could have prevented this war."

Harry shrinks from him, startled.

"What?" he blurts out.

"Yes, you could have prevented this war," Herschel says. "You and our brothers, our cousins, and our friends. You did nothing to avert this catastrophe."

Harry Hart is incredulous.

"*I* could have prevented this war?"

Even with all his knowledge, his resourcefulness, with all that the family had accomplished through the ages, with their accumulated riches, powerful associates, and world-wide influence. what could they possibly have done to alter the course of world events?

Yet, he is aware of a nagging sense of responsibility. He realizes that for many years a subtle guilt had insinuated itself into everything he had achieved. He sometimes asked himself if he wasn't leading a life built on a false premise, on conformity and hypocrisy.

Once again, he hears Herschel's voice, challenging him.

"What have you accomplished with your life?"

Harry is perplexed. He doesn't know how to answer. He really doesn't know. He really doesn't know how he came to be what he is, how he came by his way of thinking. He couldn't think of a single satisfactory reason why his life had taken the course it had. The path of his entire life, it seemed to him, had depended on happenstance, sometimes on absurdities, perhaps on a random interaction with other people, or merely on the chance convergence of events.

He stares silently at this arrogant Herschel. Bitterly, he confronts him.

"And you? What of you? What of your life?"

Here was a boy, he thinks, who was endlessly engaged in pointless striving, a boy who zealously pursued anything that was injudicious. He was a naïve boy who looked out at the world with a pompous solemnity.

"You wanted to lead a rebellion against the establishment," Harry said. "You wanted an existence that was exotic and daring. You were impatient for revolution. And where did it get you? You were severed from your family, cast out, orphaned, abandoned."

There was no reply.

Then, in a conciliatory manner, Herschel asks, "Come, tell me truthfully - however successful your life has been, haven't you always felt that something significant has been missing? What has become of all your plans and stratagems? What has become of all your lofty theories of the form of freedom, of body and spirit, of honor and shame?"

It's true," Harry thinks. He had lived a life in which every day, in his every endeavor, he was acting against his inner spirit. When he first escaped from Poland and began life anew in America, his mind overflowed with impressions and ideas. His life had been full of promise, laid out before him like a horizonless land. But then, when he became caught up in the complexities of his responsibilities, it became clear to him that his work could not coexist with the vague idealistic attitudes of his early days.

Harry Hart and this Herschel Hartenstein continued to argue passionately, bandying politics, poverty, and the decadence of aristocrats and capitalists. But there was no order, no clarity in their arguments. They contradicted each other. They contradicted themselves. It became so hard for them to distinguish between opposed positions that they couldn't even keep their opinions clear in their own minds.

Desperately, Harry Hart struggles to bring himself under control. He tries to speak, but words will no longer come. He has drifted into the mist of a world that is whirling about him. He is soaring along in a blur of surging images.

Fragments of his early life – Herschel Hartenstein's life– run through his mind like reflections in a stream. He thinks of windblown snow-painted boulevards, thatched roofs and cobbled streets, frozen wastes and mountain ranges. His gaze shifts in amazement from one image to the other. He sees a dark passionate face. Wadizlaw Franzos! He is overwhelmed by Josep Rochek's immense gusto. Intense, incredibly complicated Miriam appears before him, and Frieda, a provocative, decadent girl. Here is Tova, her dark, lonely eyes staring up at him, unseeing. The people of his past, they all emerge, glowing translucently, from some enchanted source. Mama. She stands before him in her lace-collared, high-buttoned dress, her hair white and fine, piled high upon her head. He knows that if his mother were to miraculously come back to life and stand before him now, she would forgive him; she would embrace him with joy and tears, as if he had never deserted her.

And Papa. He sees his father. From the time he had left home he had not seen his father. He had not heard from him. He had not heard a word about him. Oh yes, there was one letter: "Papa died this morning." Memories of his father's exasperation, his indifference, and his rejection are always with him. Yet he tortures himself with guilt for the inadequacy of his filial affection. He calls to his father. He laments, cries out fervent apologies and heartfelt regrets, willing his father's spirit to send him some small sign of forgiveness, some sign of approval of his years of accomplishment.

Harry remains inert, in a daze, contemplating these fragile images and studying Herschel, standing next to him.

He smiles. "I am beside myself," he says with a laugh.

Even amidst his dismay and confusion, the irony of the situation does did not escape him. He tells himself that of course Herschel is just an illusion, a chimera, a specter. He knows that his words are merely a trick of the mind. Yet his encounter with Herschel has touched something within him that was reaching outward, something elusive that he could not grasp.

He stands, lost in anxious thoughts of his fate and his future. He had survived a great tempest of emotion violent demands, formless encounters, tortured memories, experiences that merged and parted. He had been confronted by this other self, this self whose presence was so startling, who had suddenly materialized and who claimed to be him. For a brief time they had lived a masquerade, a kind of dual existence whose charm lay in ambiguity.

"Which of us is the real me?" he asked himself.

What was even more bizarre he had embraced this boy who had come to him. He and the revenant Herschel

Hartenstein had merged into an interchangeable, indeterminable state.

•

A rectangle of yellow light streamed from the undulating glass of the doors leading onto the terrace. From the drawing room comes the clamor of the family's farewells. Their voices drift out to him, the words indistinguishable, blending with laughter. As they part from each other they are smiling and embracing. The ritual Friday evening dinner has ended.

"No matter how we might cling to tradition," he muses, "no matter how mightily we strive to preserve the past, there is after all really no consistency in things. No constancy, nothing that is invulnerable to change. Though we might grasp it with all our strength, there is nothing that can insulate us from time ever-flowing."

Even as he stands there, the scene before his eyes is transfigured. It is fleeing. It has already become the past.

• • • •

ACKNOWLEDGMENTS

Most of the characters and locales depicted in *Revenant* are fictitious. However, in the context of historical events - the 1863 Polish uprising against Russian rule, for example - my fictional characters interact with authentic historical figures.

The families Hart-Hartenstein-Hyam-Hayeem are composites of the leading Jewish banking families of nineteenth-century Europe. I am indebted to several sources for information about these families and for the politics and culture of the time. Among them: *The Warburgs,* Ron Chernow's colorful portrayal of the rise and fall of one of the great banking families of the day; *The Sassoons* by Stanley Jackson, and *The Rothschilds* by Virginia Cowles. For information on the lives of America's influential Jewish families: *A History of Jews in America* by Howard M. Sacher.

Other invaluable sources include: *Faust's Metropolis* by Alexandra Richie for her depiction of the culture and lifestyle of nineteenth-century Berlin; *Gold and Iron - Bismarck and Bleichroeder and the Building of the German Empire* by Fritz Stern for his account of Prussian politics and banking; *Dreadnaught* by Robert K. Massie for information on the rivalry of the two great naval powers; *Europe-A History* by Norman Davis, a chronicle of the evolution of the nations of Europe; *Origins of Prussia* by F.L. Carstenfor, an account of Prussian and Austro-Hungarian politics; *The Birth of the Modern* by Paul Johnson; *The Jews in the History of England 1485 to 1850* by David S. Katz; and *Jewish Contributions to Civilization* by Joseph Jacob.

For information on travel in nineteenth-century Europe: *Travels in the North of Germany* by Henry E. Dwight; *The Rhine Handbook for Travelers* by Karl Baedeker; *A Steam Voyage Down the Danube* by Michael J. Quin; *The Perils of Travel Through Moldavia* by Captain_ Spencer; *On the March to Siberia* by Baroness M.DePackh; and *The Long Walk,* by Slavomir Rawicz.

Information about the Russian cavalry – its organization, armaments, barracks life, training, customs, and uniforms: *Russian Hussar* by Vladimir Littauer and *The Russian Army and Fleet in the 19th Century,* based on archives of the State Historical Museum, the Lenin Library, and the Military Academic Archive of the Russian General Staff.

Sources on anarchism, socialism, insurrectionists, and revolutionaries: *Memoirs of a Revolutionist: God and the State* by Mikhail Aleksandrovich Bakunin; *Evolutionary Socialism* by Edouard Bernstein; *The Story of an Assassination* by Marie Sukloff; and *Anarchism: From Theory to Practice* by Daniel Guerin.

The *Internet Modern History Sourcebook,* compiled and edited by Paul Halsall of Fordham University, provided essays on child labor in England in the nineteenth century, from the autobiography of Harriet Hanson Robinson; *The Philosophy of the Manufacturers* by Andrew Ure; and *The Present State of Rural Hygiene* by Florence Nightingale.

The *Geographical Dictionary of the Former Kingdom of Poland* was a vital source of information on the Polish *Shtetl,* as were the following: *The Museum of the Diaspora,* Tel Aviv; *The*

Shtetl Book – An Introduction to East German Jewish Life and Lore by Mark Zbrowski; *Once Upon a Shtetl* by Chiam Shapiro; *A History of Jewish Life from Eastern Europe to America* by Milton Meltzer; and *The Life and Death of a Small Town and The World of Polish Jews* by Eva Hoffman.

Also, I must gratefully acknowledge the rich personal recollections and heartfelt reminiscences of *Shtetl* families, which were organized by www.Jewishgen.org under the title *ShtetlLinks*. And special appreciation is due to Dr. Itzhak Zee'ev Yunis for his remarkably detailed and deeply moving stories told in *The Old Hometown*.

Finally, my apologies to Bob Landau's redoubtable Lift and Lunch Crunch Bunch, for taking some of their names in vain.

David Hanna
Sandisfield, Massachusetts
January 2011

• • • •

8937927R0

Made in the USA
Charleston, SC
27 July 2011